I0565458

Sutherland House

A five-episode series

The Complete Series

Large Print Edition

by David R. Beshears

Greybeard Publishing
Washington State

www.greybeardpublishing.com

Sutherland House –
the Complete Series

Greybeard Publishing
P.O. Box 480
McCleary, WA 98557

Table of Contents

Page 005 – Episode 1: Andover
Page 125 – Episode 2: Gryphen
Page 195 – Episode 3: the Summit
Page 301 – Episode 4: Threads
Page 387 – Episode 5: Silhouettes

Episode 1
Andover

Prolog

Sharon stood in the center of the forest clearing, bright moonlight shining down upon her. She was attractive, with long brown hair, was wearing a long, flowing white dress.

A dozen men and women stood along the perimeter of the clearing, half hidden in the shadows of the surrounding fir trees. They were dressed in contemporary street clothes, some loose fitting and fluttering in a slight breeze.

They were looking in at the forty year old woman dressed in white. They showed no emotion.

Sharon looked frightened. She turned slowly about. Those standing in the shadows continued to look into the center of the clearing, their focus on Sharon growing

steadier, more determined, yet with no
passion.

A woman slowly laid her head back,
closed her eyes.

A second observer laid his head back and
closed his eyes.

Sharon continued to spin slowly about,
looking to those in the half-shadow with
increasing desperation. Her long hair
fluttered and flowed, caught in the twisting
breeze that grew steadily stronger.

A cloud drifted in front of the silver
moon and the night grew dark. Shadows
pushed into the clearing from the black of
the forest.

Chapter One

Matthew Sutherland drove his twenty year old Lincoln slowly through the automated gates of the Sutherland House estate, up the wandering drive through the estate grounds and toward the house itself.

Matthew looked to be about forty, but his eyes revealed that he had seen much more than four decades. He had a kind face. He wore the black armband of mourning.

The estate grounds were a mix of different styles, with a variety of shrubs, plants, walks and short garden walls, as if it had all been put together piecemeal over many years as moods changed and as the gardener discovered new things and came up with new ideas; all of which were true.

The two-storey house itself was modest and surprisingly small considering the expansive grounds and high walls that surrounded it. It was unpretentious, while at the same time stately.

Matthew came into the front foyer and tossed his keys into a dish on a small table beside the front door, walked into the living room. The house was clean and comfortable; the furniture quality without being ostentatious, a mix of styles and periods, collected over the span of many years.

He dropped down onto the couch, slid back and tiredly rubbed at his face. He struggled to hold onto his emotions, fighting back grief. He wasn't ready to give into it.

He sat up then, leaned forward, elbows on his knees. He looked around him at the home that he had shared with Sharon for so many years.

It all threatened to fall in on him.

He ignored the sound of the front door opening and closing. Moments later, Jennifer Sutherland came into the room from the foyer. She moved quickly to the easy chair and sat, stared at Matthew. She looked a bit irritated with her father.

She was twenty, attractive in a very natural way, being that there was nothing artificial in her looks or her manner. She was wearing a full black dress and shawl.

"You can't just walk out like that," she said. Yes. Definitely irritated, but restrained.

"Sure I can."

"No. You can't."

Matthew turned to face his daughter, his gaze lost.

"You learn that in college, did you?"

"That's rude. It was rude."

"Yeah." Matthew slid back in the couch, laid his head back and stared up at the ceiling. "I wonder if the panels are shrinking or the house is settling."

"Dad—" Jennifer tried her best to ignore the ceiling.

"Do you see that?" He asked. "There's a gap between two of the panels."

"It's been there since I was three," said Jennifer, without looking up.

Matthew brought his head forward again, straightened with a sigh. He wore a studious frown.

"School break must be about over," he said. "When do you head back?"

"I told you. I've taken leave. Jorgenson said that I can pick it up again whenever I'm ready."

"Jorgenson thinks he owes us something."

"He does owe us something."

Matthew rubbed his face again, sighed.

"You shouldn't have done that, Jen. You don't want to fall behind."

"Don't worry about that, Dad. I'll be fine."

"This is your senior year."

"I'm fine."

Matthew stared at Jennifer for a long moment, then turned away. He stared absently up at the ceiling, at the gap between two of the panels.

"What a crappy day."

Jennifer leaned forward, rested her elbows on her knees. She looked carefully at her father. She appeared about to cry, pushed it back.

"I love you, Dad."

The room fell silent; the house was suddenly very empty.

"I guess it's you and me now, Jen," said Matthew.

Jennifer stood then and went over to her father. She sat beside him. They held onto each other.

"We'll be all right," she said, consoling.

"I know," he managed to say. "I know."

Matthew took the narrow stairs down to the basement. To one side were free-standing shelves filled with neatly labeled home-canned jars of fruits and vegetables. The other side of the basement contained a small workshop. There was a workbench with a set of shelves beside it.

Matthew reached into the set of shelves and released a hidden latch. There was a metallic click. The shelves swung open,

gliding easily, revealing a shaft with a ladder
leading down.

He stepped into the shaft, onto the ladder,
started down.

He climbed off the ladder and into "the
Apartment". The lights came on
automatically as he walked into the room.

The Apartment was comfortable
contemporary, high-tech mixed with the
every day. There was an opening in the wall
behind him with the shaft leading up to the
main house. On either side of the shaft
opening were built-in shelves filled with
books. A door along the wall to Matthew's
right led to the armory, another to the
bathroom. There was a counter beyond,
behind which was a small kitchen.

Set into the wall on Matthew's left was a
large viewing screen, beside that a bank of
computer monitors, five across and four
rows high.

A door in the far wall opened to a long
hallway leading to an underground garage.
To the left of the door were racks of
computer network, server and

communications equipment. Beside these was a computer station with desk and chair.

There was a living area in the center of "The Apartment", with couch and chair, a round kitchen table and chairs.

Matthew took off his jacket and tossed it onto the couch, revealing that he was wearing a shoulder holster and weapon. He walked across the room to the armory closet as he slipped out of the holster. A mix of sophisticated weaponry and standard weapons were mounted on one wall of the closet. He hung up his holster, unloaded and set the pistol into its slot.

He came out of the armory and went into the small bathroom. He spoke as he washed his hands and face.

"Computer," he said, impassively.

"Yes, Matthew?" came from hidden speakers. The computer voice sounded almost human, but with a lack of true emotion behind the words and an almost too perfect quality to the syntax and pronunciation.

Computer did strive, however, to inject familiarity into the conversations that it held with Matthew and Jennifer, previously with Sharon.

Matthew quickly dried his hands and returned to the main room, started into the kitchen.

"Anything more on Sharon's death since your last report?" he asked.

"All three regional newspapers carried the obituary," stated Computer. "No additional articles. No newspapers outside the local area contain any reference. There has been no mention of Sharon Sutherland in any monitored television broadcast, radio broadcast or Internet news feeds.

Matthew took a can of iced tea out of the refrigerator and returned to the main area.

"Items of interest," he requested flatly.

"Forty-eight items identified for your review."

Matthew frowned, moved slowly to the couch. He sat down, opened the can of iced tea.

"Any that could possibly relate to Sharon's death?"

"No possible connections identified."

"Are any of the items Red Priority?"

"I have identified six items identified as Red Priority."

Matthew hesitated, absently rubbed at his temple.

"Not now." He stretched out on the couch, set the can on the floor. "Dim lights."

The lights dimmed, leaving only a faint glow in the room. Tiny red indicator lights inset into the computer equipment all about the room occasionally flickered.

Matthew rolled onto his side and immediately fell asleep.

Jennifer stood over her father, asleep on the couch. She placed a hand on his shoulder. He woke, sat up.

"Good morning," she said.

"'morning…" he looked curiously at the blanket that had been covering him, set it aside. "Morning?"

Jennifer turned away and started toward the kitchen. She obviously knew her way around the Apartment.

"I'll bet you're hungry," she said.

"A bit."

Jennifer began rummaging about cabinets and the refrigerator.

"I'll fix us something while you get cleaned up."

Matthew mumbled unintelligibly on his way to the bathroom.

Jennifer began cutting up fruit. She heard the shower running.

"Computer?" she asked.

"Hello, Jennifer," came the voice of Computer. "I am pleased to hear your voice. I have missed you."

"Thank you, Computer. I've missed you, too,"

"How is your education coming?"

"I have no doubt that you know exactly how I am doing."

"Grades are not fully representative of how someone is doing, Jennifer."

Jennifer smiled, put the plate of fruit on the counter.

"I'm doing fine," she said.

"I am pleased to hear that," said Computer.

"Anything new on Mom's murder?"

"No, Jennifer. I am sorry."

"Thank you."

There was a long pause then. The only sounds came from the running computer equipment and the low thrum of the running shower.

"I liked your mother very much," said Computer.

"Me too, Computer," said Jennifer.

Chapter Two

Jennifer was standing in the kitchen, opposite Matthew sitting at the counter. They were eating a breakfast of fruit and toast, with juice. Matthew was dressed comfortably, refreshed after his shower.

"Nothing new on Mom," said Jennifer.

Matthew only nodded, continued eating.

"Dad, I've been thinking." Jennifer started then, cautiously. "I think I should come into the business right away."

Matthew put down his fork, a chunk of cantaloupe still speared, and picked up his glass of juice.

"You need to finish school," he said. He took a drink.

"I can help you."

"No." Another swallow of juice.

"I was going to join you and Mom soon enough anyway."

"Things have changed."

"They certainly have," she said.

Matthew stared down at his glass, fought a number of emotions, all of which threatened to show themselves on his stone face.

"You coming into the family business… it wasn't supposed to—"

"I understand that, Dad. I do." Jennifer started to reach a hand across the counter, pulled it back. "You can't do this alone."

"Jen…" Matthew let the thought fade.

One of the red indicator lights beneath the monitor set into the wall next to the counter began to flash. A small label under the light read 'Main Gate'.

A moment later the monitor activated. It showed a young man, about twenty years old, standing near the communication box at the gate. He had the look and manner of the kid next door.

"It's Sam," groaned Jennifer.

"I doubt he's here to see me," said Matthew.

"Computer… activate," said Jennifer, her tone surrendering. "Hello, Sam."

"Jennifer," said Sam, leaning nearer the communication box. His voice sounded tinny coming through the speaker. "I wanted to make sure you were all right."

"I'm fine, Sam."

"When your dad left like that… and then you—"

"We're okay, Sam. I'm sorry we ran out."

"No!" Sam said quickly. "That's all right. Everyone understood."

There was a long pause. Sam looked about, looked to the camera.

"Are you going to let me in?" he asked then.

Jennifer looked irritably over at Matthew, who had miraculously regained his appetite and was busily finishing up the fruit.

"Sure," she sighed. "Computer, monitor off."

The monitor went blank. Jennifer pushed away from the counter and started out of the kitchen.

"Main gate open," she said, starting toward the ladder.

"Thanks for breakfast," said Matthew, his focus across the counter, as he picked up his juice glass. "You kids have fun."

"And another thing, Dad," she said, climbing onto the ladder. "A ladder? A lousy ladder?"

She disappeared into the shaft. The sound of her voice became muffled, only her legs visible.

"All the money spent putting this place together, and you couldn't spring for an elevator?"

Matthew's smile came and faded. He pushed away from the counter, walked around and into the kitchen. He put the breakfast dishes into the dishwasher, cleaned the counter. He drifted into the center of main room and stood behind the couch. He looked at the rows of inactive monitors, then at the large wall display, currently dark.

"Computer," he said.

"Yes, Matthew?"

Matthew stared dully at the wall.

"Nothing," he said.

Matthew felt very, very alone.

§

The Academy grounds were eerily empty of people, despite it being mid-afternoon, the day sunny and warm. There were several old, stately buildings of brick and ivy. The grounds themselves were green lawns and wide, winding walkways. Several hundred feet from the main building stood a large, ancient oak tree, hovering over a wide walkway running from the small parking lot to the main administration building.

A nine year old girl was standing in the window of her room in the dormitory, looking out at the grounds and the large oak tree. Mary's face was reflected in the glass. The quarters behind her were small; a single narrow bed, a desk and chair; there was a door to the closet, a larger door leading out to the hall.

Mary continued to look contemplatively outside. There was a sadness about her.

She lifted her gaze slightly. Despite the fact that there could be no breeze, her hair began to flutter.

She closed her eyes.

Her hair brushed back from her face against a breeze that did not exist.

The lights of the Apartment had gone dim. Matthew was standing behind the couch, looking across the room at the far wall. He slowly turned his head, lifted his gaze and looked up and to one side.

There was something…

He sensed… something.

Chapter Three

Jennifer stepped off the ladder and into the Apartment. The lights were on. Several of the monitors in the far wall were on, displaying nebulous scenes from security cameras located in unremarkable office buildings.

"Computer, where's Dad?" she asked.

"Matthew is in the garage, Jennifer."

Jennifer walked across the room and opened the door in the opposite wall. She entered a long, narrow hallway, lit by several ceiling light panels evenly spaced along the hall.

She opened the door at the far end of the hall and walked into the underground garage.

It looked much like an auto service center. Along the left side were six stalls containing an assortment of vehicles: a 64 Comet, an old Bronco, a small converted school bus, a late model BMW, a 97 Ford pickup, a pair of dirt bikes, and a Harley-Davidson Sportser.

On the right was a line of service bays; a chest-high counter spanned the length of the wall.

At the far end, an opening to a tunnel that curved away and out of sight.

Jennifer moved along the line of vehicles until she found Matthew under the hood of the immaculate 1964 Mercury Comet.

"Dad?"

Matthew answered from under the hood: "Yeah."

"Dad, what are you doing?" She sounded disheartened.

"I'm walking the dog."

"Dad…"

"Jennifer, I'm working on the car." He continued to speak from under the hood. "The car needs work—I'm working on it."

Jennifer watched Matthew work for several seconds before trying again.

"Listen, I'm not trying to push you, but it's been almost two weeks. I'm not asking that you to take on anything major, but at least let Computer run you through the Red Priorities."

"Computer will let me know if there's anything vital."

"Isn't that what 'Red Priority' means?"

Matthew remained under the hood.

"Not this week, it doesn't."

Jennifer folded her arms and looked sympathetically at her father, half his body under the hood. When she spoke again, there was a quiet desperation in her voice.

"I'm sorry, but I'm not going to let you just walk away. The Business is too important. Like it or not, you have a responsibility that you can't ignore."

Matthew finally came out from under the hood. He picked up a red rag and began cleaning the open-end wrench that he brought out with him.

"I'm not walking away from anything. I know how important the Business is. I did start it, after all. The work isn't stopping just because I spend a few days taking care of some things I've been neglecting.

"Is that what you're doing?" she asked, flatly.

Matthew looked coolly at his daughter, spoke now in a lecturing tone.

"Computer continues its daily scan of every newspaper to hit a computer system or news item to hit the wires. It continues its twenty-four hour a day monitoring of three hundred forty-three television stations and six hundred twelve radio stations."

"I know that," Jennifer stated precisely.

Matthew put down the wrench and picked up another, continued cleaning his tools.

"As we speak," he went on, "it is monitoring security systems of key locations throughout the United States and select International locations. It is monitoring Internet sites and Internet communications. It's monitoring the telecommunications activity of one thousand two hundred and four key people throughout the world. It is also tracking stock markets, financial markets, monetary values and agricultural markets, as well as numerous financial institutions."

He paused, put on a sardonic smile.

"And it is managing our portfolio. I do believe we are quite well off."

"I lack for very little," Jennifer said in a low grumble.

Matthew put down the second wrench, began methodically cleaning sockets.

"Computer continually bounces all that data around; storing, rearranging, collating, filing, processing, recalculating... and when two or more items come together just right, Computer puts it on the list. When I'm ready, Computer shows me that list. Now... when it's important enough, Computer hits me over the head with it, whether I'm ready or not."

"You have Red Priority items," said Jennifer, determined. "That makes them important."

"They'll keep." Matthew began putting his clean tools into the tall, red tool chest beside him. He indicated the nearby Bronco. "Right now, I need to realign the Bronco."

"I'll do it."

"I like doing it."

"So do I," said Jennifer.

Jennifer pulled the Bronco into one of the service bays. She climbed out of the vehicle and began hooking up the alignment equipment to the front, left tire.

She stood when she heard the sound of the Comet starting, watched as it backed out of the stall and headed for the tunnel.

The tunnel was several hundred feet long, wide enough and tall enough for a small bus and not much more. Security cameras were mounted at several locations along the way. A sensor along the route activated and a red light turned off, the green light turned on. The access door opened.

The Comet passed through, started out onto an isolated dirt road, grassy foothills and scattered oak trees and brush. The metal access door glided smoothly and quietly closed behind it.

Back in the garage, Jennifer knelt and began making adjustments to the alignment apparatus.

"Computer, where is Dad going?" she asked.

"Indications suggest Rydel Ridge." Computer directed his voice to the nearest speaker. "Would you like me to ask him?"

Jennifer continued preparing the alignment equipment.

"No," she grumbled.

Rydel Ridge was a lookout point with a small picnic area and parking lot. It was surrounded on several sides by a grove of trees. Downslope below the ridge was a meadow frequented by deer.

Matthew was sitting on the hood of the parked Comet. His was the only car. He was alone.

The silence was interrupted by the sound of another vehicle approaching. A small car came into the lot and pulled up near Matthew.

A teenager climbed out.

"Excuse me," he said. "Did you order the pizza?"

Matthew slid off the hood.

"You're new," he said warily.

"Sir?"

"Never mind."

The delivery person walked around to the passenger side of his car and pulled a pizza box out of a red warmer sleeve. He also came up with a small cardboard box.

"Medium combination, potato salad, and a liter of root beer."

"Did you remember the ice and a cup?" asked Matthew.

"Right here, sir," indicating the cardboard box. "Also, napkins and a fork."

Matthew took the pizza box and set it on the hood. The delivery person set the cardboard box down beside it and pulled a receipt out of his pocket.

"Your receipt," handing it to Matthew.

Matthew dropped it into the box, then handed the teenager a ten dollar bill.

"Everything looks to be here," he said.

"Aim to please." The teenager shoved the bill into his pocket and hurried back to his car.

Matthew watched him until the car was out of sight, then climbed back onto the hood. He slid the pizza box to one side of him, the cardboard box to the other.

He brought out the container of potato salad, dug around for the fork. He sat back then and continued to enjoy the day.

Finished with the alignment, Jennifer returned to the Apartment and cleaned up, then sat at the computer station. She brought up the vehicle maintenance log, began entering information on the work she'd done.

"Computer?" she prompted as she worked.

"Yes, Jennifer?"

"Sorry to bother you again…"

"Jennifer, you know very well that I am capable of carrying on conversations and responding to your requests and queries while simultaneously performing my other duties."

"Yeah, yeah, yeah… is Dad still at the Ridge?"

"The sensor indicates that Matthew is not in the vehicle. Once he left the immediate area surrounding Sutherland House, visual surveillance was discontinued. Monitoring indicates, however, that a delivery of pizza, potato salad and Mug root beer was made to Robert Matthews at the Rydel Ridge picnic grounds approximately twenty-three minutes ago. Robert Matthews is one of Matthew's current aliases."

Jennifer continued typing while half-listening to Computer.

"Sounds like his diet," she said.

"Would you like me to attempt to establish visual surveillance of the Rydel Ridge area?"

"No." Jennifer leaned back in her chair. "Let him know that I'm watching him."

There was a long pause as Computer relayed her message through the communications system in the Comet, then waited for a reply.

"Your father conveys his deep appreciation for your concern regarding his wellbeing."

Jennifer snickered at this, gave the maintenance log a final onceover before closing it, then stood and pulled a wireless keyboard from a shelf. She activated it as she started toward the couch.

"Transfer to main display, please," she said. "Bring up my game project."

The main wall display lit up as she reached the couch, her application development screen filling the display. She plopped her body down and set the keyboard in her lap.

"I am pleased to see you working on your game again, Jennifer."

Jennifer looked at one and then another of the windows on the display, each filled with C code. She moved one to the side, then another, expanded a third.

"Not much chance at school," she said. "And here… well, lately... you know."

Chapter Four

Dianna Broderick came down the stairs to the front foyer of the fine home. She looked to be in her forties. She was trim and well-maintained, wore a well-tailored dress, and had the look and air of a woman born to the life of refinement.

Two young children stood in the foyer beside their nanny. Robby was six, Thomas five.

Dianna bent down and gave each child a gentle hug. She straightened then, gave a nod to the nanny.

"Mrs. Evans," she stated flatly.

"Good morning, Mrs. Broderick," said Mrs. Evans.

"Mr. Broderick is waiting for them in his office."

"Yes, ma'am. I'll take them up."

§

Victor Broderick stood in front of his desk, his eye on the door. He was a tall, distinguished gentleman, looked to be in his fifties, with all the air of a high-placed, well-bred individual, fully accustomed to being in control and in charge.

Just now he was nervous.

The door opened and Mrs. Evans ushered in the two young children. They stood quietly before Victor.

"And whom do we have here, Mrs. Evans?" he asked.

Mrs. Evans placed a hand on one shoulder of each child.

"Robby, Thomas… say hello to your father."

Robby spoke in a calm, polite tone. "Hello, Father."

Thomas looked up at Victor but said nothing.

"Hello, boys," said Victor. "I've missed you."

There was an awkward silence. Victor finally clasped his hands behind his back and looked calmly down at his children. With only the slightest indication from him, Mrs. Evans moved into action.

"Off we go now, boys," she said. "You'll see your father at dinner."

Victor watched the nanny shuffle them through the door and out of sight. He stared at the open doorway.

There was absolute silence.

With a twitch of two fingers of his left hand, the door closed with a soft thump.

He stood alone in the quiet room.

Matthew was alone in the Apartment. The lights were dim.

He walked to the couch but remained standing.

"Computer. Activate main screen."

The wall screen lit up, though there was no data. Matthew didn't move. He stared at the wall, now faintly aglow.

"Computer…" The word drifted away into silence.

Computer waited.

"Computer…" said Matthew. Again he hesitated. Finally then, "What say we review the Red Priorities?"

"Yes, Matthew."

The picture of a young woman appeared on the display.

"The first item is the murder of Marli Reynolds."

A series of police crime scene photographs then displayed one photograph at a time.

Matthew sat down as Computer continued to review.

"Age seventeen, her body found along the bank of the Sacramento River. She was murdered elsewhere, her unclothed body dumped at the discovery site."

"Reynolds?" asked Matthew. "Doesn't ring any bells."

"Miss Reynolds' cousin, Karen Lawrence, with whom she had a close relationship, is married to Mark Gryphen."

"Son of Phillip Gryphen," stated Matthew.

"That is correct."

The photo displayed on the wall was of Marli Reynolds' naked, bruised and broken body twisted among smooth, rounded river rocks.

Matthew calmly studied the photograph.

"How was she murdered?"

A new photo displayed on the screen, this one showing Marli Reynolds on an autopsy table.

"Reports state that there was minimal bruising on the neck, yet severe internal damage."

A series of newspaper articles displayed.

"That fact was not made public," Computer continued. "There was mention of the murder on each of the local television news programs immediately following the discovery of the body, with an accompanying statement that cause of death was yet to be determined. Similar news stories were broadcast on the local radio stations."

"Just another murdered kid," said Matthew.

"Three regional newspapers carried the story, two of which had follow-ups several days later. Once again, however, the circumstances of the death were never revealed."

"The current status of the case?"

Marli Reynolds' high school picture displayed.

"Open," said Computer. "No activity. One detective assigned, and she is also working on several other cases."

Matthew stood, walked toward the picture of Marli.

"Give me the autopsy report," he said.

The first page of the report displayed. It wasn't the image of a hardcopy, but rather a computer template populated with data. Matthew read, his face shimmering against the glow of the display.

"The authorities didn't get all this, did they?"

"No."

The display changed, showed a printed hardcopy of the report. A few moments later, the hardcopy and the computer template displayed side by side.

Matthew took a moment to compare them.

"If the M.E. was trying to hide something, why bother entering one set of data into the computer and then send out a hardcopy with a different set of data?" He turned away from the display. "Have you checked to see if the data on file has changed since you first acquired this information?"

"The data on file has not changed," said Computer. "It is not consistent with the data received by the authorities."

"The difference between the two?"

"The hardcopy report contains no mention of the severity and peculiarities of the neck injuries. While the computer data identifies these injuries as the cause of death, the hardcopy report lists the cause of death simply as strangulation."

Matthew returned to the couch and sat down.

"I didn't see possible method," he said.

"None was specified."

"So, we have Marli Reynolds; tenuous connection to one of the Families. Said young lady is found murdered. Her body is obviously meant to be discovered, and in front page, albeit brief, fashion. Cause of death is unusual, and said cause is hidden from not only the public but also from the authorities."

He quickly corrected himself…

"Although the true report may have reached the authorities and was subsequently switched."

"A plausible supposition," said Computer. "Given the current facts."

"A rather violent way to get rid of a problem, isn't it? The Gryphens are nothing if not subtle."

"They may have been hoping a connection would be made to several similar murders that had been committed in previous weeks," said Computer. "A possible connection was investigated and ruled out."

"Or perhaps someone in the family did a little independent activity," said Matthew.

"Members of the Gryphen Family are not known for independent activity."

"Oh, you can bet Phillip Gryphen is seriously peeved." Matthew grew thoughtful, then came to a decision. "Continue this one on your own, Computer. You're probably right about a Society tie-in, and I would certainly like to take a crack at the Gryphens, but—"

"I will keep you informed," stated Computer.

"Next item."

The display now showed a photograph of a middle-aged man. The picture could easily be a driver's license photograph.

"Cult leader John Cutler," said Computer. "Government sources have identified his true name as Jon Willeby."

The display changed, showing John Cutler speaking before a crowd.

Computer continued.

"There have been numerous reports of Cutler performing miracles."

"That certainly wouldn't draw your attention, and most definitely not flag it as a Red Priority. I therefore assume there is a lot more going on here than simply a miracle worker at work."

"Of course," said Computer.

"Oh… I sense annoyance."

"On the contrary. I am nothing if not content… and patient."

"Okay…" Matthew said slowly. "Go on."

The reflection from the display showed on Matthew. The pale shadows on his face shifted as the display changed.

Mary's dormitory quarters, the Academy; the rays of the setting sun were streaking in through the window, brushing across her face as she sat in her chair.

There was a sense of timeless calm in the room.

That calmness shown on Mary's face.

§

The Academy Headmaster eased into the chair behind his desk. He had a kind look about him. In his fifties, he had begun to gray about the edges and had a bit of late middle-aged spread.

The same sunset colors shone through the small window of his office.

There was a light on in the outer office that shone through the frosted glass pane set into the only door. The word "Headmaster" was stenciled on the glass, reverse image as seen from this side of the door,

As the Headmaster sat, the glow of the computer monitor before him reflected on his face. He stared at the words that he had written.

He spoke then, and his words appeared on the screen.

"Mary is progressing faster than we anticipated; faster than we dared hope. I sometimes sense that she is actually holding back so that we can keep up with her. As you will see in this week's enclosed report, she continues to show tremendous advancement in all six Abilities. As you well know, such is almost unprecedented. While ten percent of Society members do in fact possess talent in all six Abilities, very few of that ten percent have evidenced such latent power in all of them—and I have never witnessed such potential."

There was a long, ominous pause.

"Sir, I believe…" he paused again, began again. "I believe that Mary is much greater than we originally assessed."

The Headmaster grew silent, stared uneasily at the words on the screen.

Chapter Five

Matthew walked around the couch with a can of iced tea in hand. He climbed onto the couch and sat on the back, always with an eye to the main display on the wall. Spreadsheet text was displayed in a data window on the display; data on the third Red Priority item that Computer had presented.

Or was it the fourth...

Matthew opened his tea and took a long drink.

"All right, let's go on to the next one," he said. "This one bores me."

The displayed cleared.

"I will continue monitoring this item and keep you apprised of any developments," said Computer.

"You do that," said Matthew. "Next."

A photocopy of a newspaper article appeared on the display wall.

"The community of Andover, located in Washington State."

Matthew slid down on the couch, took another swallow.

"Make it interesting."

"Andover has a population of just over two thousand," said Computer. "It has its own hospital, doctor, dentist, water district, K-8 school, retirement center, police force, volunteer fire and emergency station, as well as a handful of stores and restaurants. There is also a lumber mill, a dairy, and several farms."

"Nice setup," said Matthew. "Nothing sinister, though. There must be hundreds of little empires just like it."

"Many small communities manage to establish some level of self-sufficiency. Few, however, have realized the level of independence as has Andover."

Photographs displayed in sequence, showing a small town nestled in the woods. These were followed by several official documents that looked to be permits, ownership certificates and business licenses.

"Can you tell me what drew you to some three-inch fluff story that a bored cub reporter dug up at county records?" asked Matthew. "And just how it has anything to do with us?"

"It is true that the item first came to my attention as a result of a small story in a weekly newspaper. It described the turnaround and subsequent success of the town of Andover. Further investigation subsequently revealed this to be in fact a Red Priority item."

Jennifer was behind the wheel, driving the small bus down a rural, county road. There were no storefronts or homes; only an occasional lone vehicle that passed in the opposite direction.

Computer's voice disrupted the sense of solitude, coming from a speaker set in the dash.

"Jennifer?"

"Yes, Computer?"

"Your father would like to speak with you."

"Patch him through," said Jennifer.

"Jennifer." Matthew's voice sounded distant, hollow.

"Yes, Dad."

"I hear you're doing a bit of tinkering. How's the bus?"

"The rebuild on the carb did the trick," she answered.

"It just needed your magic touch," said Matthew. "Will you be coming back soon?"

"I'm about ten minutes out. Is there a problem?"

"Not at all. I think we may have an assignment."

"We?"

"If you're interested."

"I'm on my way."

Matthew and Jennifer were sitting at the table, papers scattered about on the tabletop, along with a can of iced tea and a half-full glass of water. The wall display behind them showed one of the exterior shots of the town of Andover.

"Andover was just another mill town," said Matthew. "It had a grocery store, a gas station, VFW hall, tavern, and a few hundred houses all about half a century old. But a couple of things it had going for it that most other towns of a couple of thousand people didn't have was a hospital sitting on one hill, and a school on another."

Jennifer picked up and studied a document.

"I'm guessing things started to change about… four years ago."

"About the time the mill was bought up." Matthew tapped at the document in Jennifer's hands. "It had been privately owned, but was closely allied with one of the big lumber companies. The purchase price wasn't publicly disclosed, but it was rumored, and Computer has verified, that the new owners considerably overpaid for the mill."

"Why?"

"Don't know." Matthew picked up his iced tea, took a swallow, set it back on the table. "Once they had it, they began making changes. They severed all the original ties, and lost the mill's customer base. The employees really started sweating it, especially when the mill shut down for retooling. But the new owners kept the workers on, using them to help with the renovation. They even gave raises when they reopened a few months later. The mill began bringing in its raw materials from outside the traditional markets, and began acquiring customers from the Midwest.

"So the new owners brought their suppliers and their customers with them."

"Seems that way."

"Society?"

"The connection isn't as strong as it might be, but Computer leans to yes."

"Why?"

"Not there yet," sighed Matthew. "But here are some interesting tidbits. At about the same time the mill was changing hands, the town council began changing hands as well. An overworked group of six community leaders paid a token salary of one dollar a month each. Nonetheless, they wielded what power there was in town. The town mayor had held leadership of the council for twenty-two years and showed no signs of ever letting go. Then, in a sudden and surprising turn of events, he and two others of the council were voted out, replaced by relative newcomers."

"And these have been identified as Society."

"Not yet, but…" Matthew spoke then over his shoulder. "Computer, time for some pictures."

"Please be more specific, Matthew."

"Let's start with the Addisons and go on from there."

A moment later the display showed a photograph of Robert Addison. The photograph moved to one side, allowing room for Linda Addison. Both looked to be in their thirties.

"Robert and Linda Addison," Computer stated.

Matthew turned to Jennifer.

"The Addisons showed up in Andover about four years ago."

"The same time as—"

"Right," said Matthew. "Robert is a freelance computer expert, occasionally consults to big business, writes tech books. Linda is a teacher, and it is this that is supposed to have brought them to Andover. There was an opening at the school."

The display changed. A photograph of an older man appeared. This photograph moved to one side, allowed room for a photograph of a woman. Both appeared to be in their sixties.

"Daniel and Emma Chandler," said Computer.

"Both retired," said Matthew. "Showed up in Andover a week after the Addisons. Daniel Chandler was a city planner, and Emma had been an administrator for a retirement community.

"Sounds ominous," said Jennifer, a mocking tone.

"It's all very innocent. A rundown mill gets a lift, a town council gets some new blood, a few new folks move in, breathe life into a stagnant community." Matthew stared at his can of iced tea. He took another drink. "But there's more going on. The revitalization of Andover has been carefully orchestrated. The people coming into town aren't random. Their talents mesh just a little too perfectly with the needs of the town, always at just the right time."

"Interesting," said Jennifer. "And?"

"And... Remember that I said there's been a slow influx of new people over the years. Most small towns get the occasional newcomer, but Computer has identified a point in time, beginning about six years ago, when Andover began a steady, consistent migration of new people."

"Preparing the way?"

"Which means the work actually began six years ago, not four. But the more interesting part of this is that the actual population has remained about the same."

"Oh. Very sci-fi," said Jennifer. "The town's being replaced."

"Uh-huh."

"You brought up the Addisons and the Chandlers. They've been identified as Society?"

"Still working on it," said Matthew. "I brought them up in particular because they seem to be at the center of a lot of what is going on there; as mundane and ordinary as that activity appears to be. Computer has their new names and backgrounds, their photographs, and the dates they showed up. The names and backgrounds are forged, the faces may or may not have been altered, but there are paper trails starting the day they entered Andover. Computer is working on that."

Computer displayed another picture on the wall. It was of a middle-aged man, nondescript, with no supporting text.

"Walter Carlson," said Computer.

Matthew glanced up at the image.

"Carlson, the mayor of Andover," he said. He hesitated then, looked away.

"Dad?" asked Jennifer.

Matthew's thoughts were taking him down an uncomfortable path. He looked down at his iced tea, pushed the can aside with two fingers.

"What is Victor up to?" he asked, as much to himself as to Jennifer.

Victor stood at the second floor window of his home office. Looking through the glass, he watched the two children, Robby and Thomas, in the playground that took up the left side of the backyard. The yard contained a Jungle Jim, swing set, clubhouse, and assorted bar and climbing apparatus.

The children were playing on the bars as Mrs. Evans sat on a nearby bench reading a book.

Thomas suddenly fell from the bars. Mrs. Evans was up in an instant, but almost immediately sensed that the child was unhurt. She calmly sat back down and returned to her reading.

Robby hurried to help his little brother.

Victor turned from the window. He noted a message box flashing on his computer monitor. He returned to his desk, pushed aside the chair and stood before the monitor. He clicked a key on his keyboard. The message box disappeared. He looked over at the speaker phone.

He activated the phone with a thought. A light began blinking and the sound of the dial tone could be heard.

"Get me Carlson," said Victor.

The sound of the dial tone was replaced with the sound of numeric tones as the phone dialed.

There were two rings and the phone picked up.

"Yes?" came over the phone.

"Mayor Carlson," Victor said, harshly. "What the hell is going on in Andover?"

"Mr. Broderick—" Carlson started.

"There continue to be inquiries into our activities," said Victor. "I need your assurance that all is being done that can be done to guarantee our anonymity in Andover."

"All is being done that can be done, sir."

Victor walked back to the window, looked out at his children. He spoke over his shoulder in the general direction of the phone.

"The Andover community presents the greatest threat of exposure that we have ever faced. The peril is not only of our detection, but of our destruction."

"From Andover will come our greatest power," said Carlson through the phone's speakers.

"It is not power that we seek from Andover. It is the survival of the Society." Victor turned from the window and returned to his desk. "I've been looking over the latest reports. The conclusions from the most recent research are not as encouraging as I would hope."

"The arrival and integration of several families of… *minimal*… Abilities. This distorted the results of some of our experiments. You may also have noted the misguided directions of several Members in regards to the research. I have talked with them."

Victor responded with forced patience: "I encourage exploration, Mayor. And understand this—every member of the Society holds equal value. No one's Abilities diminish our strength—we are made stronger."

"Yes, sir," the mayor said hesitantly.

"Your reports will reflect factual data, not pretentious snobbery," Victor said sharply. "Phone off."

The light on the phone went off. Victor walked around his desk. He held out a hand and his coat came floating to him from across the room in a rush. He grasped it.

The door opened as he approached it.

Walking the second floor mezzanine, he "spoke" in *thought talk* to his wife, his words reaching out to her mind-to-mind.

"Dianna, I am more than ready for lunch. How about you?"

His wife's voice came to his mind as he reached the stairs.

"I'll be ready before you get downstairs," she said.

"On my way."

Chapter Six

Jennifer was sitting on the couch in the Apartment, reviewing the data on Victor Broderick with Computer. She was not unfamiliar with the information, but had not been around it much over the last few years.

There was a photograph of Victor on the display wall. Beside the photograph was a data window filled with text describing his Family.

Computer was providing details.

"Victor Broderick. Born 1878, Boston Massachusetts. Current residence, Boulder Colorado. He is the third Father of the Society, taking the position twenty-eight years ago upon the death of Albert Broderick, who was in turn the protégé of Jonas Westerman, the First Father and one of the three brothers who founded the Society three hundred and sixteen years ago."

The photograph on the display wall changed to one of Dianna Broderick.

"Dianna Broderick is Victor Broderick's second wife," Computer continued. "They have been married twelve years. Victor has three grown children from his first marriage and two young children from this, his second. All are Society, with his two youngest children only recently showing signs and subsequently gaining membership."

The display changed again, now showed two photographs: one of Robby and one of Thomas.

"There had been some concern," said Computer, "as both Robby and Thomas were late in showing sign."

"What are their Abilities?" asked Jennifer.

"I have yet to access information regarding the nature of their Abilities."

"Victor has four," recalled Jennifer. "How many does Dianna have?"

"Dianna Broderick has two—thought talk and telekinesis, both at high levels."

Jennifer nodded slowly, her mind drifting. Possessing two of the six Abilities was fairly common among Society members. Victor having four was rare; possessing four at high levels was very rare.

"Victor's grown children… if I remember right, they're not that much older than I am."

Three photographs appeared on the display, one at a time, each making way for the next until they were all showing side by side.

"Vincent, Carl and Anna," said Computer. "All are in their thirties."

"Which means Victor waited quite a while before having children."

The displayed changed again, this time to a candid photograph of Victor and an unidentified woman walking on a beach. By their apparel and the look of the photograph, the era was dated to nineteen twenties.

"By traditional standards, yes," said Computer. "However, many Society members choose to wait. As you may recall, Jennifer, no Society member can live under the same roof with an outsider, not even if that outsider is the Member's child. Until that child shows sign and also becomes a member, it must live elsewhere, and remain unaware of the existence of the Society."

"Or… the family can be Grey Caste," said Jennifer.

Matthew climbed off the access ladder and entered the Apartment as Computer and Jennifer continued their conversation. He quietly went into the kitchen.

"That is true," said Computer. "A special status was created approximately twenty years ago that allow Society members to live with non-Society, but only under special circumstances and under very severe restrictions. Such level of Society membership is known as Grey Caste."

"How many Grey Caste are there?" asked Jennifer.

"I do not have the most current information," said Computer. "I will begin the research and attempt to extrapolate an approximate number for you. I am afraid there is a high probability that I will not be able to acquire an exact figure."

"Don't sweat it. Cancel that research; it isn't important."

Matthew came up behind the couch, a can of iced tea in hand.

"Society population, twelve thousand, of which fewer than two hundred are Grey Caste at any one time," he said matter-of-factly. He opened his can of iced tea with a loud pop.

"Geez, Dad." Jennifer jumped, startled. "Where'd you come from?"

Matthew climbed up onto the back of the couch and sat with his feet on the cushions.

"History lesson?"

"All morning. I thought it was time for a review." She settled back. "You hang out with a scary bunch of folks."

"You can't choose your family."

There was an awkward pause, after which Matthew slid down and sat beside Jennifer. She laid her head back.

"Even growing up with this, it all seems way too bizarre. I can study the story of the Society from its very beginnings, and I can make myself believe that it all makes sense.

But when I climb up that ladder and go back into the real world, none of it makes sense. None of it seems right. None of it…
belongs. We don't belong; up there or down here."

The display showed another photograph of Victor.

"Like it or not, we were born of the Society," said Matthew. "Whether Victor Broderick likes it or not."

"Not," Jennifer stated.

"The Sutherland family was, and is, one of the seventeen Primary Families of the Society." Matthew fell into a calm melancholy. "Whether we like it or not, you and I have to somehow live in both worlds."

After a moment of appropriate silence, Computer spoke up.

"Eleven thousand, three hundred and fifty five."

Matthew glanced up. "What?"

"Society population is eleven thousand, three hundred and fifty five, of which three thousand, two hundred are of the Primary families, the remainder are of the Lesser Families."

"Have you been sulking?" asked Matthew.

"I do not sulk. Your figure of twelve thousand was imprecise."

"I do worry about you."

"There is no need," said Computer. "I continually monitor the status of all my components and perform scheduled diagnostics. Any deviations are corrected and any requiring human interactions are always reported to you in a timely manner."

"Now you're being deliberately obtuse," said Matthew.

Chapter Seven

Victor helped Robby and Thomas out of the large sedan while looking with satisfaction at the grounds and stately buildings of the Academy. They walked from the car and onto the grounds proper, followed the walkway that would take them beneath the great oak tree in the center of the grounds.

"The Academy is a wonderful old institution," Victor said to his children. "While you have attained society membership, all members must complete their instruction here prior to attaining full rights."

He indicated a new building off to their right.

"That building over there is the dormitory," he said. "For many, it is easier to stay here on the campus while attending.

You of course will be coming home to your mother and me each afternoon."

They passed beneath the tree. Victor saw Mary sitting high up in the branches. He spoke to her using thought talk, mind to mind.

"Good morning, Mary."

There was no immediate response. However, as they continued on toward the Academy main building, her words brushed his mind:

"Good morning."

Victor and his children continued to the administration building, climbed the steps and entered the foyer.

The security guard, a large, broad-shouldered man, was sitting behind a desk. He watched the new arrivals approach.

"Good morning, Father," he said. "The Headmaster is expecting you."

"Thank you, Jim," said Victor.

Victor led his children down the hall. They passed through the outer vestibule and into the Headmaster's office. The Headmaster stood behind his desk, gave a deep nod and waved a hand for Victor and his children to be seated.

"Good morning, Father," said the Headmaster.

"Good morning, Headmaster." Victor sat down, watched his children take their seats. He turned again to the Headmaster. "I saw Mary outside."

"In the tree again?" Headmaster said aloud, continued then in thought talk, mind to mind. "You saw my report?"

"I agree with your assessment," Victor answered in thought talk.

He looked to his children, again to Headmaster, spoke aloud.

"You remember Robby and Thomas?" he asked. "They are very excited about getting started."

"We've talked many times." Headmaster smiled at the children. "So, you are looking forward to beginning your classes, then?"

The children gave obligatory nods and Headmaster turned his attention back to Victor.

"They will do very well here, Father. They are quite bright and very talented."

Headmaster placed his forearms on his desk and his expression grew fixed. He and Victor spoke now in thought talk.

"You've read the details on Mary's signs?"

"I am quite pleased by the reports," Victor sent back.

"You are not concerned?"

"Concerned? Not at all. She may well be everything we hoped for."

"And then some."

"All the better."

"I of course bow to your judgment, Father."

The boys looked first to Victor, then to Headmaster, then back again. They knew there was a conversation going on that they weren't witness to.

Victor looked side-glance at them. He gave them a wink, then spoke aloud to Headmaster.

"Continue to voice your concerns, Headmaster. And by all means, proceed with due caution. Do not, however, attempt to inhibit her growth in any way."

He looked again to the children, smiled broadly.

"I am quite proud of my children. I have no doubts regarding their success at the Academy."

"You may leave them in my care, Father."

"Yes. Yes, of course." Victor showed no indications of leaving.

Headmaster smiled patiently.

"They will be waiting for you when you return for them this afternoon," he said.

"Yes."

It took another few moments for Victor to stand. Headmaster stood then, his expression sympathetic.

"No easier the second time around, is it?" he asked.

"Was I as anxious with the other children?"

"I had quite the time getting you to leave," said the Headmaster.

"Well… I'll not cause a scene this time around." He knelt before the children and spoke warmly to them. "I'll be back this afternoon. And don't forget… the most important thing is to enjoy yourselves. You pay attention to what you are told, and do your best; but do not forget to have fun."

He stood again and looked back to the Headmaster.

"Until this afternoon."

Headmaster watched Victor leave the room, then smiled comfortingly at the children, sitting patiently in their chairs. He sensed both anxiety and anticipation from them.

Good.

Victor came out onto the front steps of the Academy main building. He stopped to admire the view and take in the moment. The sun was shining, the air was fresh and clear. He heard the sound of children laughing somewhere in the distance.

He looked over at the large tree in which he had seen Mary, then took the steps and starting along the walk toward the tree.

He reached out to Mary in thought talk while still some distance from the tree.

"Mary?"

There was no response. As he came nearer, he could see that she was still in the branches.

"Good morning to you again, Mary," he sent to her.

He was within a few steps of the tree.

"Good morning, Father," she sent to him, mind-to-mind.

Victor passed under the tree, continued walking.

"And how are you doing?" he asked her. "Are you enjoying your time here?"

"I have no complaints."

"I am very glad to hear that." Victor was getting near his car. "Shouldn't you be in class?"

"I am in class."

"I see," said Victor. "I do like your classroom. But I recall that mornings are usually devoted to more traditional activity; reading, writing, arithmetic."

"I am special."

Victor smiled to himself, though he suspected she could sense that. He reached his car. There was a moment of silence.

"Father… would you like me to keep an eye on your children?"

"Thank you, Mary. I would be honored."

There was a pallet of bricks sitting on the walkway. Matthew was on his knees in front of a partially completed retaining wall that bordered the walk and enclosed a raised flowerbed.

It was another nice day, but there were clouds on the horizon.

Sam came up with a wheelbarrow load of prepared mortar mix. Matthew looked in the wheelbarrow, pushed a trowel into the mixture.

"It looks good, Sam."

"You really ought to get a mixer," said Sam.

Matthew gave Sam a devilish grin, turned back to his work without responding.

"Yeah, yeah… I know," Sam sighed. "You already have one."

"It's good for you," said Matthew.

Jennifer came down the walkway from the direction of the front of the house. Sam turned his attention to her. Seeing Sam's distraction, Matthew turned his head enough to see his daughter coming.

He gave a knowing glance to Sam, returned to his work.

Jennifer looked vaguely perturbed at Sam's presence.

"Hello, Sam."

"Hi, Jen." Sam indicated their work. "What do you think?"

"Not bad." She looked to her father then. "Are you going to run it all the way down the walk?"

"I'll enclose this bed." He used the trowel to point to the other side of the walkway.

"Can't make up my mind about the other side, though."

Sam spoke up: "I told him he should do the same to both sides of the walk."

Jennifer studied the walkway, trying to give her father's dilemma the attention it deserved.

"Yeah, well, you know my dad," she said. "Once he's built, planted or grown something, why do it again?" She indicated the grounds all about them. "These grounds are testimony to his 'now let's try it this way' philosophy."

"I like it here," said Sam.

"I know." Jennifer folded her arms across her chest, turned her attention back to her father. "How much longer are you going to be, Dad?"

Matthew didn't miss a beat, continued working.

"Something up?" he asked.

"Nothing that can't wait a few minutes." She glanced up, away, to the house. "Some info has come in on one of the projects we've been working on."

"Right. Let me get through this last batch of mortar. I'll be in once we get things cleaned up."

Sam took a look at the approaching clouds. They looked dark.

"We should cover this wall in plastic, Mr. Sutherland. It looks like it might rain later."

"Good man, Sam," said Matthew. "See what you can find in the shed."

Sam hesitated. He knew that Jennifer would be gone when he got back.

She made it easy for him by turning and returning to the front of the house. At that, Sam headed to the shed in the yard at the back of the house.

Matthew looked to his left and then his right at the receding figures of Sam and Jennifer. He allowed himself a chuckle, as if he had somehow done something.

Chapter Eight

Matthew stepped off the ladder, walked across the Apartment and stood beside Jennifer, before the wall display.

"Computer has more info on Andover," said Jennifer.

"Give it to me, Computer," said Matthew.

"Please specify, Matthew."

Matthew rubbed his forehead, his temple.

"You know what I'm asking, Computer. It's not like you weren't listening."

There was a long, awkward silence. Matthew waited for Computer to begin the review, Jennifer watched Matthew grow more impatient, and Computer stubbornly waited for Matthew to be more specific.

Matthew finally surrendered.

"Computer. Jennifer tells me that you have more information regarding the

Andover situation. When you have a
moment, will you fill us in?"

"It is one of my functions, Matthew."

"It certainly is."

The display wall before them lit up with a
photograph of Carlson, the mayor of
Andover. The picture moved to one side,
making room for a data window of text.

The display lasted for several seconds,
after which the photo and text disappeared,
to be replaced with a photograph of Robert
Addison, which slid to one side, making
room for its data window of text.

Computer spoke as these and then
additional displays came and went.

"The fabricated pasts of the Society
members in Andover are quite thorough.
There are completed life histories for each
of them."

"I'm sure that didn't slow you down
much," said Matthew. "You've ID'd them?"

"All have been identified."

"Good work."

"Thank you, Matthew," said Computer.
"Each new arrival in Andover coincided

with the disappearance of a Society member elsewhere, sometimes to within several weeks."

"Then it should have been fairly easy for you, shouldn't it?"

"Once my research made a connection between the disappearance in one location and an appearance in Andover, it was not difficult to make a positive match."

Matthew looked side glance to Jennifer.

"Computer keeps track of as many Members as he can, but it's impossible to always know where every individual is at any given moment. When one drops out of sight and doesn't surface again…" he leaned near his daughter and whispered, "… it drives him a little batty."

Matthew was sitting on the couch, looking up at the wall display. It was showing a photograph of the street intersection in Andover that made up the downtown.

Jennifer was standing behind the couch, leaning back against it, facing away from the display.

"It will be just a quick trip," said Matthew.

"To do what?" asked Jennifer. She folded her arms, stared down at her feet. "We still don't have any idea what it's all about."

"Exactly."

Jennifer shook her head, pushed off the couch, turned around and climbed onto the back of the couch.

"Then what good will it do? Dad, we need to get more info before we start poking our noses around up there."

"I gotta see what the fuss is about."

"Then I'll go with you."

"It's a simple recon." Matthew shifted on the couch to face Jennifer. "I'll be in and out of there in a day. Better if you're here to keep Computer from getting lazy. You said yourself—we need more info. You stay here and keep digging."

"Am I in the Family Business or not?"

"Up to your armpits. Don't you worry. There will be ample opportunity for you to risk your neck. First Recon is a one-person job. This time out, that's me."

Jennifer frowned, slid down from the back of the couch to the seat.

"Yeah, well, I don't like it."
"Neither did your mother."

Chapter Nine

Matthew guided his pickup alongside the pumps at the Andover Quickstop, stopped and turned off the engine. He climbed out and moved to the pump. He took in the community as he filled the tank.

The downtown area consisted of a handful of retail storefronts and a long building housing the town hall, police station, mayor's office and volunteer fire house.

The scene was a strange mix of the normal and the surreal, everyday sights and sounds filtered through an ethereal haze.

A police car pulled up along the other side of the pumps and the police chief climbed out and began pumping gas. He glanced warily at Matthew. There was a visible air of barely suppressed enmity in the way he looked at this stranger to his town.

The gas nozzle clicked off. Matthew returned it to the pump, put the gas cap back on, and walked to the open door of the store.

A young woman stood behind the counter near the register. Matthew got in line behind two men and a woman. The two men stepped up to the counter together.

"Hey, Meg," said one. "Give me the chicken and Jo-Jos."

"Me too," said the other. They were on a lunch break from the mill.

"You got it." Meg moved to one side to put together the baskets.

The first man leaned a hip against the counter and frowned.

"Man, I don't wanna go back in there today."

"What do you got to whine about, Carl?" said the second. "All you do is sit up there and bitch all day. You don't do a damn thing."

"Yeah? Like you got it so tough."

"I'm not the one doin' the whining."

"Yeah?" Carl tried to hide a grin. "How 'bout I kick your ass? We'll see some whining, then."

"Don't tire yourself."

Meg brought the two baskets over, started to ring up the totals. Carl put a bill on the counter.

"I got 'em, Meg," he said.

"Thank you, Carl." She picked up the money, opened the register and put the bill into the slot.

The police chief came into the store, stood in line behind Matthew. There was a sudden, definite change in the air; a heavy silence, though no one outwardly acted any differently.

Carl and his buddy picked up their lunch baskets and started toward the door.

"I say we grab a coupla' beers to go with these and head in the opposite direction," said Carl.

"Sounds great," the other said doubtfully. "And do what?"

"Anything. Anything we want."

"Yeah… you gotta give me more than that."

Outside, they started across the parking lot and in the direction of the mill.

The line at the counter moved forward and the woman put her few things on the counter.

"Is this it for you, Angie?" asked Meg.

"All for today, Meg."

Meg rang up the items and began putting them into a bag.

"Nine forty," she said.

Angela handed Meg a ten dollar bill. Meg looked past Angela and Matthew to the police chief as she gave Angela her change. Angela smiled uncomfortably as she quickly gathered her things.

"Thank you," she said. She started toward the door.

Matthew moved up to the counter, pulled his wallet out and held it ready. The police chief was close behind him.

"Welcome to Andover," said Meg. She seemed distracted.

"Thank you," said Matthew. "Pump one."

"Anything else?"

"Just the gas, thanks."

"Eighteen even," said Meg, not looking at the pump register.

Matthew pulled out eighteen dollars. Handing it to Meg, he glanced back over his shoulder. The police chief stood silent, looking directly at him.

Matthew turned back to Meg.

"Where's a good place for a sit-down lunch?" he asked.

There was a long moment of heavy quiet when nothing appeared to happen.

"Sally's," Meg said at last. "Right around the corner."

"Thank you." Matthew moved away from the counter.

"Sure thing. Come again."

Matthew started away from the counter, hesitated as he reached the door. Looking back into the store, the police chief hadn't moved to the counter, was watching him. Meg, her hands resting on the counter, managed a smile in Matthew's direction.

"Thanks, Meg," said Matthew. "I'll do that."

Matthew turned the pickup into an available parking space in front of Sally's Café, a low structure with a flat roof, a wall of windows with the front door at one end of the building. He took a leisurely look around before slowly walking to the door.

The café was two-thirds full. Jan, the waitress, approached and directed Matthew to an open booth.

Robert Addison and his wife Linda were in the booth next to his. Robert watched Jan fill the stranger's water glass and take his order.

"Carlson's right," Robert said in thought talk. "It's him."

"Probably," Linda sent back, mind-to-mind.

"It's him," Robert returned. "Did you see the way he took in the room? He picked out every Member here, almost instantly. Who else could do that?"

Daniel and Emma Chandler came into the café. Robert watched as Matthew quickly took in the Chandlers, then appeared to ignore them.

"Daniel! Emma!" Jan said, coming up to them. She called back in the direction of the kitchen. "Sally! Come out here!"

Sally, a middle-aged woman dressed in black slacks and a brightly colored blouse, came out from the back to greet them. Robert divided his attention between Matthew sitting in his booth and Sally greeting the Chandlers.

"Did you see how he reacted to the Chandlers coming in?" Robert sent to his wife.

"No, I'm sorry. Not really," Linda said aloud, in a low voice.

Matthew was absently watching Sally talking with the Chandler's at their booth when Jan came with Matthew's lunch of burger, fries and iced tea. While not overly friendly, Jan was polite enough.

"Will there be anything else?" she asked.

"Not just now. Thanks."

"Enjoy your lunch, hon," she said, starting away.

Matthew took a bite of his hamburger, munched on a couple of fries. He took his time. As he ate, he listened.

In addition to the normal sounds of people at lunch, there was something else; an undercurrent of sound. There was a noise, a hissing sound of thoughts and words, all just under the surface. Matthew was able to snatch a word here and there.

He casually glanced at the Addisons in the next booth. He caught Robert glaring at him before he slowly turned away.

Matthew continued eating, observing... and listening.

§

Robert turned his head, slowly, until he was looking directly at Matthew. He reached down and took hold of Linda's hand. She looked at him, then looked around the room.

There were occasional bursts of static in the background. The subvocal whispers grew suddenly louder… then stopped.

Robert continued looking at Matthew. He watched Matthew slowly put down his hamburger and take a drink of his iced tea.

There were several sudden, flashing images of Matthew's past, pictures of Matthew Sutherland: with his daughter, with Computer, with his vehicles, with Sam; with Sharon, his wife.

Sudden, rushing close-up of Matthew's face Present Time; a barely perceptible movement of his eyes. At that instant, Robert was visibly thrown back into his seat.

Linda and several others turned quickly and looked at Robert; Robert sat stunned.

"Did you see that?" He asked aloud, a harsh whisper. "Did you feel that? He did that on his own!"

Matthew calmly finished his hamburger.

The subvocal hissing whispers continued to intensify. Matthew caught quick words of violence among the static.

He finished his French fries, took another drink from his iced tea.

He caught then, very clearly, Robert saying subvocally: "We should kill him now."

Matthew calmly took another drink from his iced tea.

Chapter Ten

Jennifer came from the back of the main house, turning off lights along the way. Coming into the foyer, she made sure the front door was locked. She glanced out the window before heading down the hall toward the door to the basement.

She worked her way down to the Apartment. The room was quiet but for the faint hum of the computer equipment.

"Any word, Computer?"

"Your father left Andover thirty five minutes ago," said Computer. "He should be checking into the hotel in Olympia within the hour."

Jennifer slid onto the couch, pulled her feet up and wrapped her arms comfortably around her legs.

"Why didn't you tell me?"

"I am not permitted to communicate with you while you are upstairs unless there is an emergency or I am specifically directed to do so. I monitor the grounds for intrusion or other danger, but am programmed to disregard all personal—"

"Stop," Jennifer cut him off. "Ya' know, I think there's a lot more going on in those vacuum tubes of yours than you let on."

"As you are well aware, Jennifer, vacuum tubes have not been used in the manufacture of compu—"

"I know that."

There was a long pause. Both were silent.

"And you know that I know that," said Jennifer. Another pause. "Computer?"

"Yes, Jennifer?"

"You always know the right thing to say."

"It is the way Matthew programmed me."

"Sure." Jennifer smiled nostalgically. "You and I have both done some growing since then."

"Yes, Jennifer," Computer stated matter-of-factly. Several moments later then: "Upon his departure from Andover, Matthew stated that all went well. He will be making a full report once he checks into his room."

"Anything else?"

"He asked how you were."

"You can tell him that I'm all alone in a hole in the ground, getting ready to eat leftovers."

"Sensors indicate that Matthew is no longer in the vehicle. I will attempt to deliver your message when—"

"Stop toying with me."

"Jennifer, I—"

"He's out of the pickup?"

"The sensor indicates that no one is in the vehicle."

"How long ago?"

"I cancelled constant monitoring of that sensor once Matthew left the Andover community, whereupon I returned to intermittent check mode," said Computer. "I sought current sensor status immediately prior to attempting to deliver your message."

"Then he must be—"

"Excuse me, Jennifer. Matthew's John Marshall credit card has just been used to register into the hotel."

Jennifer let out a sigh of relief. Computer continued.

"John Marshall is the identity selected to indicate that all is well and that there is no duress."

"I need something to eat," said Jennifer.

She stood and went to the kitchen. Opening the refrigerator, she brought out a bowl of leftovers, shook her head in bewilderment.

"If there hadn't been computers, Dad would have had to invent them," she said. "There's no way he could have played these games without you to keep track of all this crap."

Computer responded calmly and without emotion, as always.

"I keep your father alive."

Jennifer was numbed by the statement. She stood before the microwave, bowl in hand.

The silence hung heavy in the air.

"Matthew has made Internet contact," said Computer. "Report begins."

The hotel room was clean, comfortable, but nothing special. Matthew was sitting at the desk. The report finished, he turned off his laptop. He stared at the darkening display a moment, then slid the chair back and stood up.

He walked across the room, leaned a shoulder tiredly against the wall beside the draped window; he looked absently back into the room; something was brushing at his mind; something nearby... something... bad.

Outside, the night was dark, wet. Across the narrow parking lot, Robert Addison was sitting on the hood of a car. He appeared calm, his feet on the bumper, elbows on his knees and hands clasped.

§

Victor's home office was lit only by a single lamp. Victor was sitting at his desk, a photograph in his hand. It showed Matthew Sutherland standing in line at the counter in the Andover Quickstop.

He tossed the picture onto the desk. He rubbed his face with his hands, turned his chair until he was facing the dark window.

"Damn," he grumbled.

Dianna was standing in the doorway, little more than a silhouette.

"What does he know?" she asked.

"Enough." Victor turned about in his chair and pulled the photograph to him. He stared at it, frowning. He pushed it aside again. "His way of letting us know that he's onto us. But it was recon. He knows we're up to something, but not what or why."

"Victor…" She moved into the room.

"Damn him."

"This project is too important to let Matthew—"

"Yes, yes," Victor said irritably. He turned away from Dianna. "As Father, my first duty is to protect the Society. My second duty is to the prosperity of the members of the Society." He turned back. "By inference, my third duty is to ensure the survival of the Andover project."

"He has left you with no alternative."

"For decades, he has been little more than a thorn in my side, never really a serious threat. Lately…"

"If only—"

"Yes," said Victor. "When Sharon…"

"What else could we do?"

"I know. And now…" Victor rested his head against the back of the chair. "That damnable computer creation of his. If anything happens to him or his daughter, everything they know about the Society will be sent out to dozens of news organizations around the world."

"So, what do we do, Victor?"

"As you said, we have no choice. And the longer we delay, the more difficult it will be. It's obvious that his daughter is being groomed to join the family business." He let out a tired sigh. "How did we come to this?"

"You can't blame yourself, my love," said Dianna. "You have done everything possible to avoid what Matthew has made inevitable."

Chapter Eleven

The Andover Elementary School was little more than a handful of administration offices, a row of classrooms, and the auditorium, which also served as cafeteria and school gym.

There were eight cars in the small parking lot. To the east, the horizon was just beginning to turn a predawn pink.

A ninth car pulled into the lot. Daniel Chandler and his wife Emma got out, walked across the lot and approached the front doors.

The police chief stood in the foyer. The Chandlers said nothing as they passed him.

There were several dozen people in the auditorium, gathered in groups of three and four. Some were talking aloud, others subvocally using thought talk.

The mayor was in deep conversation with Linda Addison, Meg and Angela. Linda looked anxious, yet excited. When the mayor saw the Chandlers enter the auditorium, he waved them over to join them.

"Welcome," he said, shaking Daniel's hand.

"Good evening, Mayor," said Daniel.

"Hello, Tom," said Emma.

Daniel quickly scanned the room, looked briefly at each of those gathered. He turned again to the mayor, spoke to the entire group.

"I'm glad to see that Victor has finally decided to put an end to the Sutherland problem."

Meg and Angela bristled at the comment. The mayor, however, maintained his vague political face.

"It had to have been a difficult decision for Father to make, Dan."

"Quite," Emma agreed. "Everyone knows how close Victor and Matthew once were."

"Everyone also knows the threat that he poses to the Society," said Daniel.

Linda Addison pushed aside her anxiety.

"He shall be dealt with tonight," she said.

"We all hope so," said Daniel.

"No time for doubts, my friend," said Mayor Carlson.

"Matthew Sutherland is not a threat to be dealt with lightly."

"We were recently witness to that," agreed Emma.

Linda gave a sharp, sure nod.

"We will not be caught unawares again, Emma," she said.

Emma gave Linda a faint smile, spoke with a barely hidden patronizing tone.

"Of course not," she said.

"Robert is not totally without his own strengths," said Linda. "With mine to support him, and through me all of yours, Matthew Sutherland will not be a problem."

Meg stepped into the conversation for the first time.

"What about that AI of his?" she asked.

The mayor responded with an air of authority.

"The Father will make contact with it the moment Matthew has been dealt with. A truce will be offered—Jennifer will remain unharmed so long as the computer does not release Society information."

Daniel nodded agreement, "Victor is certain that Matthew has made his daughter's safety the computer's number one directive."

"Once the truce is made," said the mayor, "we will have all the time we need to complete the Andover project and find a way to deal with Jennifer Sutherland and the threat the Sutherland computer holds over us."

The police chief came into the auditorium then, ceremoniously closed the doors behind him. It took several moments for the room to grow quiet, during which time everyone in the room grew introspective.

Linda Addison wound her way through the people and into the middle of the room. The others in the room began to drift toward her. She calmly and unhurriedly turned about in a circle and stopped. She moved her feet apart, held her arms slightly out, palms out.

She closed her eyes…

Robert Addison slid off the hood, stood beside his car. He looked over the hood to the hotel, the outside room doors even spaced, alternating with large, draped windows. Behind him, a wall of trees bordered the parking lot.

He took a long, deep breath.

In the Andover Elementary auditorium, Linda smiled. She breathed deep, moved her arms further away from her body.

She made contact.

Eight people in the auditorium formed a circle around her. Holding their arms out, their hands just touched. As others in the auditorium began closing in around the circle, the eight laid their heads back and closed their eyes.

In the hotel parking lot, Robert Addison took in strength, swallowed energy.

§

An old neighborhood in Andover, just before dawn; it was wet outside.

A middle-aged woman came out onto her porch. Next door, another stepped outside, onto her porch.

Half a dozen homes, half a century old… neighbors came out onto their porches. They looked up into the predawn sky. They spread their arms, hands, palms out.

They closed their eyes…

In the auditorium, those outside the circle of eight had formed a larger outer circle.

In the parking lot, Robert Addison moved away from the car.

Matthew stood in the middle of his hotel room. The only light was that leaking in from around the sides of the drapes, sending shadows across Matthew's face and frame.

He gave a glance to his laptop, which was still sitting on the desk across the room.

With the casual flick of two of his fingers, the display shattered and whorls of smoke came up through the keys.

He went to the door, opened it and stepped outside.

Arms loose at his sides, he twitched a finger. The door closed behind him.

There were seven vehicles in the lot, including his pickup. The predawn air was wet, the asphalt and cars shimmering with the damp.

Robert Addison was standing near the treeline bordering the parking lot.

Matthew took a step from the porch of his hotel room.

Suddenly then the parking lot, the hotel, the surrounding world... all spun dizzily... all went fuzzy...

The world cleared then, refocused; the hotel, the parking lot.

Robert Addison was looking down the treeline... to where Matthew now stood, some forty feet away.

They eyed each other, studied each other...

Robert twitched a hand, almost imperceptibly. The large tree beside him ripped from the soil, uprooted, and was tossed toward Matthew.

With a tilt of the head, Matthew shattered the tree in midair. A thousand large splinters rained onto the parking lot.

Five of the largest splinters lifted up from the asphalt and rushed at Matthew.

He casually lifted a hand. The wood exploded into a cloud of powder in front of him.

He tilted his head, twitched. Six medium sized trees, still standing upright, rushed toward Robert, surrounded him, closed in tightly around him.

Robert flicked two fingers. The trees exploded into thick chunks of sawdust, leaving Robert standing unharmed in the dusty cloud.

In the elementary school auditorium, Linda was standing inside the circle of eight, the larger circle beyond. Her hair was limp, her skin shiny and pasty. Her arms trembled slightly.

On the porches of the old neighborhood, men and women stood unmoving, arms out, hands out, heads back with eyes closed; faces pasty, hair hanging damp.

Robert turned his head, looked back to his car. He spun his head back then. The car lifted off the ground, turned on its side and rushed at Matthew.

Matthew looked at the car and the metal of the vehicle was crushed in midair. The car spun about and rushed back toward Robert.

Robert swung his arm and the car was flung back into the parking lot, crashing down onto its wheels.

Matthew took the moment to look sharply at Robert. Robert was pushed violently back, as if from a blow. He stumbled but remained standing.

§

In the auditorium, Linda's eyes opened wide and she sucked in a throaty breath.

On a porch in the old neighborhood, a middle-aged woman fell to her knees, clutched at her chest. She reached out to the porch rail, her face taut with surprise and pain.

In the auditorium, tears ran down Linda's cheek.

She was suddenly afraid.

Matthew took a step nearer Robert, then another. He ignored the trees and cars. He focused on Robert.

Robert cried out in pain. He twisted in distress. He tried to fight back, but Matthew easily tossed the attempts aside. Matthew took another step, and another, moved methodically closer to Robert. Robert shuddered at every slight twitch or flick from Matthew.

Robert fell to his knees.

Matthew took a final step, six feet from Robert. Matthew's expression was calm but determined.

Robert let out a piercing mind scream.

In the elementary school auditorium, Linda fell to her knees and let out her own mind scream. Those around her were thrown violently backward, some stumbling to remain standing, many thrown hard to the hardwood floor.

On the porches of the old neighborhood, neighbors thrown back against the wall fell to their knees, fell forward.

Matthew looked away from Robert Addison's body. He started across the parking lot. The debris that littered the lot moved out of his path as he walked to his pickup. Debris that covered his pickup was thrown clear.

He climbed in behind the wheel.

There was a clear path out of the parking lot.

Victor stood at the window, gray early morning light glowing dully on his face. It streamed past him and into the room, his office in heavy shadow.

He turned to his wife, standing in middle of the room. She held her arms stiffly at her sides, a look of desperation on her face that she tried to hide with a false calm reassurance.

Something bad had happened. They both sensed it, felt it.

Victor set his own expression…

He was Father.

They would overcome whatever was out there.

He turned back to the window, clasped his hands behind his back.

§

Mary was sitting in the wooden chair in the middle of her small room. She was looking in the direction of her window. The curtain was pulled aside, the gray light of early morning streaming in.

While there was a calmness in her expression, there was little emotion visible on her young face

Chapter Twelve

The lights of the Apartment were set to dim, the glow from the rows of active security monitors pushing into the middle of the room. Matthew was sitting at the kitchen counter, his back to the room, absently dunking a tea bag in a cup of hot water.

Jennifer stepped off the access ladder and into the room. She walked across the room and came up behind Matthew. She hugged her father about the shoulders, moved around beside him and climbed onto the empty stool next to him.

"Feeling any better?" she asked.

"I'm fine," said Matthew.

Jennifer nodded slowly, not completely convinced, but decided to let it go.

"Sam came by today," she said. "Looking for you."

Matthew lifted the tea bag out and set it on the saucer.

"He's a good kid," he said.

"Uh, huh."

"What time is it?" He rubbed at his tired eyes.

"About eleven thirty."

"Night?"

"Uh, huh."

"Damn." He turned and slid off the stool.

He reached back, picked up his cup of tea and carried it over to the table. He sat down and leaned back in the chair.

Jennifer followed and sat in the chair opposite. She studied him a moment.

"Well?" she finally asked.

Matthew looked up, looked across the table to his daughter. Their eyes locked and each seemed to be searching out the other. He finally leaned forward, however hesitantly, and set the cup of tea on the table.

"Everyone was watching, Jen," he said. "Everyone. Pushing. I wasn't fighting just Addison. I was fighting the whole town. They were feeding him."

"I've never heard of that," said Jennifer. "I mean, I've heard of linking, but it's always one member supporting another; never a group."

"Me either. A few with the ability to support, like Addison's wife." Matthew frowned. "This was more. She... funneled. Like a conduit. I was facing all of them; from all over Andover."

Jennifer reached out and rested a hand on her father's forearm.

"And you won."

"I don't think we won anything."

"I don't understand."

Matthew leaned back again, spoke into the air.

"Computer," he said. "Update, please."

"Andover population is eighty three percent evacuated," said Computer.

"Current location of evacuees?"

"Unknown."

Matthew turned again to Jennifer.

"They began leaving almost immediately; most likely following a pre-established emergency plan."

"So you won," Jennifer stated again. "Whatever they were planning, it's not happening."

"Delayed, maybe," he said, sighing. "And we don't know what *it* is. We have no idea what their goal was for Andover, or if this funneling had any part in it."

"We know that you have the strength to stand against a whole town."

Matthew shook his head and leaned further forward.

"Nope. That's just one more question," he said. "It shouldn't have been possible. Not even close."

Jennifer had no response to that. She knew that he was right. There was no way her father should have been able to take on an entire town, whatever the inherent strength of his Abilities.

"We can assume the few folks remaining in Andover are not Society," she said, redirecting the conversation. "They have to be confused right about now. And there are going to be a few stories hitting the wires."

"So true."

"We can also assume that Computer will be in Batty Mode for the next few weeks, looking for signs of where our Andover refugees went."

"Also true." Matthew reached out and picked up his tea. He took a sip. It was already getting cold.

He set the cup back on the table, pushed it aside.

"Let's put ourselves in Victor's shoes," said Jennifer. "We may not know the goal they've set for themselves, but we may be able to extrapolate what Victor's next step might be."

"Maybe." Matthew leaned back, fought back a yawn. "But not tonight."

Victor climbed out of his car, looked up into the sunny sky as he gently closed the door. He turned about then and started across the Academy grounds, following the winding concrete walk. He slowed as he reached the great Oak tree, stopped once he was beneath its wide branches.

He stepped up to the gnarly trunk, leaned against the bark.

He spoke aloud, without looking up into canopy.

"You were there," he said.

Mary didn't respond at first.

"I was," she said finally, also speaking aloud.

"Mary…" he started. "Why did you help him?"

"I did very little."

"It was enough."

"Yes," she said. "I had no choice."

"That isn't true," said Victor. "You had a choice. You could have stayed out of it."

Mary said nothing.

"I thought we were friends, Mary."

"The Society must come first, Father."

"Always," said Victor. "Absolutely."

"Everything that happened, had to happen."

"Your Sight is not developed, Mary," said Victor, frowning and shaking his head.

"It is untrained. Taking actions on it now is dangerous."

"I know what I know."

"And what is it that you know?" Victor asked. "Must Matthew live in order for the Society to survive?"

"No."

"Then what? We have been set back months, maybe years. Is that a good thing?"

Mary hesitated.

"What happened, had to happen," she said then, basically repeating what she had said a moment before.

Victor pushed away from the tree and started slowly away.

He spoke to her then in thought talk, mind-to-mind.

"Perhaps the next time you choose to side against us, you can do me the honor of letting me know."

Up in the tree, Mary turned her head and glanced up, glanced away.

"If it serves the Society to do so," she sent, mind-to-mind.

Mary turned her face to the sun, closed her eyes. She let the warmth of the rays soothe her.

The 64 Comet was parked in the small lot of Rydel Ridge. Matthew was sitting on the hood, leaning back on the windshield, eyes closed.

He was taking in the same sun as young Mary.

End Episode One...

Episode 2
Gryphen

Chapter One

The narrow two-lane highway wound through the low mountains, gentle slopes of evergreen and alder bordering the dark gray asphalt. Yellowish-gold rays of sunlight shone through the trees, creating stripes of light and shadow across the road.

The converted school bus rounded a tight curve much faster than it should, straightened from a slight fishtail and continued on. Jennifer was sitting behind the steering wheel, her focus divided between the road ahead and the wide strip of rearview mirror attached to the sun visor above her.

Her father was sitting in a comfortable, upholstered chair some six feet behind her. Matthew appeared calm and matter-of-fact despite what should have been tense circumstances.

There was little of the school bus origins left of the interior of the bus: bench seats had been removed, interior walls were covered in quality, light-colored paneling; the floor was covered in a light-colored deep pile carpet. There were a few small tables and upholstered chairs scattered about; a couple of cupboards and cabinets were set against the walls between or beneath small, dark windows.

Matthew shifted about and looked out the back window: nothing but the tree-lined road behind them.

He tilted his head, closed his eyes. Several long moments passed. His mind reached out. His vision stretched out behind them.

The droning sounds of the vehicle's engine, tires on rolling on asphalt.

"Half a mile," Matthew said calmly, his eyes closed. "Getting closer."

"No doubt, Dad," said Jennifer. "We're a bus."

Matthew opened his eyes then, turned about and looked forward through the front window. Ahead was the county road winding through the hills, a mix of evergreen and deciduous trees blanketed the slopes on their left and right.

"We're not going to make it," he said casually, continuing to study the road and forested terrain. "We need to change the circumstances."

Jennifer glanced again at the rearview mirror: quick view of a vehicle on the road behind them, it disappeared when the bus rounded the next curve.

"We should do that sooner rather than later."

Up ahead, the slope of evergreen trees on their left, bordering the road steepened, pushed up close to the asphalt.

Matthew glanced up at the rearview mirror. The vehicle closing in on them appeared again around the curve. It was drawing nearer.

The bus rounded another curve.

Matthew again tilted his head, closed his eyes. He lifted a hand, held it just in front of him. His hand twitched; two fingers twitched.

Behind them, hidden now beyond the curve, a dozen of the evergreen trees nearest the road shuddered. Suddenly then, they uprooted from the ground, swept down from the slope and down across the roadway directly in front of the approaching car.

The sedan came to an abrupt, fishtailing stop. One of the passengers hurriedly jumped out of the car. He waved his arms as he rushed forward, causing the fallen trees to shudder and begin to slide from the road.

"I bought us a minute at best, Jen," said Matthew. "Make the most of it."

"You got it."

The bus rounded a curve, then another, hurrying along the winding mountain road.

Jennifer came out of apartment's kitchen area with a can of iced tea and a glass of water. She set the can onto the table in front of Matthew, sat down beside him and took a swallow of her water.

"You went out of your way not to hurt them back there, Dad," she said. "You took a chance; it could've gone south on us."

"It worked out." Matthew took a drink from his iced tea. He looked across the room to the large monitor screen mounted on one wall, surrounded by narrow shelves of high-tech equipment. Another wall was filled with shelves of computer equipment, a built-in desk, and the door to the hallway leading to the garage.

He looked back to Jennifer, took another swallow from his tea.

"Hard to track them if they're lined up in hospital beds," he said.

"Equally difficult if it's us lying in those beds," she answered. "Or worse."

"It worked out," he said again. "Computer will keep an eye on 'em."

He spoke to Computer, then, "Right, Computer?'

Computer's almost but not quite human voice came over speakers set inconspicuously yet strategically about the underground apartment.

"I shall advise you of any changes in status regarding this project."

"Thank you, Computer," said Matthew, then gave Jennifer a half-smile.

Jennifer leaned back in her chair.

"But… Dad… Cutler's got Society in his cult?" she asked critically. "And Computer missed that?"

"Kids playing outside after the streetlights come on," said Matthew, dismissively.

"Kids with nuclear weapons."

"They shall be disarmed; and sent to bed without their supper."

"Dad." Jennifer frowned. "You need to take this seriously."

"Oh, I take John Cutler's deranged cult very seriously, Jen. In particular his human followers, as they are true believers. But his Society friends…" Matthew slowly shook his head. "They're there because they are bored."

"And?" Jennifer encouraged.

Matthew nodded curtly, took another long swallow from his iced tea.

"And we'll deal with this one pizza slice at a time," he stated matter-of-factly.

One of the ceiling light panels above them flickered.

"Can't go ten minutes without something," he grumbled. He spoke full-voiced then to the air. "What is it, Computer?"

"Sorry to bother you, Matthew," said Computer. "You have an incoming call."

"Must be important."

"It is Victor Broderick."

At that, Matthew looked over at Jennifer. Jennifer shrugged...

"The distinguished Father of the Society." She took a drink from her water. "I suppose that qualifies as important."

"We shall see." Matthew slid his chair back and stood up. He walked around to stand in front of the couch. He faced the wall monitor.

"All right, Computer," he stated flatly. "Put him on the screen."

The wall monitor flickered to life. Moments later, it displayed Victor Broderick, a man of graying sophistication.

"Victor," Matthew said, guardedly. "You're looking well."

Behind him, Jennifer came from the table and sat on the couch. She was focused on Victor Broderick's image.

"Hello, Matthew," said Victor. He looked to Jennifer. "Jennifer. All grown up. In college, I hear."

"I'm currently on leave of absence," said Jennifer.

"Family obligations, no doubt. If there's anything I can do, please, just let me know."

"Thanks," Jennifer stated flatly.

Victor gave a brief nod of the head. "Of course, my dear."

"Victor," said Matthew. "You've never been one to dance around the important stuff. So, what's up?"

"Yes, well..." Victor pursed his lips, set his jaw. "I would rather not get into it over the phone. It would be better if we met."

"Really. To what purpose?"

"As I said, I would rather not discuss it over the phone."

"Right, right... as you said." Matthew took a moment, considered. "Okay, Victor. Where would you suggest?"

Behind Matthew, Jennifer shifted forward on the couch.

"Dad," she said, obviously concerned.

Matthew ignored his daughter, waited patiently for Victor's response.

"How about the Academy?" asked Victor.

"That would be a bit of a drive for me, Victor. I'll have to cross several states."

"Perhaps, but you haven't visited the Academy since we remodeled the dormitory. I could give you the tour." Victor looked to Jennifer. "And I don't believe Jennifer has ever seen the place. She never took advantage of the school's services."

Matthew hesitated, looked back to Jennifer. She was frowning her darkest frown. He gave a slight, conciliatory smile and looked forward again to the monitor, to Victor's image.

"You'll have to give me time to clear my calendar," he said at last. "And then there are the travel arrangements."

"Of course," Victor stated.

"Computer will be in touch."

"Thank you, Matthew. I look forward to your visit."

Matthew gave a vague nod. "See you then."

Victor gave an acknowledging nod in answer. A moment later, the wall monitor went dark.

Matthew let out a heavy breath, turned then to Jennifer.

Jennifer was not happy.

"What is wrong with you?" she demanded, standing.

"Jen?" he asked, feigning innocence.

"You willingly meet the head wolf… in the wolves den."

Matthew gave a sympathetic smile as he moved to step up beside her, turned about then and sat on the couch. He looked side-glance up at his daughter, still standing.

"Victor knows where we live, Jen; where we go to lunch, where we shop. It isn't hiding from Victor that keeps us safe."

"I know, I know," she droned. She dropped down to sit beside her dad, waved her hand at the apartment in general. "He who watches…"

"Right," said Matthew; a swallow from his can of iced tea. He gave a nod to Computer: a network of wires and circuits and boards hidden within the walls. "Anything happens to either one of us, Computer will let everyone and his grandmother know all about the Society and provide all the necessary particulars."

Jennifer slid back into the couch, smirked as she looked at her water glass. She chose not to take the last swallow.

"Yeah?" she asked. "How's that working for you, Dad? They tried to kill you three weeks ago."

Matthew grew thoughtful.
"I should ask him about that."

Chapter Two

Matthew turned the pickup into the small lot, pulled it into the parking space. He and Jennifer climbed out of the well-cared for 97 Ford. They stepped away and quietly took in the Academy grounds.

The campus included several stately buildings of brick and ivy. The grounds themselves were green lawns and winding walkways. An ancient oak tree hovered over the wide walkway that ran from the parking area to the admin building.

Matthew and Jennifer stepped from the lot and onto the walk, started across the grounds.

The campus was noticeably quiet.

"It feels old," said Jennifer.

"It's almost as old as the Society itself," said Matthew. "It's bound to it; integral."

"I know. Understanding the history doesn't do it justice," said Jennifer. "There's something ominous about it."

"In the end, it's just a school."

"You don't believe that."

Matthew pushed back a smile and let the matter go. They approached and passed under the great oak tree. Matthew glanced up into the branches.

Just branches; there was no sign of Mary.

They continued on toward the administration building. Drawing nearer, the front double-doors opened and Victor Broderick stepped out. He waited at the top of the steps.

To their left, a young girl was sitting on a bench that was set along the walk that ran the length of the building, some thirty feet from the main entrance: Mary.

Mary appeared to be ignoring them.

"I think I'll hang out here, Dad," said Jennifer. "You let me know how it goes. Assuming they don't disappear you."

Matthew noted Jennifer's focus of attention.

"Give Mary my best," he said.

Jennifer gave a final glance up at the man standing at the top of the steps.

"I'll do that." She started toward Mary on the bench. "Say hey to Victor."

Victor descended the steps. He and Matthew shook hands.

"Matthew," said Victor. "Thank you for coming."

"Victor." Matthew indicated his daughter's receding figure. "Jennifer sends her best; says hey."

Victor gave a knowing glance to Jennifer, then turned and started back up the steps.

"We'll let the young ladies get acquainted."

Matthew followed Victor. They crossed the porch and Victor opened the door. He indicated Matthew should enter.

"Please…"

§

Jennifer reached Mary on the bench. She hesitated, looked out across the grounds rather than directly at the young girl.

"Good morning, Mary," she said. "I'm Jennifer Sutherland; Matthew's daughter."

"Yes," Mary said calmly. "Good morning, Jennifer."

There were a few moments' awkward hesitation, then Mary rested a hand on the bench beside her.

"Join me," she stated.

Jennifer stepped back and sat down. She gave Mary an uncomfortable smile. Both looked out across the Academy campus at the lawns and shrubs and walkways.

The Academy headmaster's office was small, cluttered with overstuffed bookshelves, a side-table with a lamp and stacks of papers. A small window was set in the wall behind an old desk with office chair. On the desk was a computer monitor and keyboard. Two guest chairs sat in front of the desk.

Feeble light shone dimly through the frosted glass of the door leading to the outer office. "Headmaster" was stenciled on the glass, reverse image as seen from the office side of the door.

The door opened; Victor stepped through. He moved around the desk as Matthew followed him in and closed the door behind him. He sat in the chair behind the desk, indicated one of the guest chairs for Matthew.

"Headmaster was kind enough to offer us the use of his office," he said. He spoke as he watched Matthew take a seat. "I believe he's meeting with staff regarding the progress of several of our children."

"All good, I trust," said Matthew.

"Quite."

Victor studied Matthew for several long seconds. Matthew said nothing, waited for Victor to let him in on the reason for the get-together.

Victor leaned back in the chair, let out a quiet sigh.

"Matthew," he said. "A bit of a set-to last month."

"Uh, huh."

Another several seconds of silence. Victor's face shifted slightly, his displeasure almost showing through.

"You certainly put a crimp in things."

"You're just saying that," said Matthew, a hint of a smile. "And I'm pretty sure that's not why we're meeting like this."

"No." Victor shifted forward, the chair creaking. He set his forearms on the desk. He studied the man across the desk for a few moments. "You and I have known each other long time, Matthew. We got along well enough. Maybe not friends, but…"

"Close enough to fool anyone looking."

"Quite. And, of course, the Broderick and Sutherland families have a history going back to the founding of the Society."

"I am well aware."

"The Society…" Victor said thoughtfully, "was diminished by the loss of the Sutherland Family."

"I could not in good conscience remain," said Matthew. "You know that."

"I do not. Had you chosen to stay, you could have helped direct the final configuration of the Agenda."

"We both know that is not so." Matthew indicated their surroundings. "The purpose for this… our little get-together."

"Yes. So…" Victor's chair creaked as he leaned back. "Mary."

"The girl?"

"She is quite the young lady."

"I'm sure she is. And?"

In answer, Victor put on a slight, indefinite smile.

"Ah," said Matthew. "You are unsure of your protégé."

Mary appeared distant, lost in thought. She turned slowly then, looked back in the direction of the admin building, to Headmaster's office window. She betrayed no emotion.

She turned forward again, remained silent.

Jennifer looked for a way to broach the subject, finally simply stated her thoughts.

"Mary... Mary, my father believes that he was not alone when he faced the citizens of Andover."

"Matthew Sutherland's death at that time would have not benefited the Society."

"Good news for Matthew Sutherland," said Jennifer.

"It was not about Matthew," stated Mary.

Jennifer turned to look directly at Mary.

Mary looked to Jennifer...

"Matthew Sutherland will become necessary to the Society."

Jennifer wasn't sure how to take that comment. "I understand," she said finally.

"I believe you do," said Mary, again looking forward. She grew increasingly distant.

Jennifer's body language and expression hinted at increasing discomfort.

"Where is this going, Mary?" she asked. "I mean, in the end."

Mary said nothing at first, turned slowly to look again to Jennifer.

"I regret that your objective and mine will not always align."

"I'm not sure I know what my objective is."

"We have growing yet, you and I," said Mary. "With that will come greater insight."

"No doubt," said Jennifer. She watched Mary again shift about to look back at the Administration building, in the direction of the Headmaster's office window.

Matthew came into the apartment from the garage hallway. Jennifer was sitting on the couch, frowning as she studied a screen of text displayed on the wall monitor.

"Computer. Monitor off," said Jennifer. The monitor went blank. She continued to frown at the now blank screen. "How's work going on the bus?" she asked Matthew.

"Good to go." Matthew started toward the kitchen area. "And what are you working on?"

Jennifer gave a dejected sigh.

"I can find nothing. It's as though Mary doesn't exist."

"Yes. Mary." Matthew filled a glass with water, started back in the direction of the couch. "She doesn't. Exist, that is. Society made sure of that."

"They did a good job," said Jennifer.

Matthew sat on the arm of the couch. "Computer thinks so."

Jennifer lifted her leg onto the couch, tucked her foot under her butt. She studied her father.

"Dad. That kid… I felt it. The strength; I mean, wow…"

"Mary is a very powerful, very dangerous little girl," said Matthew. "For the moment at least… supportive."

"That support has nothing to do with any sense of admiration for Matthew Sutherland.

She could as easily crush Sutherland House if she felt that doing so would be to the betterment of the Society."

"Ah, right," said Matthew, nodding. "The uh, '*interest of the Society is all that matters*' line.

"Something like that," said Jennifer.

"Well, whatever her history, she has Victor on his toes."

"His creation, good luck to him."

Matthew grew thoughtful, spoke calmly.

"He needed to know she and I didn't coordinate what happened in Andover; to know that Mary hadn't taken sides with me against him."

"So it seems," said Jennifer. "And?"

"And… that he would ask the question, however veiled, means that he's not fully in control."

"Good."

"That depends, Jen. The devil you know."

"I don't like the devil I know."

"Good point," said Matthew. "And this devil is nervous; always unsettling."

Jennifer slid her feet off the couch, shifted about and turned to look up at her father.

"Okay..." she said thoughtfully. "Andover. Mary. Connection?"

Matthew considered his response.

"Two key points when it comes to Andover," he said. "First. We know that it served as a lab for developing a tool, a methodology, to be incorporated into the Agenda. Second. We were witness to funneling taken to the next level."

"Next level. Right," said Jennifer. "They channeled the entire town against you. A helluva funneling two-point-oh."

"Exactly," said Matthew. "Not something I want to see utilized within the Agenda."

"Nor I." Jennifer gave a knowing nod. "And Mary's role in all this?"

"Mary, once trained, serving as funneler, targeting anyone standing in the way of the Agenda?"

"Okay... better she sit on our side of the table."

"And that, my daughter, is something that Victor will not abide."

The wall monitor activated, as if on its own. Moments later, several images from the Marli Reynolds case displayed: a photograph of Marli, autopsy photos, text document.

Jennifer glanced up at the screen; the images serving as a reminder.

"Ah. Right," she said. "Thank you for the subtle reminder, Computer."

"The Marli Reynolds case?" asked Matthew.

Jennifer gave a single curt nod.

"Murdered teenager, vague ties to the Gryphen House."

"I remember," said Matthew. "Her body was left on the banks of the Sacramento."

"You asked Computer to follow up on his own, to let you know if he came up with anything."

"And so?"

"He came up with something," said Jennifer. "So he said an hour ago."

"Computer?" asked Matthew, glancing up and away.

"Yes, Matthew?"

"Don't start. You're the one gave the nudge. What's up?"

The images on the monitor winked out, moments later were replaced with new images: a snapshot of Mark Gryphen and Marli Reynolds coming out of a restaurant together, another of Mark holding a car door open at a hotel vale station, Marli climbing out of the car. There were several images of receipts.

Computer's voice was clear and precise.

"Significant effort was made to remove all evidence of a relationship between Mark Gryphen and Marli Reynolds."

"Apparently they were not completely successful," said Matthew.

"They were not. I was able to locate a number of records that directly tie Mr. Gryphen to the young lady, including receipts, photographs and videos; several from the week prior to the incident."

"But nothing directly connecting Mark to the murder."

"Nor have I been able to place them together the night of the incident."

"Scrubbing their shared history is awfully suspicious," said Jennifer.

"Yes," said Matthew, frowning. "It is possible that Phillip was attempting to prevent unfavorable attention on the Gryphen family by removing any connection between his innocent son and a murdered girl."

"You don't really believe that."

"No," said Matthew. "Marli was killed by someone with telekinetic ability. That makes it Society, which brings us back to Mark Gryphen."

He spoke then to Computer: "Computer. Anything suggesting a motive?"

"I am afraid not, Matthew."

"No, that would be too easy," Matthew grumbled. He spoke then to no one in particular. "I suppose it's time I have a chat with Phillip. A bit of tit for tat."

"The patriarch of Gryphen House is not one to be trifled with, Matthew," said Computer.

"Oh, of that, you are absolutely right, Computer."

"Dad," said Jennifer. "I know that you and Phillip Gryphen used to be close."

"We respect one another."

"You were friends."

"Our Houses got along well enough, but I wouldn't call us friends," said Matthew. "We were often on the same side in Society affairs, but… let us just say that we are very different people."

Jennifer considered for a moment, then…

"I was young when we left the Society, but I always had the feeling he liked you."

"As may be; that doesn't make him any less dangerous. He is obsessively protective of Gryphen House."

"I never got that," said Jennifer. "What I got was self-assured, aristocratic, maybe overbearing."

"All true, and then some. The thing to remember with Phillip… Gryphen House comes first, the family comes second, the Society third."

"Okay. Good to know," said Jennifer. "Isn't that like the absolute opposite of Victor's views?"

"Sure. And it might explain how Phillip and I were frequently on the same side in Society matters." Matthew frowned. "However, Phillip's objections to the Agenda notwithstanding, and his unwavering devotion to Gryphen House, his commitment to Society remains resolute."

"The fact remains…" Jennifer wondered aloud. "He doesn't approve of the Agenda."

"Should the Agenda be fully realized, the Society will no longer be the Society."

The two grew quiet. Matthew again glanced outward.

"Computer," he stated. "Please contact Phillip Gryphen. Offer my regards, request an opportunity for us to meet."

"Yes, Matthew."

Chapter Three

The Gryphen House grounds were five acres enclosed within a stone wall, accessible via a double wrought-iron gate with twenty four hour security. In the heart of the grounds, near the Gryphen mansion, was a small, high-walled garden of winding walkways and raised beds of flowers and shrubs.

Matthew and Phillip Gryphen casually followed the central walk, working their way in the general direction of a glass-walled conservatory set in the center of the garden. Phillip had a fatherly appearance, was confident in manner, gray hair and gray eyes.

"Your garden has matured since I was last here, Phillip," said Matthew, admiring their surroundings. "All the more beautiful for it. I have always admired your proficiency in the garden."

"It has been much too long, Matthew," said Phillip. "I have missed our exchanges."

Matthew slowed, regarded a flowering shrub, continued on then.

"It is unfortunate that events have led us down divergent paths," he said.

"Your quarrel with the Society does not interest me," Gryphen said dismissively. "That is no reason for us not to get together now and then."

"It was a bit more than a quarrel, Phillip. The fact is, Sutherland House is estranged from the Society."

Gryphen stopped before a thick, green shrub, reached out and cradled a bloom. He spoke matter-of-factly while admiring the flower.

"I do not involve myself in Society politics."

"And yet you keep yourself abreast of all that is going on."

"No more than is absolutely necessary," said Gryphen.

There was an uncomfortable pause, then Matthew's expression darkened.

"They murdered Sharon," he said.

Gryphen stared coolly at the flower in his hand.

"So I was given to understand." He looked up from the flower, looked up the walk. He started forward again. "I don't believe you've seen my new conservatory."

The conservatory was a small, domed structure of glass panels set into a metal framework. The interior was filled with greenery and narrow walks.

Gryphen and Matthew approached a chest-high counter, freshly made of rough wood planks. There was pitcher of juice and several glasses on the counter.

Phillip Gryphen poured juice and handed a glass to Matthew.

"You're A-I's exchange with my assistant was rather cryptic; something about a murdered girl."

"Marli Reynolds," said Matthew.

"Yes." Gryphen took a drink from his juice, stared down at his glass. "I heard of the case, of course. There was a tenuous connection to the family; friend of a friend and all that."

"Come on, Phillip. Your son's wife was Miss Reynolds' cousin. Tenuous is not the word I would use."

"As you say," Gryphen said hesitantly. He looked up from his glass to Matthew. "In any event, I am aware of the case. People in our circumstance must stay alert to potential unwanted attention. You understand."

"I do."

Gryphen took another short sip of his juice, looked up and away, to their green and flowery surroundings, again to his glass of juice.

"A tad bitter," he said. "I must speak to Bedford."

Matthew said nothing, silently observing his host. Gryphen looked to Matthew and gave a faint smile, then indicated their surroundings.

"So… what do you think?" he asked.

Matthew looked about as if examining the conservatory, spoke in a soft sigh.

"Now of course I will have to build one."

"Highly recommend," said Gryphen. "And how are your grounds these days, Matthew?"

"Quite ordinary by comparison."

"Don't be so modest. I've always appreciated your estate. You need to allow me a visit. It's been a while."

"Any time, Phillip." Matthew stared down at his juice, spoke without looking up. "Now. About Mark's involvement in Miss Reynolds' murder."

"Yes," sighed Gryphen. "Beyond Gryphen House itself, I do fear that my son often draws unwelcome attention to the Society."

Matthew hesitated, looked up then from his glass, gave Phillip Gryphen a sympathetic look.

"I'm going to follow this wherever it leads me, Phillip," he said. "I will do whatever needs doing."

"But of course, Matthew." Gryphen looked closely at his guest. "Mark has brought this upon himself, but do not doubt, whatever comes of this, Gryphen House will be protected."

"I understand that. And that is why I am here." Matthew set his glass on the counter. "I wanted to let you know, in person, that my investigation will likely lead to an uncomfortable meeting with your son."

Gryphen considered. He finished off his juice, set his empty glass on the counter beside Matthew's.

"Come," he said. "Let me give you the full tour."

The visit ended, Matthew and Gryphen stood together near Matthew's pickup, which was parked near the wrought-iron main gate of the Gryphen House estate. The silhouette of the security guard passed into and out of view beyond the gate, inside the grounds.

Gryphen took a moment to silently admire Matthew's pickup. He reached out then and shook hands with Matthew.

"You watch yourself, Matthew."

"Always."

"Really…" said Gryphen, clearly dubious. Reflective then, "I've known you for a very long time, and I have seldom known you to be sufficiently cautious."

"Phillip, I'd swear you've been talking to Jennifer."

"A smart girl, that one," said Gryphen.

"It <u>has</u> been a while," said Matthew, raising a brow. "She is quite the grown woman these days. You must drop by."

"That is clearly an invitation. I'll have Bedford arrange something."

They shook hands again, and Gryphen watched Matthew move to the driver's side of the pickup.

"Matthew…" he said.

Matthew held the driver's door open, looked to Gryphen and waited.

Gryphen continued.

"They'll not forgive what happened in Andover. You set the Agenda back months, maybe years."

"Good news," said Matthew. "I could only hope."

"Yes, well," Gryphen stepped nearer. "Some may sympathize, but none are willing to stand beside you. Not yet. Victor's hold on the Society remains strong, and more members support the Agenda than do not."

"And you?" asked Matthew, considering. "Where do you stand?"

"With Gryphen House. Always."

"So I've heard."

"Matthew…" Gryphen said, and then, "Gryphen House will take no action that assists in furthering the goals of the Agenda. That is so. Such would take the Society in exactly the wrong direction."

"But…?"

"Yes," said Gryphen in a long breath. "As I said, Victor maintains a strong hold on the Society. There are grumblings, but they remain muted."

"So, nothing new then." Matthew readied to get into his truck. "Got it."

Gryphen reached out and placed his hands on the door.

"I will do what I can."

Matthew gave a slow nod, then climbed into his pickup and closed the door. Gryphen stepped back and watched Matthew start the pickup. He took another step back, watched the pickup back out of the parking space, back out and onto the road and start away.

He slowly walked to the wrought-iron gate. The security man came into view beyond the gate. He opened the gate, patiently waited for Phillip Gryphen to pass through, then closed the gate and continued his watch.

The apartment was dark but for the many tiny red indicator lights on the computer equipment and a single ceiling light panel that was set to low and spreading a dull glow across the room.

Jennifer climbed down from the access ladder. Ceiling lights activated as she stepped into the room. She started across the room toward the kitchen area.

"Computer. How's Dad?"

"Matthew left Gryphen Estate three hours ago, Jennifer," said Computer. "Most recent sensor readings suggest that he is heading for Rydel Ridge."

Rydel Ridge… one of Matthew's favorite get-away spots.

Jennifer opened the refrigerator, took out a food container and tossed it into the microwave. She pushed the reheat button, went back to the refrigerator and took out the milk.

"Sounds like good news." She filled a glass, returned the milk to the refrigerator. "No doubt ordering pizza to celebrate."

"Not as yet," said Computer. "I am monitoring his accounts."

The microwave went '*ding*'. Jennifer took the food container, the glass of milk and a fork to the table. She sat and opened the container.

"You do that," she said. "Meantime, where are we with the Mary investigation?"

The large wall monitor activated. A moment later, one portion of the screen displayed a window containing a blur of small text, unreadable from this distance.

"There is some as yet unverified data per preliminary research," Computer stated.

Jennifer stood, took the food container and fork with her as she moved unhurriedly several steps nearer the monitor. She stopped behind the couch, furrowed her brow as she studied the text.

"How certain are you of this, Computer?"

"It is preliminary," said Computer. "As I stated."

"Right," Jennifer said absently.

"Further investigation is required."

"Right," said Jennifer. "Do that."

Mary's room was lit only by the lamp on her desk. She was sitting in the high-backed upholstered chair in the corner of the room. The night shown through the one small window.

All was quiet.

She shifted her head slightly then, her mind reaching out…

Focus to: a black sedan in the small parking lot on the academy campus grounds. Dusk had slipped into night. Victor climbed out of the car. He closed the door, started across the grounds toward he dormitory building.

Mary shifted her head again, betrayed no emotion.

She spoke in thought-talk then… "Good evening, Victor."

Victor continued on the walk, nearing the building. He responded to Mary in thought-talk.

"Hello, Mary. How are you this evening?"

"I am fine," said Mary, still in thought-talk. "Are you well?"

"I am. Thank you for asking." Victor approached the steps. "Is it all right if I come up? A brief visit?"

"Of course. You are always welcome."

"Thank you, Mary. That means a lot to me."

Victor climbed the building's front steps. The door opened as he approached.

Focus back to Mary… she shifted her attention to her dorm room door. Moments passed as she waited.

She gave then a twitch of two fingers of her hand; the sound of the door lock clicking. The door slowly eased open.

Mary's attention returned to the center of the room.

Victor appeared in the open doorway; he stepped through, glanced back to the door, then to Mary.

Mary's expression changed only slightly, and the door closed behind Victor. She watched as Victor looked casually about the room, moved to the small desk. He pulled out the desk chair and sat down.

"Mary," he said in open voice. "How go your studies?"

"They go well enough," she answered, also in open voice. "Do you not know that?"

Victor managed a thin smile.

"Yes. I do," he said. "Headmaster tells me that you are in fact doing very well."

Mary watched and waited.

Victor continued then...

"All six Abilities. Quite impressive. Your progress with several has been very impressive indeed."

"Thank you," she said flatly.

"I follow Headmaster's regular reports with great interest."

Mary tilted her head, let her mind reach out as she looked calmly at Victor.

Victor felt it. He furrowed his brow. He slowly lifted a hand, gently rested two fingers against his temple. A moment later, he brushed his hand away, pushing back, pushing aside Mary's reach. His faint smile returned.

Mary gave a curious look.

"You have concern that you won't be able to control me," she said.

"Telepathy," he observed. "With training, you will be able to reach in surreptitiously."

Mary ignored the observation. "Your concern grows," she said.

Victor grew more thoughtful, his words more considered.

"It does. Headmaster has the same concern." He shifted in his chair. "And that is why I am here."

"Yes?"

"Should we be concerned, Mary?"

"Do you intend to control me?" she asked, her tone without emotion.

"Insofar as we all have our place in the Society, it will be incumbent upon us to guide your talents to best serve."

"My actions will always serve the Society."

"I have never doubted that." Victor gave a long considered pause, deciding how to continue. "Headmaster has advised me that you have been showing significant sign of Social Sight."

He waited then, waiting for Mary to comment. She did not.

He continued.

"And you see the direction of the Society using the Sight."

He again waited. Mary continued to remain silent, her expression unchanged.

"You are very talented, Mary, and you possess all six of the Abilities." Victor shifted forward in the chair, rested his elbows on his knees. "But your training has only begun. We will continue to guide you. That training will serve Society, will it not?"

Rydel Ridge was a lookout point with a small picnic area and parking lot. It was surrounded on several sides by a grove of trees. Downslope below the ridge was a meadow frequented by deer.

Matthew's pickup was parked beside the bench at the edge of the hilltop park, the bench overlooking the valley below. Matthew was sitting on the bench, an open pizza box beside him, along with a bottle of soda. He had a slice of pizza in hand.

He took a bite, looking absently out at the scene below.

Rydel Ridge was only a few miles from the Sutherland House Estate, and was a favorite spot of Matthew's.

He took a drink from his soda.

There came a *beep beep* sound…

Matthew put down the soda bottle, picked up and put on a small headset. He pushed a button.

"Yes, Computer?" he asked.

"Good evening, Matthew," said Computer through the headset. "I monitored the use of your Robert Jansen alias credit card for the purchase of pizza and soda."

"And you felt the need to inform me of this," stated Matthew.

"And you are having this meal at Rydel Ridge."

"That I am."

"I am sorry, Matthew," said Computer. "Jennifer has concerns regarding your decision to not come directly home, as you are so close."

Matthew took a bite of pizza, spoke while chewing.

"I like it here," he said. "Jen knows I like it here. You know I like it here."

"I do not believe that she will consider that to be an adequate answer."

"And I am meeting Mark Gryphen here."

"Mark Gryphen," Computer stated flatly.

"That's the guy."

The sound then of a vehicle approaching. Matthew half-turned on the bench, looked side-glance back over his shoulder.

"Sorry, Computer. Gotta go."

Matthew touched the button on the headset, removed the headset and set it on the bench. He stood then when he heard the crunching sound of tires moving across gravel.

The black sedan pulled up beside Matthew's pickup.

Chapter Four

Mark Gryphen climbed out of the black sedan. Mark was in his thirties, was slim, medium height. He was dressed smartly in slacks, a button shirt and light jacket.

He took a moment to look out across the valley below. He turned then and walked toward the bench. He wore a frown, didn't appear all that pleased to be there.

Matthew picked up the pizza box to make room for Mark, set the box down on the other side of him.

He took another bite of his slice.

"Mark," he said. "Pizza?"

"Already had dinner," said Mark.

"Too bad. Good pizza."

"Yeah." Mark sat, leaned back and folded his arms. "How about we get this over with?"

"Always so impatient. Don't be in such a rush. It'll get ugly soon enough."

Mark gave a heavy sigh, frowned darkly as he looked outward.

"What do you want, Matthew?" he asked.

Matthew picked up a napkin, wiped his hands clean, folded the napkin and set it in the open pizza box.

"Marli Reynolds," he stated matter-of-factly.

"That much I got," said Mark. "What of it?"

"You and the young lady were quite involved; had quite the relationship."

"Yeah? So?"

"So, something went wrong. It turned sour. She became more trouble than she was worth. Worse yet, it could have blown back on the family."

"Ya' got me trembling in my loafers. What are you going to do? Tell my daddy?"

Matthew picked up his soda, took a swallow. He set the bottle carefully down beside the pizza box.

"I was talking with your father just today."

"Of course you were," Mark said in a groan. "The great Matthew Sutherland, defender of the little people."

"When I see the need," said Matthew, calmly.

Mark slowly leaned forward and stood up, stepped away from the bench. He looked out across the valley. Evening was quickly settling in.

"One of the little people comes to a grizzly demise and somehow it's my fault," he stated. "Is that it?"

"Don't give me that crap. You murdered an innocent girl and dumped her body."

"We are not little people." Mark looked back to Matthew, his gaze sharp. "We can't be tried and judged by little people laws."

"It is because of what we are that we must be held to an even higher measure. With greater power comes greater responsibility."

"Sutherland House sentimentality. How sweet."

Matthew didn't respond. He picked up his soda bottle, looked briefly again to Mark, and took another swallow.

Mark Gryphen gave a tired sigh.

"This is a waste of time," he said. "Why am I here?"

"I suspect you are here because you are curious as to my intentions. Not so?"

"Why did you ask me here?" asked Mark, clearly exasperated.

Matthew took his time, set the bottle back on the bench. He absently turned the bottle as he studied it. He stood then, stepped up beside Mark. He looked out across the valley as he spoke.

"It is important that you understand. I intend that you be held to account for your actions." He looked directly at Mark. "I do not know what form that accountability will take, but it will happen."

"That's it?" Mark's apparent surprise wasn't at all genuine. "I come all the way out here to the middle of nowhere so that you can shake your finger at me?"

"I'm checking all the boxes," said Matthew.

Mark studied Matthew a moment, then…

"This is about my father," said Mark, matter-of-factly.

Matthew's subtle expression suggested that Mark's comment was close to home.

"I put you on notice, Mark," he said. "That shadow you see? It is the anvil hovering above your head." He turned about, took a step back to the bench.

Mark gave a nod.

"Ah," he said. "It is a threat, then."

"An observation." Matthew said as he reached down and picked up another slice of pizza.

"So. There is to be a confrontation." Mark looked about. "Is it to be now?"

Matthew faced Mark. "I wouldn't want to spoil my dinner."

He took a bite of his pizza.

§

Headmaster was sitting at his desk, working at his computer. He tapped at several keys, hesitated, stopped. He sat back.

He looked over at the window; the view beyond the window revealed evening.

Hearing as sound from the outer office, he casually turned about in his chair, looked across the desk to the door. A shadow appeared beyond the frosted glass inset in the door.

The door opened. Victor came into the office, closed the door behind him. Headmaster started to stand, Victor waved him to sit.

"Good evening, Headmaster." Victor crossed the small room, stepped around the desk, stood at the window. He looked out on the campus grounds, graying now with the coming dusk.

Headmaster turned about in his chair to look over at Victor.

"Your meeting today with Matthew…" he started.

"Well enough." Victor turned from the window to look at Headmaster. "I am not here to discuss Matthew Sutherland."

"Of course not, Father."

Both were silent for several moments, each to their individual thoughts.

"My visit with Mary last evening was… disquieting," said Victor.

"She said as much."

"Did she?" asked Victor, more a statement than a question.

"I spent some time with her this morning between her classes," said Headmaster. "She mentioned your visit."

"And what did she have to say?"

"She was quite clear regarding her devotion to the Society."

Victor turned back to the window, frowned. He spoke Headmaster's earlier statement back to him:

"She said as much."

"I do not doubt her commitment, Father."

"Her level of commitment is not the cause of my disquiet, Headmaster." He turned from the window, stepped back into the center of the room. He turned about to look across the desk to Headmaster. "Mary is very young, at times quite naïve. Her siding with Matthew at Andover demonstrates as much. She has set the Agenda back months."

Headmaster leaned forward, rested his arms on the desk and clasped his hands together.

"From my time with the young lady these past months, I do not believe she fully accepts the premise of the Agenda," said Headmaster. "She has not stated so directly, but such is my observation."

"I agree with your observation," said Victor. A moment's thought, then, "We must refine our approach to her continued training. Mary's role in the Society may yet realize its full potential, but if she were to outwardly turn against the Agenda, she could as easily become the Society's greatest threat."

"You've read the reports, Father. I've never seen anything like it. Mary's skills in

all six Abilities are advancing so quickly;
alarming, to be honest."

"I share your concern."

"Father, we may already be beyond
controlling her should she not see the
Agenda favorably."

"And so…" Victor said slowly. "We
should prepare alternatives to controlling the
girl, should it become necessary."

Jennifer walked across the main house
living room and entered the foyer. She
double-checked the front door's lock, turned
away and started down the hallway, flipping
the light switch as she went. She opened a
narrow door and started down the stairwell
to the basement. To one side were free-
standing shelves with neatly labeled home-
canned jars of fruit and vegetables. The
other side of the basement contained a small
workshop. Directly ahead was a workbench
set against the far wall with a set of shelves
beside it.

She reached into the shelves and released a hidden latch. There was a metallic click. The shelves swung open, gliding easily, revealing a shaft with a ladder leading down. She stepped into the shaft and onto the ladder.

She stepped down from the access and into the underground apartment. The overhead lights came on as she started across.

"Computer," she stated, standing behind the couch. "News on Dad."

"At last communication, Matthew waits," stated Computer.

"I don't like this." Jennifer frowned, stared across the room at the blank wall monitor. "How long?"

"Mark Gryphen departed less than half an hour ago. If he intends something, it will be soon."

"Real soon," said Jennifer. "He can't expect Dad to remain there much longer. Not once the pizza runs out."

Jennifer turned about, sat on the back of the couch.

"I wish I was there."

"I have confidence that Matthew will be fine," said Computer. "His skills are significantly above those of Mark Gryphen."

"But an ambush—"

"Anticipated, and therefore not truly an ambush." Computer gave an appropriate pause. "Should one in fact be attempted."

"I don't get it." Jennifer folded her arms. "What's the purpose?"

"While Phillip Gryphen has stated his intentions regarding Mark Gryphen, an attempted attack on Matthew will require that Phillip Gryphen take immediate action."

"No. I do understand it. I just don't get it." Jennifer considered. "Never mind."

"Yes, Jennifer."

Matthew stood near the trash bin and folded the empty pizza box. He stuffed it into the bin. He heard a sound then, looked in the direction of the narrow access road to the hilltop park.

The sound of an approaching vehicle and tires on gravel; moments later, a long black sedan came into the parking lot. It pulled up and parked near Matthew's pickup. A tall, thin man in his sixties slid out of the driver's seat.

Bedford was in his sixties, gray, serious in manner and appearance.

Matthew approached.

"Good evening, Bedford."

Bedford nodded in acknowledgement, opened the back door. Phillip Gryphen climbed out of the back of the car, looked carefully about as he stepped away.

Matthew managed a quick glance into the back of the car before Bedford closed the door. Mark Gryphen was sitting in the shadow of the back seat, dark and dejected.

Matthew turned to look at Phillip.

"Hello, Phillip," he said, pleasantly enough. "Gotta admit, I'm surprised to see you."

Phillip Gryphen looked about their surroundings. "I do have certain abilities, Matthew."

"Yes. Of course," said Matthew.

Gryphen looked over at Bedford, said nothing but appeared to give him a silent order. He turned forward then and started away from the car.

"Let's walk."

They started casually toward the bench and the lookout. They reached the bench, stepped around it and stood before the slope.

"Your intention was obvious, Matthew." Gryphen frowned, tapped a temple. "As were Mark's."

Matthew looked to Phillip with a thin smile, again looked out across the valley.

"Loud, huh?"

"Mark lacks subtlety," said Gryphen.

"Yeah, I get that."

The valley below fell into heavy shadow as the evening grew darker.

Gryphen gave a nod outward. "Nice view."

"I like it," said Matthew. A long pause, then. "And so?"

"And so…" Gryphen looked back to the sedan, where Bedford stood waiting. He looked again to Matthew. "Stepping in when I did, I likely saved the boy's life."

"Please," said Matthew. "I would have kept damage to minimum."

"And then turn him over to me for final disposition."

"That was kinda' the plan."

"Assuming the uh, plan, went as planned," said Gryphen. "Also assuming you haven't underestimated the power of Mark's abilities."

"Assuming."

A long, uncomfortable pause, neither looking at the other.

"He can't walk away from this," said Matthew. "He must be held to account."

"I will take care of the boy, Matthew," said Gryphen.

"Phillip…" Matthew considered. "Phillip, this goes beyond family. He has committed murder."

"The boy will be dealt with." Gryphen's expression hardened. "Out of the light of general society."

"Phillip…"

"This I swear," Gryphen said firmly. "Matthew. Allow me this."

Matthew studied Gryphen, looked to the black sedan, again finally to Gryphen.

"All right, Phillip." Matthew gave the man a grave look, heavy with meaning. "I will step aside."

Phillip gave a slight acknowledging nod. "I understand."

Jennifer stepped down from the access ladder and into the apartment. The ceiling lights activated as she started toward the kitchen area, spoke over her shoulder to her father, who was following after her.

"He knew what happened, Dad," she said. "There is no way that Gryphen could not have known."

"Of course he knew," said Matthew. He watched her fill two glasses with water.

"Then why—"

"And he tried to cover it up." Matthew took one of the glasses. "Oh, the boy tried to make it look like one of the serial killings, but it was Phillip who changed the paperwork, shuffled things around."

"Then how can you—"

"As he said: he wants this taken care of out of the glaring light of civilians. Keep it in Society. Keep it in Family. Mark Gryphen will be dealt with, and it won't be a slap on the wrist."

They moved to the table and sat down. Jennifer gave Matthew a hard glare.

"He could have dealt with him long before now," she said. "It took you stepping in for something to happen."

"True enough." Matthew took a swallow of water, stared then at his glass. "That's Phillip Gryphen. Mark murdered an innocent girl, but what he'll be punished for is putting the Family at risk. For Gryphen, there is no greater offense."

Jennifer gave a long, dark frown.

"And… it won't be a slap on the wrist," said Jennifer plainly, a long, dark frown.

Matthew took another drink from his water. He set the glass back on the table.

"We shall see."

Chapter Five

Jennifer appeared comfortable, settled on the couch, her feet up, the computer keyboard on her lap. The apartment was quiet but for the hum and clicks of computer equipment. She was studying text that was displayed on the wall monitor.

Her expression grew increasingly curious. She slowly slid her feet off the couch, leaned forward and looked more carefully at the screen.

She set the keyboard aside. She stood, took a step nearer the monitor.

She stepped back, looked from the monitor to the door leading to the access hallway.

One more glance at the wall monitor, then she turned and stepped to the door.

The narrow hallway led to the underground garage. It looked much like an auto service center. Along the left side were six stalls containing an assortment of vehicles: a 64 Comet, an old Bronco, the small converted school bus, a late model BMW, the 97 Ford pickup, a pair of dirt bikes, and a Harley Davidson Sportster.

Along the right side, opposite the stalls, was a line of service bays.

At the far end of the garage was the opening to a tunnel that curved away and out of sight.

Jennifer walked down the center of the garage, found Matthew working on the Comet. The hood was up and he was leaning into engine compartment.

She stood quietly beside the car, watching.

Matthew pulled his head out from the engine compartment, socket wrench in hand. He picked up a blue cloth with his free hand and closed the hood.

"What's up, Jen?" He leaned back against the narrow counter running along the wall in front of the vehicles, begins cleaning the wrench with the cloth. There were a handful of tools on the counter.

Jennifer took a step nearer Matthew, looked from the Comet up to Matthew.

"Computer and I have been digging into Society genealogy," she said. "We've come up with something that you should find interesting."

Matthew set the wrench on the counter behind him, next to the other tools.

"Society genealogy is nothing if not interesting." Matthew walked past Jennifer out to the center row of the garage. Jennifer followed. They started up the center of the garage toward the access hall door.

"I was finally able to get some info on Mary," said Jennifer. "Not easy. Not meant to be found."

They stopped at the door. Matthew looked to Jennifer as he finished wiping his hands.

"You have my attention," he said.

"Mary," said Jennifer, a long pause. "She is the granddaughter of Jonas Westerman."

Matthew looked genuinely surprised. "That's some lineage."

He opened the door, followed Jennifer into the hallway. The narrow passage led them back into the apartment. They moved into the center of the room. Jennifer looked back to her father.

"I find it equally interesting that Victor chose to hide the granddaughter of the first Father of the Society in plain sight."

"Interesting that no one knew that Jonas Westerman had a granddaughter."

They moved into the center of the room.

"Computer is following several lines of investigation on that," said Jennifer. "We should have something before long."

"I wait with bated breath," said Matthew. He sat on the back of the couch, folded his arms across his chest. "This may all come to a head soon. The Summit is in three weeks; should be exciting."

Jennifer put on a sly smile.

"Guess our invites got lost in the mail," she said.

Matthew returned Jennifer's smile with a grin.

"I'm sure they'll show up," he said.

Jennifer studied her father for a few moments.

"We're going," she stated. "Aren't we?"

Matthew gave wink to his daughter, unfolded his arms, turned about to look at the wall monitor.

"While we wait…" He spoke then to Computer. "Computer. What say we have a look at your list of red priorities, find something interesting to work on?"

The wall monitor turned on.

"Yes, Matthew."

Matthew turned to look at Jennifer.

"Well?" he asked, raising a brow.

Jennifer started around the couch.

"Yes, sir."

End Episode Two…

Episode 3
the Summit

Chapter One

It was a clear day, the midmorning sky a bright blue. Tall evergreen trees threw shadows across the narrow, winding road. Matthew Sutherland absently navigated the 64 Comet around the gentle curves, his mind wandering.

His daughter Jennifer was in the passenger seat, staring out the side window, lost in her own thoughts.

"What's wrong, Jen?" asked Matthew.

Jennifer shook her head, said nothing. She continued staring out at the high mountain surroundings.

"It should be fun," Matthew urged. "Did you check out the agenda?"

"Thrilling," she grumbled.

Matthew lost the smile he had been trying to keep pasted on his face.

"You didn't have to come, Jen," he said. "You're a grown woman. There was no pressure."

"Yeah. I did."

"You skipped last year's summit." Matthew kept his eyes on the road. "And the year before that."

"Times, they are a changing."

"That's true enough."

Another uncomfortable silence filled the car, leaving only the low thrumming of the engine, the rumbling of the tires on the asphalt.

"A lordly get-together of the Primary Families," Jennifer said then. She turned finally and looked at her father. "Sutherland House is no longer a Primary Family, Dad. I don't see the purpose. What are you hoping to gain?"

Matthew focused on the tight curve up ahead, guided the car around the bend.

"It may not always seem so, Jen, but we do have friends in the Society; allies, to one degree or another. We don't want to lose them."

"Out of sight, out of mind?" she asked, not buying the assertion.

"Let's just say this is our chance to touch base."

Jennifer turned her gaze again to the passing terrain.

"An annual opportunity to put your head into the lion's mouth," she said.

Not far wrong, thought Matthew.

The conversation again drifted into relative silence. There was a series of tight curves in the road ahead and Matthew thought it best to focus on his driving.

Half an hour later, most of it in silence… the vehicle slowed, turned off the road and into a vista point, little more than a small dirt parking lot. Matthew and Jennifer climbed out of the car, casually walked up to the low wall that bordered the edge of the lot.

The vista point looked out across a deep valley. Set into the mountainside across the valley, midway up the steep slope, was a sprawling castle-like structure. The stone walls shimmered in the sun.

"Well," grumbled Jennifer through a tired sigh. "There it is."

"We wouldn't be going if I didn't believe we would be all right," said Matthew, his gaze on the grandiose structure across the valley. "We always gain something from these gatherings."

"Victor's invitation didn't spook you?"

"Being on the outs, an invite is the only way we get in."

"Not the point," she stated firmly.

"Victor…" Matthew considered, started again: "Victor is ever hopeful of bringing this lost sheep back into the fold."

Jennifer turned from the view and started back toward the car.

"We both know that's not the reason." She continued to the car, opened the door and climbed in.

Matthew half-turned his head and glanced briefly back to the car. He looked forward again, quietly taking in the view.

§

The light blue 64 Comet approached the stone wall that enclosed the castle-like villa. A guard stood at the station beside the open gate. He waited, eyeing the vehicle rolling to a stop.

Matthew rolled down the window, handed his ID card to the guard. The guard set the ID on his clipboard, studied the list against the name on the ID. He gave a glance to Mathew, hesitated longer than necessary, finally gave the card back to Matthew.

He leaned down and gave only a cursory glance to Jennifer sitting in the passenger seat, stepped back and waved them to continue through. Matthew put the car into gear and slowly rolled through the gate.

The courtyard was a large, open expanse enclosed by centuries' old brick and stone buildings and rough stone walls. Matthew guided the car across the plaza toward what appeared to be the drop-off area near the steps of the main building.

He brought the car to a stop, put it in park and turned off the engine. He looked across to Jennifer, then reached for the door handle.

They climbed out of the car. Matthew looked over the roof of the car to Jennifer, then looked about the courtyard. He took calm note of the security personnel standing at well-camouflaged security stations monitoring the goings-on both within the villa and beyond its walls.

He gave a smarmy half-smile and looked side-glance back to Jennifer.

"Now don't tell me you're not feeling the warm and fuzzy," he said.

Jennifer chose not to look directly at her dad.

"It's all just so lovely," she answered.

The door of the main building opened and two men came out onto the porch. The footman was in his fifties, dressed in long coat and knee-high boots. Beside him was the car valet, much younger, dressed more casually.

They took the wide front steps down to the ground and approached. The valet stood to one side as the footman stood silent before Matthew, waiting with an expectant eye.

Matthew handed him the car keys.

"Bags are in the trunk," he said.

"Thank you, sir." The footman gave a nod and went to the back of the car.

Matthew turned his attention back to the courtyard. A middle-aged couple was casually working their way toward one of the buildings, arm in arm, in quiet conversation. Two men in slacks and jackets followed several paces behind the couple, stone-faced, silent, watchful.

Private security…

Matthew turned his attention to the now open trunk of his car. With the two suitcases retrieved, the footman closed the trunk, handed the keys to the waiting valet. The valet stepped around toward the driver's door. Matthew had to step aside, allowing the valet to open the door and climb in.

Matthew and Jennifer moved back, away from the car. The vehicle started, rolled away, tires crunching hardened gravel.

Matthew watched the car move slowly toward a side gate.

"It'll be fine," said Jennifer. She took a step toward the waiting footman, who had the two suitcases in hand. She gave the man a silent call to lead the way.

Matthew watched as his car, disappeared through the breezeway. He turned then and followed his daughter and the footman up the steps and to the front door of the villa's main building.

The main foyer was a high-ceilinged room. The front desk was set into the center of the opposite wall, winding staircases set to either side. A number of passages were visible through open doors along the walls to the left and right.

Jennifer gave a tired glance about the room.

"It hasn't changed much," she said. "It does smell a little more self-important, if that's possible."

"You wouldn't think so," said Matthew. "But yes."

The footman continued across the foyer and set the suitcases down before the front desk. He looked back to Matthew and Jennifer, still standing in the middle of the room. He gave a nod to them and left the counter.

Matthew and Jennifer stepped up to the front desk. The desk clerk gave a welcoming nod to Matthew.

"Mr. Sutherland. Welcome," he said. Carl was tall, ageless with just a hint of gray. He was formal, reserved. "How was your trip?"

"Hello, Carl. Pleasant, as always. Thank you."

Carl took a few moments to check them in. He then handed a booklet to Matthew, another to Jennifer.

"The schedule of meetings and events," he said. "There are a few on the calendar this afternoon, but most of the activities will begin tomorrow."

"Thank you, Carl."

Carl reached back to the wall of room key cubby holes. He took keys from two and turned again to Matthew and Jennifer. He slid a key across the counter to each of them.

A bellhop appeared as if on cue and picked up their suitcases.

Carl spoke to the bellhop.

"The young lady's bags to room 212, Mr. Sutherland's to 213."

Jennifer indicated one of the suitcases to the bellhop.

"That one's mine."

The bellhop acknowledged Jennifer and then started to the staircase.

"Upstairs and to the right," Carl said to Matthew. "Your bags will be waiting for you."

Matthew gave a thank you wave with the booklet as he and Jennifer stepped away from the front desk.

Starting across the main foyer, a middle-aged woman approached.

Catherine Gray, matriarch of Gray House, was a youngish sixty year old woman, physically small, while her presence exuded strength, self-assuredness, confidence.

"Matthew, so good to see you," she said. "And here I was fretting that our pompous little gathering was destined to be another yawner."

"Hello, Catherine," said Matthew. "It will undoubtedly be as lethargic as ever, despite my presence."

"You are probably right," said Catherine, laughing lightly. She looked to Jennifer. "My, my. This is Jennifer? Haven't you bloomed into a full-grown young woman?"

"Time has a way of doing that to a person," said Jennifer.

"And then some!" Catherine studied Jennifer more closely. "I haven't seen you in, what? Three or four years?"

"Good to see you, Miss Gray." Jennifer turned back to Matthew. "I should head upstairs, get settle in. See you later?"

"Meet for lunch."

"Okay," she said. She turned again to Catherine. "It was nice to see you again."

Catherine smiled in answer. She watched Jennifer head for the stairs.

"I understand that she moved back home: left college," she said to Matthew.

"I hadn't realized the private lives of Sutherland House were so public."

"Don't give me that crap, Matthew. Keeping an eye on you is one of our few guilty pleasures. Damn near impossible to look away, truth be told."

"Good ratings, then?"

"Oh, the best," said Catherine. "I hear tell you've been picked up for another season."

"And I was afraid we were going to be cancelled."

"My dear." Catherine leaned nearer Matthew, her tone now serious. "That is always a possibility, the ratings be damned."

"I see," Matthew stated calmly.

Catherine straightened and brought back her warm smile.

"So good to see you, Matthew," she said then. "I do hope to see you in a few of the workshops. Yes?"

"But of course, Catherine."

"Very good, then." As much a good-bye as any, Catherine turned and started away.

She stopped midway across the foyer, looked back and watched Matthew starting up the stairs. She gave a thin smile, turned about and continued across to one of the narrow passageways.

The upstairs hallway had an air of times long gone. Wide and high-ceilinged, thick carpet, old light fixtures mounted on the walls between dark, heavy doors. It was quiet, any sound there was coming from downstairs muffled to silence.

Matthew unlocked the door to his room. Stepping through, he stood just inside and took a moment to look about. The small room was sparsely furnished, the highest quality. There was a twin bed, a dresser, a small desk and chair. There were two doors set into the left wall: a bathroom and a closet. His suitcase was sitting on the bed.

He went over to the one window and looked out. There was a small courtyard below, bare ground with a few shrubs, a web of flagstone paths.

He left the window and went to the desk. He took comm gear from his inside pocket, flipped it open and set it on the desk.

"Computer," he stated. "You there?"

"Yes, Matthew. One moment, please," came the voice of Computer. A moment later: "Communication secure."

"Thank you." Matthew moved again to the bed, opened his suitcase. He took another device out of a pocket in the suitcase. He pulled four tiny plastic legs from the base of the device and set it on the desk.

He pushed a button on the device. An indicator light flashed several times, eventually glowed solid.

"Room secure," said Matthew.

"One moment," said Computer. "Verified."

Matthew returned to the suitcase and began unpacking, placing closes into the dresser drawers, hanging shirts in the closet.

"How are things back home, Computer?" he asked.

"Secure, Matthew."

"Progress on our active priority items?"

"Nothing to report." There was a long pause, then. "You have only been gone a few hours, Matthew."

"Don't get cute, Computer." Matthew flipped his empty suitcase closed, picked it up and took it to the closet. "I met up with Catherine Gray. Our brief exchange supports our background on Gray House."

"A good sign, then," said Computer.

"As close to an ally as we have, but…" Matthew let the thought drop. They both knew that Catherine Gray's true feelings were always shrouded in subtlety and diplomacy.

"Yes. A good sign," he finished at last. He returned to the window, absently watched several people following the flagstone walks. "I expect this will be an interesting few days," he said distractedly.

He turned back into the room at the sound of a knock at the door.

"Hold one, Computer." Matthew went to the door and opened it.

The bellhop was standing in the hall. He handed Matthew a note, turned and left without speaking.

Matthew closed the door as he turned back into the room, opening the note.

"Sad news, Computer," he said, more than a hint of sarcasm. "The 'Positive Career Moves' meeting has been cancelled."

Chapter Two

Matthew walked the second floor hallway and turned onto the staircase. He passed a middle-aged man on the way down. He recognized the face, but couldn't remember the man's name. From the man's dark side-glance, he apparently recognized Matthew.

Matthew slowed as he neared the bottom stairs, noting Saul Morgan checking in at the front desk. Saul was about fifty years old; he dressed casually, had bushy brown hair, his beard well-trimmed. He wore a broad, genuine smile as he spoke with Carl.

Matthew walked across the foyer to one of the side hallways, took the passage to a set of double doors. The dining room was an open, cafeteria-like setting, cluttered with numerous tables and chairs. To the left was a wall of windows, the wall ahead lined with a row of buffet counters.

A number of the tables were occupied, and several of the diners glanced up at Matthew as he passed them on his way to the buffet. He heard the faint background noise of thought-talk.

He nodded to some, gave a friendly smile to others. Reaching the buffet, he picked up a plate and looked over the food choices.

Catherine Gray joined him, picking up a plate for herself.

"Matthew," she said, looking over the assortment of food items.

"Catherine," said Matthew. He gave a quick glance behind them, focused again on the buffet counter. "Two encounters in one day. Folks will talk."

"Not a problem," said Catherine. "I'll talk smack about you behind your back."

"You are a smart woman, Catherine. I've always said so,"

"And you, Mr. Sutherland, genius that you are, can be quite naïve. I have always said so."

She looked back over her shoulder, noted several in the room looking their way. She gave one of them a playful wink, turned again to the buffet. She placed a dinner roll on her plate.

"Nonetheless," she said in a sigh. "I do miss Sutherland House. Gray and Sutherland, standing side by side."

"And frequently all alone," said Matthew.

"Ah, yes. Those were the days."

Catherine's tone and expression held a nostalgic air. Both continued to search the buffet and make careful selections.

"So," Catherine continued then. "Have you had a chance to look over the meetings? Filled up your schedule?"

"Wondering which meetings to avoid, are you?"

"Not at all, not at all." Catherine again looked behind her at those gathered around the cafeteria tables. The background thought-talk noise rose imperceptibly. "I'd love for us to have a few meet-ups," she said.

"Maybe we can compare our meeting choices," said Matthew. "Two hours freed up today… a cancelled meeting."

"I heard. Positive Career Moves, wasn't it?"

"I think that was it."

"I expect we'll see a few more folks in the off-schedule side-meets," said Catherine. "Should be more exciting than the leaders conferences."

Matthew considered, then, "The Steering Council's Seat Appointment meeting?"

"For one," she said. "Almost as thrilling as the 'Upcoming Directives' session."

"Ah, yes." Matthew grinned. "Maybe I'll make an appearance."

"Oh, would you, dear? Please, that would so liven things up."

Jennifer came into the dining hall. After a brief look about the room, she noted her father and Catherine Gray walking from the buffet to a nearby table. She came up to them as Matthew set is plate on the table.

"Ah, there she is," he said.

"Dad," said Jennifer; a smile to Catherine. "Miss Gray."

"Hello, Jennifer." Catherine stood with lunch tray in hand. "I do hope you're finding enough to hold your interest."

"Always on my toes, keeping my head up, Miss Gray."

"Very good, dear." Catherine looked to Matthew. "You could learn something from this one, Matthew."

"It's why I keep her around, Catherine." He pulled out a chair and readied to sit down. "Please. Let's eat."

Catherine gave a smirk as she looked about the room.

"Oh, I'd love to, but I do have matters to discuss with Everett," she said, indicating another table.

And best not push things too far... thought Matthew.

"Very wise," he said. "As always."

Catherine gave a brief nod to Jennifer and turned to leave.

Jennifer spoke quietly to Matthew as she watched Catherine move to the other table.

"What was that all about?" she asked.

"Society politics," said Matthew as he sat down and pulled his tray near. "A living, breathing mutation of our own creation." He stabbed a piece of fruit with his fork and put it in his mouth. "Be sure to get the cantaloupe. It's very good."

"I'll do that," she said absently, looked down then to her father. "She's one of those *allies* that you don't want to lose… right?"

"I would much rather have her on our side as not."

"Yeah, yeah… I get that." She looked again at Catherine, sitting at the other table, talking with Everett. "I do remember Gray House supporting us back in the day, when we were still in the Society."

"That is so."

"So where was she during Andover?"

"She picks her fights very carefully." Matthew took another bite of his meal. "You bother me standing there. Go get your lunch."

§

A long, dark sedan crossed the courtyard and came to a slow stop near the front steps of the main building. The driver got out and opened the back door. Victor Broderick and his wife Dianna got out of the car and looked about. They watched a second sedan pulling up behind their own.

The summit manager hurried down the steps, the footman following immediately behind.

"Mr. Broderick. Father," said the manager. "Welcome. How was your trip?"

"Fine," said Victor, his attention on the second sedan. The driver had opened the back door. Mrs. Evans, the Broderick's nanny, climbed out. She helped the two children out of the car.

Meanwhile, Dianna reached out to shake the manager's hand.

"Our apologies for being late," she said. "It's always the one thing you don't anticipate. By design, I expect."

"Not at all, Mrs. Broderick." He looked from Dianna to Victor. "As requested, the council meeting has been moved to this evening."

"Yes," said Victor. "Very good."

Mrs. Evans approached, allowing the children to follow beside her. There was no doting by this nanny.

Robby and Thomas, six and five years old, were quiet, calm, dressed in button shirts and slacks, wearing light jackets.

Dianna gave a supportive smile to Mrs. Evans, then looked to Robby and Thomas.

"Children, did you enjoy the trip?"

"Yes, Mother," said Robby, a flat statement.

Thomas gave a look to his brother Robby, looked up then at his mother and gave a nod.

Victor Broderick gave a subtle indication that he was ready to head inside.

"Shall we?" he asked absently, ostensibly to the summit manager, though not directly.

"Of course," said the manager. He stepped to one side and indicated the steps. "Please. This way."

He gave Victor and Dianna a moment to start toward the steps, then hurried up beside them. Mrs. Evans and the children followed behind, leaving the two drivers and the footman to take care of the luggage.

The manager spoke as they continued up the steps.

"Matthew Sutherland arrived this morning," he said. "With his daughter."

"Any problems?" asked Victor, distractedly. His thoughts had already gone elsewhere.

"None, sir. Everyone is well-behaved."

"Fine then."

They reached the top of the steps. The manager stepped ahead and opened the doors, quickly stepped aside. Once the Father of the Society and his wife had gone inside, the manager took a moment to look about the courtyard. He took a calming breath, then followed Victor and Dianna

Broderick inside, leaving Mrs. Evans and the children to follow after.

Chapter Three

The only furniture in the small meeting room was a rectangular table and eight chairs. Most of the chairs were occupied.

A tall, narrow window was set into one wall. Saul Morgan was sitting at the head of the table, the window behind him.

"That's it then, folks," he said, closing a binder. "A most successful discussion. Thank you all for coming."

With the meeting adjourned, the handful of attendees stood and gathered together what few materials they had brought with them.

The door opened then and Matthew came into the room. He stood to one side as the attendees began leaving. Several looked uncomfortably at Matthew as they passed by. One did acknowledge him.

"Matthew," he said, not much above a mumble.

Matthew gave only an acknowledging nod in return, not wanting to draw attention to the man.

Saul was the last in the room. He spoke to Matthew as he gathered his papers together. The exchange wasn't unfriendly, but there was an underlying hint of concern at seeing Matthew at the summit.

"Hello, Matthew. And how are you this fine day?"

"Saul," said Matthew, watching Saul gather the last of his papers together. "Not bad, all considered."

"I was a bit surprised that you decided to attend, all considered."

"Yeah, well… I was invited."

"So I understand. Victor has a curious sense of humor."

"I doubt that was behind the invitation."

"You are probably right." Saul stepped around and sat on the corner of the table. "To be honest, I doubt the Father of the Society has a sense of humor, curious or otherwise."

"Oh, I've known him to chuckle now and then," said Matthew. A thin grin and a shrug, "Sort of. Now and then."

Now it was Saul's turn to give a slight grin.

"You sure it was chuckling?" A long pause, and then Saul's expression grew serious. "You watch yourself, Matthew. Victor's orders or not, some with grudges may choose to act on them."

"So then, much like every year."

"Not so. A lot has happened recently to make this year very much not like every year."

Matthew moved from the wall, moved to the table. He sat on the edge, beside Saul.

"How ya' been, Saul?" he asked, pushing the change the subject.

"Not bad. Family's doing well. How are you holding up? I'm sorry I missed the funeral."

"I understand," said Matthew. "Probably best."

"Yes, well…" Saul stated down at his hands. "I was very fond of Sharon."

"I know that."

Saul now looked up, looked to Matthew.

"Why are you here, Matthew?"

"I was invited."

"That's not good enough."

"Okay... No better place to gather intel."

"Okay… And just what are you looking for?"

"Whatever I find." Matthew pushed away from the table. He took a step toward the door, then another step. He looked back to Saul. "I saw your name on the schedule, just dropped in to say hello."

"Hello," said Saul.

"Hello." Matthew hesitated, considered. "While I'm thinking about it, what do you know about a member named Jon Willeby?"

"Not a thing."

"The Family?"

"Willeby? Not much. One of the Lesser families, but not without powerful friends. Why do you ask?"

"He's been causing problems in the real world, going by the name John Cutler."

"Oh, right…" Saul grew thoughtful. "Some kind of cult; pushing his Society Abilities as miracles."

"That's the guy," said Matthew. "Ordinarily I wouldn't bother, but he's hurting folks. I may have to do something about that."

"Go for it," Saul said in a shrug.

"I wasn't exactly seeking your approval, Saul."

"Whatever." Saul looked directly, sharply, at Matthew. "I doubt what friends you have here are going to turn on you over this, but then I don't think that's ever really been a deal-breaker for you."

"No, but I'd rather not lost those few friends. Not if I can help it."

Saul put on a genuine smile. "Good to hear," he said.

Matthew put a hand on the door jamb, prepared to leave.

"Good to see you, Saul."

"Yeah…"

Matthew gave a nod, turned into the hallway.

Saul watched Matthew disappear from the doorway.

Jennifer was standing at the buffet counter, using tongs to place assorted slices of fruit on her plate. It was mid-afternoon, the lunch crowd long gone. The dining room was about half full, some diners having a late lunch after meetings, others looking for a snack.

Phillip Gryphen, patriarch of the Gryphen House, came up beside her and picked up a plate. At sixty plus years, Gryphen had a fatherly appearance, with gray hair and gray eyes. He wore casual, well-fitting pants and shirt. He held the confident manner that sometimes came with the passage of years.

"Good afternoon, Miss Sutherland," he said, looking over the various fruit offerings. "How are you this fine day?"

"Well enough, Mr. Gryphen," said Jennifer. "Yourself?"

"Fine, fine." Gryphen began placing fruit on his plate. "And how is your father? Matthew is well? Ready to mix things up?"

"He has the stirring stick firmly in hand."

"Yes," said Gryphen, smiling. "That would be Matthew."

Their plates with assorted fruit, they stepped away from the buffet counter and moved to a table. Sitting, Jennifer settled in while the elder Gryphen looked about the room.

Several of the diners were openly looking to Jennifer, while others looked to one another, outwardly silent while internally speaking in thought-talk, creating an underlying background white-noise of internal mumblings and whisperings.

Gryphen pushed the thought-talk noise further into the background, turned and focused then on his meal and to Jennifer sitting across from him.

"So, Jennifer... do you have your schedule all worked out? Chosen your meetings?"

"I'm here mostly to keep an eye on my dad," she said. She stabbed at a piece of cantaloupe with her fork.

"I can certainly understand that, but don't let that get in way of enjoying yourself. Believe it or not, this year's agenda offers a number of worthwhile conferences."

"Yes, well…" Jennifer looked furtively about at those sitting at the other tables. "I wouldn't want my attendance to uh, *complicate* the mood."

Gryphen ran a dark gaze about the room. There was a distinct rise of unintelligible background whisperings and mumblings. Gryphen's gaze sharpened and the internal noise level as quickly fell.

He used his fork to sort through his fruit, looked again to Jennifer.

"Please don't let their issues become your issues," he said.

Jennifer offered a weak smile in answer. Both focused on their meals. Gryphen then again looked up from his plate to Jennifer.

"How are you holding up with the…" he waved his fork in the general direction of their fellow diners, "with the noise?"

Jennifer had managed to keep the background thought-talk rumblings to mostly unintelligible white-noise since their arrival at the summit, with only the occasional snippets of "father's daughter" and "Sutherland" coming through.

"What noise?" she forked a piece of apple and put it in her mouth.

"Good, good. Not worth your time," said Gryphen. "Did your father teach you that? Shutting it out?"

Jennifer offered Phillip Gryphen, patriarch of Gryphen House, a not-so-subtle knowing look, took another bite from her fruit plate.

"Are you concerned with my training?" she asked.

"I don't know what you mean."

"My not attending the Academy," she stated. "Folks seem awfully concerned as regards my education."

"Ah. I see," Gryphen managed. "No. Just curious."

They focused on their meals then, intent on slices of fruit, choosing one and then another piece. Others in the cafeteria continued to surreptitiously observe, to speak both in low voice and in thought-talk.

"And, just to get it out there…" Jennifer started then. "I don't have as many Abilities as my father, but more than most."

Gryphen returned the comment with an uncomfortable expression.

"Not really my business," he said. He managed a thoughtful smile. "Not as many as your father, you say."

Jennifer forked her last piece of fruit.

"Not yet."

The late-afternoon sun was sitting low on the horizon, splaying rays of fading sunlight across the sprawling garden of low-growing bushes and colorful flowerbeds. It was cool outside; the few people walking the garden paths wore coats and hats.

Jennifer stood alone, beside a bench. She watched as a pair of birds hopped about in the branches of a nearby bush.

Matthew came up the walk, stood silent beside his daughter. He watched the birds for a moment, turned about and sat on the bench.

"Good afternoon," he said.

"Dad." Jennifer continued to watch the birds. "I missed you at lunch."

"Sorry about that. Meeting ran over."

"And then some." Jennifer walked around Matthew and sat down beside him. "Gray Caste Policy?"

"Sad affair," he sighed. "Their idea of reevaluating the policy and mine are apparently quite different."

"I'm not sure why the subject is of interest to you."

"It's always been a matter close to my heart," said Matthew. "Did you Enjoy your lunch with Phillip?"

"It wasn't lunch. It was snack," she said quickly, and then, "Word does get around."

"In all its myriad forms, my daughter."

"Right," she said in a tired sigh. "Some real winners here."

"Don't be so hard on them, Jen. They're not all bad."

"I can probably count the good ones on one hand."

Matthew decided not to pursue that line of thought. He did manage a light chuckle and then let it go.

"You and Phillip getting along all right, then?"

"We've always gotten along."

"Yes. That's right," Matthew stated matter-of-factly. "Anything on his son?"

"The subject of Mark Gryphen never came up in conversation." Jennifer looked then directly at Matthew. "He's here?"

"So I understand."

"How?" she asked. "I mean… why?"

Matthew only shrugged in answer. He had no answer.

Jennifer faced forward, looked across the walk to the flower bed beyond. There were more important matters…

"There's danger here, Dad," she said. "It's there, behind all the cool expressions, the frozen smiles; to say nothing of the outright hostility."

"You haven't been—"

"To now, I'm getting the guilt-by-association treatment. I'm more concerned about you. The animosity here is palpable. There is a real sense of betrayal."

Matthew leaned forward now, rested his forearms on his knees and clasped his hands.

"Sad. Isn't it?"

"Scary, more like."

"Avoiding it won't help, Jen."

He straightened then, sensing movement to their right.

Ben Aldridge was coming up the walk, dressed in a heavy peacoat and black jeans. He walked with smooth confidence. He was in his forties, had broad, square shoulders, well-groomed hair.

He approached and stood before Matthew and Jennifer, looked directly at Matthew. His expression wasn't entirely unfriendly, and yet managed to betray nothing.

"It's been a long time, Matthew," he said.

"A year," said Matthew. "How are you, Ben?"

Ben glanced about, looked back to Matthew.

"I didn't expect to see you this year. Not after, you know…"

"I haven't missed one yet."

Ben accepted that; he considered then…

"It should be an interesting summit," he said after another look about the garden. "Matthew Sutherland's presence notwithstanding."

"I'll try not to be too disruptive."

"Oh, I think we're well beyond that," Ben said, chuckling. "The rumblings started the moment the word went out: hands off Matthew."

"Victor?" asked Matthew.

"It came with the room key and the agenda flyer." Ben looked to Jennifer then. "It's Jennifer, right?"

"That's right," she answered warily.

Ben took that as a dismissal, returned to Matthew.

"Meeting coming up," he said. "Family Leaders."

"Saw it in the agenda," said Matthew. "I expect I'll see you there."

This startled Jennifer, and it showed. She started to say something but held her silence.

Ben, however, put on a broad smile.

"Really?" he said. "Non-voting attendee, obviously."

Matthew sensed more movement, and looking about noted that some of those in the garden had started working their way down the paths.

"Obviously," he said, looking back to Ben.

"Uh, huh," Ben said absently, watching a couple approach, following the walk. They glanced down at Matthew and Jennifer sitting on the bench, more sharply at Ben, and continued past.

Ben waited until they were out of earshot.

"A bit frosty, I must say."

"There's a lot of that going around," said Jennifer.

"No doubt, no doubt," said Ben, giving a consoling look to Matthew

"Nothing serious," said Matthew.

"It never is until it is." Ben said, rather casually. He looked away, up the walk. "I suppose I should head inside. Gonna get cleaned up, grab a quick snack before the meeting."

"Good to see you, Ben," said Matthew.

"Right. Off then." He nodded to Matthew, then to his daughter. "Jennifer."

Jennifer watched the man start up the walk.

"I don't remember him," she said to Matthew.

"That would be Ben Aldridge, young patriarch of Aldridge House." Matthew slid back in the bench, leaned back.

"Friend or foe?"

"Neither, best I can tell."

"Okay…" she said, hesitantly.

"Let's just say that he's good at working the floor."

"Ah." she now slid back, resting against the bench back. "Got it. I think."

§

The conference room was labeled the Minor Hall. It was larger than the general conference rooms of the majority of the summit meetings, but much smaller than the Great Hall that would be the venue of the upcoming main Gathering.

There was a long, narrow table in the center of the room; a pair of tall windows were set into one wall. The leaders of most of the seventeen Primary Families were standing about in small groups, in quiet conversation.

Matthew came into the room. He looked casually about before taking a step further into the room and moving up beside one of the groups.

Ben Aldridge reached a hand out to shake hands.

"Ah. There you are Matthew. Welcome, my friend."

"Heretic," said Matthew, giving a half smile and shaking Ben's hand.

"In my nature," said Ben, winking.

Looking about again, Matthew noted several in the room glancing his way; some gave non-committal nods, though most though quickly turned away.

Catherine Gray was seated alone near the head of the table. She offered a warm smile.

Victor Broderick, Father of the Society, entered the room then. He acknowledged members as he moved toward the head of the table. He talked quietly with one member as others slowly moved to their chairs.

Victor spoke briefly then with Catherine Gray. Their exchange finished, Victor looked about the room from his place at the head of the table. He sat down and settled in.

"Good evening, everyone," he stated. "Let's get started. Shall we?"

Those not already seated moved to their chairs. Three others quietly entered the room, the door closing behind them as they found chairs set along the wall.

Victor looked patiently on, his gaze drifting about the meeting room, ensuring that all were paying attention. Looking last to Catherine Gray, he gave a friendly nod.

He opened the folder before him, looked up and across the table.

"Welcome," he stated formally. "First on the agenda this evening are the Steering Council appointments. We have two open seats."

Catherine Gray gave a silent but visible chuckle.

Jennifer came out of the small meeting room set directly off the main foyer. She stepped aside from the door, quietly acknowledged several others coming out of the meeting and passing her on their way into the foyer and toward side halls.

She saw then Mary and Headmaster coming down the staircase. Walking across the floor toward the west side hall, they stopped to exchange greetings, Headmaster holding out his hand.

"Miss Sutherland, isn't it?" he asked, shaking hands with her.

"That's right," said Jennifer. "I'm surprised you remember me, Headmaster."

"You're all grown up, but to me you're still the young lady walking proudly beside her father." He looked to Mary, then. "Jennifer Sutherland was that rare Society child not to attend the Academy."

Mary gave Jennifer a studying eye.

"I know," she said.

Jennifer in turn gave a polite nod to Mary, looked again to Headmaster.

"The situation at the time suggested alternative schooling might serve me better."

"Of course," said Headmaster. "I understood and chose not to take it personally."

"I'm glad." Jennifer looked again to Mary. "Hello, Mary. This your first summit?"

"It is."

"She wished to see what all the fuss was about," said Headmaster. "I thought it would be a great learning experience."

"Yes. Of course," said Jennifer before turning to Mary. "You're here on your own then."

"I am here with Headmaster."

"I'll be pointing out events of interest," Headmaster jumped in.

"Of course." Jennifer kept her attention on Mary. "Sorry. My fault. I meant that you are not here representing your Family, your House."

Mary gave a calm, cool expression, said nothing.

Headmaster again stepped in.

"Mary is what you might consider an independent."

"I know a bit of her background, Headmaster." To Mary then, "Just a bit."

"You do…" said Headmaster.

"I do wonder that her heritage is not more… public."

"Nothing sinister, Miss Sutherland. I am sure you can understand the impact that such notoriety would bring to the Academy. We felt that it might adversely impact Mary's training regimen."

"I see." Mary gave a gently, knowing smile to Mary. "It is going well? Your education?"

"It is," said Mary.

"Quite well," said Headmaster. "Surpassing expectations."

"No doubt," Jennifer said reservedly. She offered a more guarded smile to Mary.

Mary's expression remained blank, without emotion.

Mark Gryphen watched the exchange from midway across the foyer. Phillip Gryphen's son was in his thirties, slim, medium height. He dressed smartly in slacks and a button shirt. Seeing Mary and Headmaster move on, he came up to Jennifer.

"That is one scary little girl," he said, watching them disappear into a side hall.

"I feel sorry for her."

The younger Gryphen thought on that a moment, decided then that the subject wasn't worth pursuing.

"I'm Mark Gryphen," he said, reaching out a hand.

Jennifer stared at the offered hand, considered ignoring it before finally accepting a brief handshake.

"Of course you are," she said. "Why aren't you locked away in a dungeon somewhere?"

"That may yet be in my future, Miss Sutherland. Jennifer, isn't it?"

Jennifer ignored the question. She looked about the foyer, watching the few people in the room moving about rather than look at Gryphen directly.

"Will you be attending any of the meetings, Mr. Gryphen?"

"The Networking with Politicians meeting sounds interesting."

Jennifer tried to hide her surprise.

"You figure on getting into human politics, do you?" she asked.

"Worth a look…" he said through a half-smirk. "But then, where life takes me isn't entirely up to me, now is it?"

"Such a pity."

A short, elderly, silver-haired woman with a stiff back and sharp features came into the foyer from the nearest side hallway. She gave Jennifer a long, cold stare as she passed by.

Mark Gryphen watched the woman reached the staircase and start up the stairs. He feigned a sympathetic smile side-glance to Jennifer.

"I do hope you and your father have not been made to feel unwelcome," he said.

"Good evening, Mr. Gryphen," said Jennifer, ignoring his comment. She turned away then and started toward the side hall.

Mark Gryphen gave an acknowledging nod to Jennifer's retreating figure.

"Good evening, Miss Sutherland," he said, but by then Jennifer had disappeared into the hall.

Chapter Four

Dinner each evening was scheduled to run two hours. Midway into the evening, all the tables were occupied. A low rumble of conversation came from all about the dining room.

Matthew and Jennifer were sharing a table with two others. Matthew knew neither of them personally, though he did remember seeing them at the last summit. Both men were in their thirties, neither was particularly sociable. There was an air of awkwardness at the table, and comments back and forth were seldom and brief.

Victor and Dianna were sitting at a nearby table with their two young children. There was no sign of the children's nanny.

Don, the diner sitting on Matthew's left, absently took a bite of his dinner, spoke in a low voice to his friend Edward, both looking in the general direction of Victor's table.

"Another summit and no sign of Father's grown children," said Don. "What's with that?"

"No big deal," said Edward. "They're very private."

"Still. Weird." Don looked to Matthew, hesitated, finally asked, "You know them, right?"

"I know them." Matthew gave a nod of agreement to Edward. "They keep to themselves."

Jennifer furrowed her brow in thought, recalled then…

"Vincent, Carl… and Anna." She looked to Matthew. "About my age, a bit older. Have they married?"

"Anna married a couple of years ago," said Matthew.

"They don't come to the summits," Don pushed. "Have you seen them? I mean recently?"

"I'm afraid we don't move in the same social circles."

"Of course," said Don, uncomfortably.

The background rumble of conversation throughout the dining room grew muted. Don sensed movement, turned his head and noted Mary and Headmaster entering the cafeteria.

Shifting about, Matthew watched as Victor Broderick indicated with a wave of the hand that the new arrivals should join them.

Chairs were shifted; staff appeared out of nowhere with two more chairs. The chair placed next to Victor was held ready for Mary. Two dinners were brought to the table, one set before Mary, the other before Headmaster.

Jennifer spoke to her father while discreetly watching Mary, her voice low so that only Matthew could hear.

"So… were her heritage more widely known, her training regimen might have been adversely impacted," she stated, astutely recalling the recent observation given her. "So I was given to understand…"

Matthew picked up his water glass, took a drink. He returned the glass to the table in front of his plate and picked up his fork.

"You can be so cynical, my daughter," he said.

Matthew backed out of his room and into the upstairs hallway. Several doors down, Ben Aldridge came out his own room.

"Good morning, Ben," said Matthew. He closed and locked his door.

"Matthew," said Ben, more reservedly than Matthew would have expected.

"Okay," said Matthew. "Is there a problem?"

"Sorry." Ben put his room key in his pocket, frowning. "My bad."

"Yes?"

Ben took a single step nearer to Matthew. He gave one look up and down the otherwise empty hallway, furrowed his brow.

"You ever notice that the more interesting conversations happen after a meeting adjourns?"

"Sure," said Matthew. "I take it there was talk after I left the meeting yesterday?"

Ben looked as though he would just as soon leave.

"Ben?" Matthew urged.

"Matthew," Ben managed. "Emotions are running rather warm around here this year. Not sure if it's because of Andover or just folks stirring things up when no one's looking."

Whichever… not unexpected… thought Matthew.

"I'm sorry to hear that," he said.

"Yeah, well," said Ben, faltering. "I gotta go."

Ben stepped past Matthew and walked down the hall toward the staircase. A bellhop appeared at the top of the stairs and passed Ben. He handed Matthew a folded message.

"Thank you," said Matthew.

Jennifer came out of her room, locked her door as she looked down the hall, saw her father opening and reading the message.

"Good morning, Jen," he said distractedly, refolding the note. "Sleep well?"

"I miss by bed," she said. "You ready for breakfast?"

"You go on ahead." He held up the note and then stuffed it into his pocket. "I'll catch up."

"Problem?"

"I don't think so. An old friend wants to say hello."

Jennifer responded with a concerned frown.

"You go," said Matthew. "Save me a chair."

"Sure..." she said, more of a sigh than a comment.

Matthew absently watched his daughter walk the hall to staircase and start down. He glanced over at his door then, reached out and made certain it was locked, followed after Jennifer. Descending the stairs and stepping down into the front foyer, he passed several others as he crossed the room. Most but not all returned his nods of greeting.

He followed a long, narrow hall to a door with a plaque displaying "104". He gave a single, light knock with a knuckle and opened the door. He entered the small room, made less claustrophobic by a large window with a wide sill.

Matthew closed the door and looked over at a small, slight man with long gray hair standing at the window.

"Mister Hawthorne," said Matthew.

Edmund Hawthorne was eighty years old, looked every year of his age. His current expression was very close to a scowl.

"Sutherland," he grumbled.

Matthew took another step into the room.

"I gotta say, I was surprised to get your message."

"Of course you were." Hawthorne turned about and sat on the window sill. His bright blue eyes shimmered, contrasting the scowl and the air of gray that he wore as a cloak.

He indicated the table and chairs.

"Sit," he stated, silently watched Matthew move to the table and sit on the corner. "Sutherland. You and I have never been friends."

"Our conflicting views regarding the Agenda got in the way."

"Didn't help," Hawthorne grumbled shortly.

Matthew rested his hands on the table, considered for several moments...

"You weren't part of Andover," he said.

"Hawthorne House monitored the research. We were not directly involved."

"So, again, not much chance that we'll be rebuilding our friendship anytime soon."

"Whatever," Hawthorne waved an impatient hand. His expression grew more thoughtful. "I understand you're looking into the Cutler Cult."

"That's right," said Matthew, curious now.

Hawthorne pushed off the windowsill, stiffly folded his arms.

"Not a fan," he said harshly.

"Is that so?"

"Left to his own, he is likely to expose the Society. We cannot abide that."

"And that is where I come in."

"I would never underestimate your capabilities regarding such things."

"I see," said Matthew. "So… what would you have of me, Mister Hawthorne?"

Hawthorne offered another dark frown, his expression such that he may yet decide to end this conversation then and there. Another few moments and he chose to continue…

"I would direct your attention to Cutler's sister."

"Cutler… Willeby… doesn't have a sister," said Matthew.

"Ah. There you are wrong. He has a half-sister; non-Society. Result of a fling of his father's with a human some twenty five years ago." Hawthorne gave a snide grin. "Your know-all computer managed to miss that."

"I see," Matthew managed to say. *A chat with Computer…*

"She serves as one of Cutler's cult lieutenants."

"Thank you, Mister Hawthorne," said Matthew. He pushed away from the table, started toward the door. "I expect we'll be able to put the info to use."

"I would hope so," said Hawthorne, maintaining the scowl. He watched then as Matthew continued to the door. "Sutherland," he called to him.

Matthew turned and looked back to Hawthorne, waited.

"Despite what others may say, I know that Sutherland House is not a threat to the Society."

Matthew gave a silent nod but said nothing.

"Still not a fan," Hawthorne finished.

"Right," said Matthew. "We should work on that."

Hawthorne watched Matthew open the door and leave the room. The old man's scowl remained; a permanent feature.

§

Matthew was standing at the window, looking out at the grounds below without really looking. The overhead light in his room was turned off, as well as the table lamps, so the only light was that streaming in through the window from outside.

He turned back into the room.

"No, Computer. That's it," he said. "Kinda rounds out the background, doesn't it?"

"Yes, Matthew," came Computer's voice from the device on the desk. "This avenue of investigation may provide additional options."

There was a knock at the door. Matthew moved across the room and opened it, continued speaking to Computer as Jennifer came in, closing the door behind her.

"That's all, Computer," he said. "Get back to me."

"Yes, Matthew. I shall."

"Better yet, prep the package." Matthew moved toward the desk. "We'll delve into it when I get back. Comm off."

He looked to Jennifer as he sat on the edge of the desk. "What's up, Jen?"

Jennifer had moved into the center of the room, stood now with arms folded.

"You mean other than our coming here was very likely a big mistake? Oh, nothing much. How about you?"

"We may have more on the Cutler Cult; should know more by the time we get home." Matthew let Jennifer's tone register then, not just her words. "You haven't been threatened?"

"More subtle than that," she said. "But it's there."

Matthew looked aside, gave a slow nod and placed his hands on the edge of the desk.

"It is," he said. "Though a lot less subtle than last year."

"Dad… a lot has happened since last year."

"You're not the first to say that."

"And so?" prompted Jennifer.

"You're not suggesting we pack up and go home?"

"Of course I am," said Jennifer "That's exactly what I'm suggesting."

"I'm not ready to do that, Jen. You, of course—"

"I'm not leaving you here alone," she jumped in.

Matthew let out a long breath, folded his arms across his chest and looked calmly to his daughter.

"We have the Gathering coming up," he said then. "You do what you can to avoid situations that put you alone. And hang with those you trust."

"Here? Really?"

"Come on, Jen. You've a few."

Jennifer turned toward the door, shaking her head.

"I gotta get changed," she grumbled. "The Gathering, don't you know…"

"Hold on." Matthew pushed off and away from the desk. "I'll stand watch in the hall."

"Geez, Dad." Jennifer opened the door. "Cute."

A number of Society members were already in the Great Hall, many milling about in small groups in quiet conversation, others standing alone, eyes drifting as they communed in thought-talk.

A long table of dark, heavy wood dominated the center of the room, lined with high-backed wooden chairs. To either side were a number of smaller tables with simple chairs. Additional chairs lined the walls.

Matthew and Jennifer came into the room, moved off to one side away from the door. Jennifer looked about at the goings-on in the room, spoke aside to her dad.

"Rather pretentious, don't you think?" she asked.

"Pretentious?"

Jennifer fell into a heavy melodramatic tone, "The Gathering…"

"Ah. Yes." Matthew gave a broad smile as he studied the room. "A holdover from back in the day."

"We're all holdovers from back in the day, Dad."

And at that… Walter Fletcher, an unremarkable middle-aged man with an unremarkable appearance stepped up to face Matthew. He said nothing at first, his expression cool.

Jennifer looked from Fletcher to her father.

"Um… later." She left Matthew to go find a chair along the wall.

"Hello, Fletcher," said Matthew, his own expression giving away nothing. "Good to see you."

"I doubt that," said Fletcher. "What are you doing here?"

Phillip Gryphen joined them then, wearing a pleasant grin.

"Matthew is here as a guest of the Father," said the patriarch of Gryphen House.

At that, Matthew held a hand out to Fletcher.

"I don't like it." Fletcher gave only a fleeting glance to Matthew's offered hand. "I don't like it at all."

"How sad." Matthew lowered his hand.

"I don't like it at all."

Fletcher moved off then. Phillip Gryphen watched him go in search of his seat, spoke in an aside to Matthew.

"I expect you're getting a bit of that, eh Matthew?"

"Oh, they've been quite polite for the most part." Matthew took a step nearer Gryphen, looked casually about the room. "I understand Mark is here."

"We arrived together," Gryphen's tone grew somber. "I have yet to determine my son's penance."

"Of course," said Matthew. *Best not to pursue this...*

Victor Broderick, Father of the Society, came through a side door with his wife Dianna and several staff. Dianna moved off to one side as Victor stood near a window a few yards from the head of the table. He and his staff fell into quiet conversation.

Matthew and Gryphen watched for several moments, noting a few of the attendees ending their own conversations and drifting toward their seats.

Gryphen indicated the nearest table, one of the smaller tables.

"Shall we?"

Matthew indicated an empty chair set in amongst those along the wall.

"I think I'll, uh…"

"Of course," said Gryphen, and he moved to the table as Matthew settled into the chair.

The Gathering, the headliner meeting of the summit, was well under way in the great hall. Thomas Lawrence, a middle-aged man with bushy, unruly hair and clothes one size too big, stood near the head of the table, a step to one side of Victor, the Father sitting at the head of the table.

Thomas had a sheaf of papers in hand. He moved the top sheet to the back, took a moment to review the next sheet.

"The conference on the calendar for early next month," he began, "a pre-scheduled follow-up to yesterday's 'Infiltrations into Human Government' workshop, has been pushed out at least three weeks, revised date and location to be determined. Scheduled attendees will be notified as to new date and location per normal channels."

He paused then, looked up from the sheet.

"And that's the last of the event announcements for now," he concluded. "Are there any questions?"

There was an immediate thought-talk exchange between two of the attendees, though the sub-vocal exchange was open for all to here.

"They no doubt need time to regroup after the blistering success of yesterday's meeting," said the first in a sarcastic, biting tone. This brought simmering chuckling from many in the room.

"Hey, now. This is serious stuff," said the second, as sarcastic as the first. "You know the difficulties involved. Baby steps now."

The first attendee lost any cover of humor.

"Baby's been grown a hundred years gone now, friend. Time to put away the diapers."

The Father of the Society did not appreciate the distraction, spoke aloud in a reproachful tone.

"We shall continue," he stated firmly.

This brought a few uncomfortable chuckles and smirks from several in the room, and then the room fell quiet.

Victor gave a thank-you nod of dismissal to Thomas. Thomas acknowledged the nod and returned to his chair.

Victor took a few calculated moments to study the papers before him.

"One final important recognition before we move on," he said then. "A major thank you to Edmund Hawthorne, who has been doing a great job heading up the Phase Three research team since taking over for

Fran. I was sorry to see Fran step down, but it is good to know the project is in good hands."

Edmund, sitting midway down the main table, calmly accepted the polite applause from those in the room.

"Thanks again, Edmund. Well done," said Victor. He set the sheet of paper aside, spoke to the room without looking at the remaining paperwork before him. "The discussion on the floor is in regard to a subject brought up at an earlier meeting, a matter that we need to revisit… the policy surrounding Gray Caste criteria."

This brought about both vocal groans and a rise in background noise from sub-vocal thought-talk.

Jennifer stepped out of the Great Hall and into the hallway. She let the door close silently behind her, saw then Mary sitting at a bench several yards down the hall. She considered for half a dozen seconds, then took the few steps and stood at the end of the bench.

With no response or acknowledgment from Mary, Jennifer sat beside her. Mary said nothing, gave no sign that she knew Jennifer was sitting next to her.

"Not the most exciting Gathering I've been to," said Jennifer.

Still nothing from Mary.

"Important, I suppose, from a Society perspective," Jennifer mumbled. "Sharing of facts… consensus. All that."

"Yes," Mary stated. "Important."

Jennifer was almost encouraged.

"Have you had a chance to sit in?" she asked.

Mary turned to look directly at Jennifer.

"I am sitting in."

A moment of realization then from Jennifer. She gave a short nod and turned forward.

"Of course. Sorry."

Mary looked away then, slowly, forward again.

"No need to apologize."

Long, awkward moments passed. Seconds ticked oh-so-slowly by. It came as a relief when the door to the Great Hall opened, a distraction from the uncomfortable silence. The relief quickly faded then at the sight of Mark Gryphen.

Mark gave a cheerful smile at seeing Mary and Jennifer, stepped quickly over. He indicated the door to the Great Hall.

"I thought I was going to doze off in there." To Jennifer then, "You?"

"Just taking a break," she said.

"Right." Mark looked from Jennifer to Mary. "Hello, Mary. Are you enjoying your first Summit?"

Mary slowly turned her head to look up at Mark Gryphen.

"I am not here to have fun, Mr. Gryphen. I am here to learn. I am here to… experience."

"Right," sighed Mark. "Experience. Important. Still, no harm in having a little fun while you're at it. Right?"

Mary betrayed no emotion.

"I suppose not."

Mary looked away from Mark Gryphen, a sign of dismissal. Jennifer tried to hide a smile as she too looked away from Mark.

Mark appeared increasingly uncomfortable.

"Well," he managed. "I'm heading to the cafeteria for a snack. Would either of you care to join me?"

"Not just now," said Jennifer. "Thank you."

Mary, continuing to reveal no emotion, gave her response in thought-talk.

"No. I would not care to join you, Mr. Gryphen."

Mark, disconcerted, put on an awkward, uncomfortable smile.

"Perhaps another time," he managed. He took a step back, gave a nod and started away in the direction of the hallway leading to the cafeteria.

Jennifer waited until he had gone.

"That was a bit harsh, wasn't it Mary?" she asked. "Not that I disagree with the sentiment."

Mary said nothing for some moments, and Jennifer thought she might be through talking altogether, and then the young girl spoke, cool and matter-of-factly.

"He will bring much trouble to Gryphen House," she stated. Another few moments, then, "I like his father."

"I have fond memories of Phillip Gryphen," said Jennifer, pondering. "I think my father likes him."

Another long pause from Mary.

"Your father sees people," she said.

Jennifer had to think on what Mary might mean by that. She considered.

"You might be right about that," she said then. "Don't tell him I said so."

"The subject is not likely to come up."

"No. I suppose not."

Jennifer leaned forward, elbows on her knees. The two young women were both silent for a long time, Mary placidly observing their surroundings, content not to converse, Jennifer just lost in thought.

"Sees people," said Jennifer then, just above a whisper. "Yes… I suppose that's true."

Chapter Five

Matthew quietly, and as much as possible unobtrusively, watched the Gathering's goings-on from his place sitting in one of the chairs set against the wall. There were the occasional glances in his direction from one or another of the attendees, but these grew less and less frequent as the meeting wore on.

The meeting had just finished up one agenda item and was moving on to the next.

"Headmaster will now catch us up on the status of the upgrades to the Academy's East Wing," said Victor. He looked over at Headmaster, sitting at one of the smaller tables. "Headmaster?"

The Academy's Headmaster slowly stood, looked briefly about the room. Seeing Matthew, he managed a subtle nod in his direction before offering another to Victor.

"Thank you, Father," he said. He spoke to the room, then. "There have been a few very minor setbacks, due primarily to delays in material deliveries, but we are not far off schedule. The expansion of the first floor will complete late next month, the second floor upgrades are now near completion. The attic conversion has already begun."

"And the upcoming semester?" asked Victor.

"We are on schedule to reopen the East Wing in time for the next semester," said Headmaster. He gave another look about the room, a final nod to Victor, and sat down.

Victor responded with an acknowledging bow of the head, then spoke to the room as he reviewed the paperwork before him.

"Headmaster gave me a quick tour just last week. I was much impressed. The upgrades were much needed, and should serve our students well." Victor set aside the top sheet and looked over the information on the next. He glanced at the time as he spoke. "The next item on the agenda, evaluation of the Andover Project, status review and projections."

There was an immediate undercurrent of white-noise pushing in on Matthew as many in the room began voicing concerns and apprehensions in thought-talk. The undercurrent of noise came through as harsh, hissing whisperings; it grew louder and more intense, the words "Sutherland" and "Matthew" and "traitor" frequently coming through amongst the static.

Victor raised a hand for silence, his expression stern. It took a few moments, but quiet soon returned to the room.

Fletcher spoke up then, vocally, breaking the silence.

"He can't be here," he said, his tone severe.

More noise… both thought-talk and aloud.

Victor again held out a hand for silence. He looked again at the time.

"This would be a good time to adjourn for lunch," he said. "Return in one hour."

There was a moment's hesitation, then all in the room began to stand, chairs sliding back, attendees working their way toward the door. Vocal and sub-vocal white noise picked up yet again.

Victor stood up, managed to get Matthew's attention. Matthew worked his way through the generally less-than-friendly faces.

"Matthew…" said Victor.

Matthew noted Headmaster waiting in the background before turning his attention to Victor.

"Hello, Victor." There was the hint of snarkiness in Matthew's tone. "Thanks again for the invite."

"My pleasure." Victor noted the still-departing attendees, several of whom were looking back in his direction. "You do bring out the best in people."

"I consider that to be one of my better qualities."

"No doubt," said Victor. "Well… as much as I am sure you enjoyed this morning's session, perhaps this afternoon you should be somewhere else."

Mary was still seated on the bench, Jennifer standing beside her. The door to the Great Hall stood open as people worked their way out of the meeting, streaming past Jennifer and the young girl. Some openly stared at Jennifer, some gave her frosty side-glances.

Those looking down at Mary as they passed looked uncomfortable, uncertain as to what to expect from her.

The last of the meeting attendees passed by and there was still no Matthew. Jennifer looked expectantly to the door.

Matthew appeared then in the doorway. Seeing Jennifer, he stepped over to her, gave her a subtly humorous smile.

"I have been given the afternoon off," he stated.

"Afternoon off..."

"I'll explain later." He glanced about them, briefly to Mary, again to Jennifer.

"The sun is shining, the day is most pleasant. Walk with me?"

"Um… I guess." Jennifer was slightly taken aback; not exactly Dad's way.

Matthew looked to Mary.

"Mary?"

Mary's expression, while not open was not unfriendly.

"Another time, Matthew," she said. "I am expected for lunch."

Matthew looked back through the open door and into the Great Hall. Victor was at the far end of the room speaking to Headmaster.

"Of course," he said, turning again to Mary. "As you say, another time."

The sun was shining down on the sprawling garden of low-growing bushes and colorful flowerbeds. There were a number of people about, enjoying the lunchtime break before returning to the afternoon session.

Matthew and Jennifer strolled slowly along the garden's main path. They slowed further and stepped aside as a couple passed, walking the opposite direction. The woman gave Jennifer a cold stare.

"It's not getting any better, Dad," said Jennifer as they continued on. "Worse, if you ask me."

Matthew gave a friendly yet hesitant smile to another couple passing by.

They did not return it.

"I would say there are those whom I believe are actively organizing against us," he said.

"Have you talked with Victor about it?"

"He is no doubt aware of it."

"And yet he does nothing." Jennifer came to a stop, waited for Matthew to stop and turn back to her. "Why are we here, Dad? Why did he invite us?"

"The one for our own reasons, the other for Victor's; which, if I were to hazard a guess, has something to do with the very hostility of which you speak."

"He wants this?" she asked, her voice raised. Then, "What am I saying… he did try to have you killed."

"He's looking for resolution, and that can go either way," said Matthew, in all serious now. "Sutherland House is casting a shadow over the Society, and he doesn't like that."

Matthew looked across the garden. He could see Mrs. Evans walking with Victor's two young children.

He started forward again, Jennifer following beside her father. They worked their way to one of the gates and out to the main plaza. They walked across the courtyard and approached the front steps of the main building.

Catherine Gray was sitting on the steps, taking in the sun.

"Catherine," said Matthew as they took the first step.

Catherine gave an acknowledging nod, continuing to look out across the courtyard, the sun on her face.

"Still with us, I see," she said.

"Wouldn't miss it," said Matthew, several steps above her now.

"Matthew…" Catherine said, softly now, focus forward still.

Matthew stopped, half-turned and looked back to Catherine.

"Catherine."

"You've more enemies than friends, Matthew."

Thanks for sharing.,.

"So I do have friends, then…"

Catherine glanced down at her hands, rubbed her palms together. She looked up again and out across the courtyard.

"More than you know, fewer than you need."

Late afternoon sunlight streamed through the window and into Matthew's room, motes of dust floating in the air. He came out of the bathroom, buttoning the clean shirt he'd just put on after washing up. He was speaking to Computer.

"All right, so you've verified he has a sister and she's part of his cult. See what more you can dig up on her background, her family; anything that might give us some insight."

"I have already begun such research," came the voice of Computer.

"And we need to know what role she has in Cutler's organization; lieutenant in charge of what?"

"I will try to have something for you upon your return," Computer stated. "On that point, Matthew, I do not know what further can be gained by you remaining at the summit. Perhaps an early departure…"

Matthew tucked in the shirttail into his pants as he walked to the window. He looked out at the oncoming dusk.

"You've been speaking to Jennifer," he said.

Computer did not respond. The room was eerily quiet for several seconds.

"Dinner this evening," Matthew said then. "You never know what might come up in dinner conversation."

Hesitation, and then, "Yes, Matthew."

Matthew turned from the window.

"We'll be heading home in the morning," he said.

"Yes, Matthew."

"I'll be careful, Computer."

"Yes, Matthew."

Matthew stood in the middle of the room. Another long moment's hesitation, then his expression very slowly shifted to… uncertainty.

Something…

Matthew sensed something… something wasn't right…

Something isn't right…

He tried to push it aside, at the same time tried to sort out what it might be.

Matthew smoothed the sleeves of his tucked-in shirt, pulled at his cuffs.

"I'll talk to you after dinner, Computer. Out."

The room again fell silent. Matthew tilted his head, lent an ear, listened … something was brushing at his mind.

It was there, and then it was not.

Mathew moved to the door, rested his hand on the doorknob.

He hesitates yet again… *something*…

He opened the door then and left the room.

Catherine met Victor and Dianna midway up the lobby stairs, she on her way down, they on their way up.

"Victor. There you are." She stopped, effectively blocking his way. "I need to speak with you."

Victor frowned at Catherine, looked aside to Dianna.

"You go ahead," he said. "I'll be right there."

Dianna looked from Victor to Catherine. She raised a brow and Catherine made way for her.

"Catherine," Victor said then. "What can I do for you?"

Catherine took the step between them, looked sharply at the Father of the Society.

"You know what they're planning," she said, a statement, not a question.

"Excuse me?"

"Victor," accusing.

Victor turned and looked out across the lobby. He stuffed his hands into the pockets of his light jacket. He and Dianna had been walking out in the courtyard.

"Of course I do," he said then. "How could I not?"

"And you're going to allow it?"

"He'll be fine." He turned back to Catherine. "They're not fully ready just yet."

"Victor." Catherine appeared dumbfounded. Realization. "You're not just allowing it. You want it. It's why you invited him."

Victor turned again to look out across the lobby. There were increasing shadows, the tall windows turning gray as the afternoon sun drifted toward dusk.

Catherine moved to stand on the same step as Victor, her words falling to harsh whisper.

"But why? What would be the point now? Andover is…" she hesitated, considered. "I see. Yes. What better way to test the project?"

"We've made significant advances since Andover, despite the setback."

"But why do you need Sutherland?"

"Why not? Despite the early stage of the project at the time, he did expose several weaknesses. The incident will serve as a benchmark."

"And Mary will step in yet again," said Catherine. "You know how she feels about him."

"I'm counting on it," said Victor. "Without her intervention, how are we to compare the results of the test? Or the status of the project?"

Both fell silent for several moments. The sounds of guests moving about the lobby, speaking in low voices, drifted up the staircase.

"Nothing more than a yardstick for you now," she said, her tone surrendering. "He was once your friend, Victor."

"And he is yet yours, Catherine."

"At the moment, I like him a lot more than I like you."

Victor managed a sympathetic smile.

"Matthew will be fine," he said. "Mary will see to that. She believes the Society still needs him."

Catherine said nothing. At that, Victor set his jaw and took the next step up the staircase.

"I believe we're done here," he said, took another step and looked back to Catherine. "I'll see you at dinner."

Catherine hesitated, finally gave a curt nod. Victor smiled and nodded in response, turned and continued up the staircase.

Matthew entered the Great Hall, earlier that day the site of the Gathering. A single overhead light put the large room into shadow; there was the dark silhouette of a figure at the head of the main table, a man sitting in high-back chair.

Matthew moved over to the table, looking about the room and into the shadows as he did so. He pulled out a chair and sat down.

The man at the head of the table shifted slightly, his face now visible. It was Ben Aldridge. He wore a blank expression.

"Ben," said Matthew, working to match the empty expression. "I didn't expect to see you sitting there."

"Hey, Matthew. I volunteered."

"Really? Again, unexpected. I never saw you in the role of an assault front man."

"Not to worry, Matthew," said Ben. "I'm just here to see that we don't have another Andover incident."

"Worried? No… As for another incident, that's not up to me."

Another *something* brushed at his mind. Tendrils of thoughts, of searching? He wasn't sure. He reached out, stretched his mind outward, in all directions.

Matthew saw them; ethereal observers watching from their rooms and from other meeting halls, from staircases and hallways.

He could just hear the whispers of thought-talk.

"Is it?" he asked then. "Up to me?"

Ben ignored the question.

"We may not have been close friends, Matthew, but I've always considered us… comrades, shall we say?"

"That would suggest something shared. What might that be, Ben?"

"Despite what they would say, I know that you believe in the Society. You fear that it has gone astray." Ben gave a supportive smile. "I too believe in the Society. I too have concerns that it has veered from the path."

Matthew's expression changed subtly… something buzzing in his head, and a vibration in his chest. He shifted, uncomfortable, and rubbed at his temple, tried not show a growing anxiety.

"Be careful that you don't find yourself on the wrong list Ben."

"The schism between you and the Society is not due to your views regarding the

Agenda, Matthew. It is rather your active opposition to it."

The white noise scratching at Matthew's brain increased as the level of thought-talk rose. He lifted a hand, brushed the noise aside with two raised fingers, pushing it again into the background.

"An agenda that is diametrically opposed to all that is the Society," he said.

A knowing smile from Ben.

"And so there you are," he said.

Matthew tried and failed to return the smile. He looked to one side as if looking at the distant observers.

"And so what happens now?" he asked Ben. His level of distress rose again, he again raised a hand. It was more difficult this time. He drew his fingers to a fist. He furrowed his brow and pushed back a rising hissing sound. It didn't help the discomfort.

Ben leaned back in his chair, his face drifting back into shadow.

"A lot has changed since the Andover Project, since its premature conclusion," he said. "Much progress, if you will. Even shifts in direction."

"So I see." Matthew spoke through increasing unease and discomfort. "And have these shifts brought the Agenda back in line with the purpose of the Society?"

"Not so much, no. I bring it up only to note that the vaster project has advanced beyond the original Andover research that you were witness to."

"Then why tell me this? To get me to do what?"

"To get you… nothing," said Ben, shrugging. "I'm thinking they wanted you to know that the Agenda trudges inexorably on in spite of you."

"And just how does any of this, Andover and wherever the project has gone since, how does any of it advance the Agenda?"

"Ah!" Ben's broad smile was genuine. "And that they don't want you to know. I find it petty, but there you are." He shifted forward in his chair and indicated the room around them. "And here we are."

"Yes..." Matthew's brow furrowed deeper, his frown darkened. He shifted position in his chair.

He saw…

There came an ethereal image of three people standing in a tight circle in an empty room. They were facing inward, eyes closed, their expressions intense.

Matthew raised a hand to brush aside the image.

"This is new," he said.

Matthew's distress suddenly increased yet again, very uncomfortable now.

Ben looked on…

"The uh… *funneling* I believe you call it, has been reworked," he said. "Three working together, drawing on the powers of the individuals of the larger group, pushing it out then without the need of an initiator being present."

Matthew used his raised hand to push against the force that was threatening to overwhelm him.

Ben leaned forward, rested his forearms on the table. He managed a growing hint of concern on his face. His words carried earnestness.

"And the ability to focus telekinesis, to reimagine it, brought now to a fine precision." Ben pointed to Matthew's chest. "The ability to target specific organs within an individual's chest; to take hold…" He drew back his hand, closed his fingers. "To grip, to squeeze."

Ben relaxed then. He slid his chair back and stood up.

"Again… the project has advanced somewhat… the research continues." Ben seemed to sense something then, and he half-turned, curious, looked across the room.

The misty image of Mary appeared in the corner of the room, a ghostly figure. Motionless for several long seconds, she tilted and turned her head, appearing to look to Ben, then to Matthew, then aside to something that none in the room could see.

Matthew shifted about in his chair and got to his feet.

Mary turned forward then, facing the heart of the room, her expression revealing nothing.

"No," she said, impassive, the word drifting across the span of thought-talk. She lifted her arm from her side, held a hand out before her. Two fingers shifted and twitched.

The background whisperings increased suddenly, as suddenly fell to nothing, leaving only silence.

In some distant room, heavy in shadow, the three individuals standing in a circle each took a stumbling step back from the center.

Mary slowly lowered her hand to her side. She half-turned her head, looked to Matthew.

Matthew felt an increasing intensity building up somewhere within him. He turned his gaze from Mary, looked forward. He swiped a hand before him, brushed aside the image of the three.

Mary moved her gaze from Matthew to Ben. She cocked her head to one side.

"No more," she stated firmly, again in thought-talk.

She gave a final glance to Matthew, and her image faded… she was gone.

Ben and Matthew alone again, Ben smiled and spoke in an almost jovial tone.

"I would call that a successful test, wouldn't you?" he asked.

Matthew, regaining some composure, rested his hands on the back of the chair.

"So this was all about Mary," he said.

"Oh no… not at all." Ben gave shrug then, a smirk. "Well, a lot of it, maybe. But not all."

Matthew thought it through, considered, finally then: "She is the Society's greatest hope, , and also its greatest threat."

"Disappointed, Matthew? You're no longer number one."

"I like the company."

"No doubt," said Ben. He moved to one side and sat on the corner of the table. "That still puts you on the outside looking in, though; doesn't it?"

"I'm right where I need to be." Matthew pushed off the chair. "And where does that put you, Ben? Didn't you say we were comrades?"

"I do my part. I continue to gather the data, perform the analyses, and follow where it leads."

"And that's where you are? Taking the project forward?"

"Along the proper path, Matthew. As I said." Ben pushed off the corner of the table. He held a hand out to Matthew. "Good to see you, Matthew. We'll do this again."

Matthew studied the offered hand.

"I'd just as soon not," he said.

Chapter Six

Matthew and Jennifer strolled casually along the path winding through the garden. They had been in quiet conversation for several minutes. The evening sky was graying, the horizon losing its sunset colors.

"We saw it coming though, didn't we?" asked Jennifer.

"Yes... though the specifics were rather a surprise," said Matthew.

"That's true enough." Jennifer gave worried side-glance to Matthew. "Are you all right? You still look a bit... beaten down."

"I've been better." Matthew looked up at the evening sky. It was clear, the air cool, "They've taken what they learned at Andover to a whole new level."

"No kidding."

"Harder to fight against; more important, they can take this out to the real world, use it against whomever they want and no one the wiser."

"At least now we can tie in what they were doing in Andover to the Agenda."

"Which makes the Agenda more dangerous, and more heinous."

They walked on in silence for a time. Others in the garden, some distance away, would briefly looked their way before turning away.

"You came here to learn," said Jennifer then. "Happy now?"

Matthew said nothing, but managed a grin.

They continued their evening walk.

It was a most pleasant morning. Matthew and Jennifer stood at the foot of the steps of the main building. Matthew's attention was on the breezeway where he had last seen his car.

"I'm sure it's fine, Dad," said Jennifer.

"Sure, sure…" Matthew mumbled absently.

Behind them, the footman appeared at the top of the steps with their two bags. He started down the steps.

Matthew's Comet appeared in the breezeway and then entered the courtyard. He watched its approach and began walking around the car as it was still coming to a stop. He was looking for signs of damage.

The valet turned off the engine, climbed out of the car and walked to the back where the footman waited with the bags. The keys were passed and the footman opened the trunk.

Matthew watched the luggage being loaded into the trunk; Jennifer stepped up beside him. She quickly looked the car over.

"What'd I tell you? Not a scratch."

"Hmm…" frowning.

The bags loaded into the trunk, Matthew stepped up beside the footman, reached for the trunk lid before the footman could close the trunk.

"Thank you," said Matthew. "I'll take care of that."

The footman stepped back and away with a nod. Matthew looked over at Jennifer as he closed the trunk and started around to the driver's door.

"We've places to go, things to do, daughter."

"I just want to go home," said Jennifer.

"We'll be there by lunch."

Jennifer opened the passenger door, spoke to Matthew over the roof of the car.

"And then what?" she asked. "What are we going to do about what happened yesterday?"

"About what happened? Nothing. About what it means… I don't know." He gave a wink and nod as he climbed into the car. "For now, places to go, things to do."

Victor and Dianna stepped through the doors of the main building and moved to the top of the steps. They paused, noting Matthew's car traveling slowly across the courtyard in the direction of the front gate. Starting down the steps then, Dianna gave a nod in the direction of the Comet.

"Safely away," she said.

"Never a doubt, my dear," said Victor.

Reaching the bottom step, both looked back behind them at the sound of their children coming out of the building under the escort of Mrs. Evans. The children quickly fell silent as they descended the steps toward their parents.

Victor and Dianna turned forward then, as two black sedans moved out of the breezeway and came in their direction.

Meanwhile, Matthew's car maneuvered through the front gate. Dianna watched it leave the villa, spoke to Victor in a low voice, almost conspiratorial.

"You would consider your efforts to be successful…"

Victor looked to the now empty front gate across the courtyard; a sly grin formed and then faded.

"I believe I would," he said.

The two sedans came to a stop before them. They started toward the first, Mrs. Evans and the children toward the second.

Mary and Headmaster appeared at the top of the steps. Mary watched Victor and his family as they began loading into the sedans.

Victor looked up at Mary. Her expression remained cool and aloof at Victor's smile and nod.

She watched him climb into the back of the sedan. She spoke calmly and precisely to Headmaster.

"I will not be used again, Headmaster." She watched as the pair of black sedans started across the courtyard toward the gate. "I will do what is best for the Society."

Headmaster stood looking out across the courtyard, the morning sun shining brightly across the compound.

"I expect nothing less of you, Mary."

End Episode Three…

Episode 4
Threads

Chapter One

There was a sense of presence about the quiet stillness within the walls of Sutherland House. The rooms were filled with shadows; gray, mote-filled light from thinly curtained windows hung in the air.

The front door opened and Matthew Sutherland came into the small foyer. He closed the door and tossed the keys into the tray on the side table. He stepped further into the house, hesitated and looked curiously about. He stepped into the living room, taking in the silence.

He started down the hall then, taking off his jacket and hanging it on the wall hook as he passed it. He opened a door and took the narrow stairwell down to the basement. He flipped the light switch and crossed the room, passing free-standing shelves filled with home-canned jars of fruit and vegetables.

There was a small workshop area at the far end of the basement, a handmade workbench along the far wall, a set of shelves beside the workbench.

Matthew reached into the shelves and released the hidden latch. There was a metallic click sound and the shelves swung open a few inches. Pulling the shelves open further, they glided easily, revealing a dark shaft with a ladder leading down.

He stepped into the shaft and onto the ladder and climbed down. Reaching the bottom of the ladder, Matthew stepped out and into the underground Apartment. Overhead lighting came on as he moved into the room.

The Apartment was comfortable contemporary; high-tech mixed with the every day. The wall to either side of the access shaft behind him was lined with shelves filled with books. A door set into the wall to Matthew's right opened to a small armory, another door to the bathroom. There was a counter beyond that, behind which was the small kitchen.

Set into the wall on Matthew's left was a large monitor screen, beside that a bank of computer monitors, five screens across and four rows high. All were off at the moment.

A door in the far wall directly ahead opened to a long hallway that led to the underground garage. To the left of the door were racks of computer network, server and communications equipment.

There was a living area in the center of the Apartment between the kitchen counter and the computer center, with a round kitchen table and chairs, a couch facing the wall monitor.

There was no one in the Apartment.

Matthew walked into the kitchen area, spoke into the air as he opened the refrigerator.

"Good afternoon, Computer," he said. "Status, if you please."

He took a can of iced tea out of the fridge, closed the door and started out of the kitchen.

"Good afternoon, Matthew," said Computer, the calm voice coming from hidden speakers. "General status, nothing to report. Would you like specific update details on our outstanding projects?"

Matthew moved around to the front of the couch, popped open his can of tea and sat down.

"Not at the moment, thank you." He took a long drink and sat down. "Do you know where Jennifer is?"

"I do not know her current location. She left the Apartment approximately three hours ago without informing me of her destination. Would you like me to attempt contact?"

"Not necessary." Matthew frowned, stared in the general direction of the wall monitor. "I suppose we should take a look at where we are with the Cutler situation."

"Of course, Matthew."

The large screen wall monitor activated, displaying images and data windows. The glow from the screen spread out across the Apartment.

"John Cutler, the name used in the outside world," said Computer. "Society name, Jon Willeby."

Matthew took a few moments to reacquaint himself with the background information regarding Cutler, looking from data window to data window.

The picture displaying in the top left of the monitor was a face shot of John Cutler: in his thirties, thick brown hair, bright blue eyes, clean-shaven.

One of the windows displayed a set of data regarding the Willeby Family, a Lesser Society family. A second data window displayed a timeline detailing the timespan from Jon Willeby's move to the outside world forward, picking up the outside name of John Cutler, the rise of his cult-like organization, and on to the present.

"I would have thought the Willeby Family would have tried to rein in their wayward son by now," said Matthew.

"I can find no evidence of any such attempt, Matthew," said Computer.

"Yes. I know," Matthew said thoughtfully. "And that Victor has let this go on to now is downright puzzling."

He continued studying the data displayed in the individual windows on the monitor. He slid back further into the couch, took another swallow from his iced tea.

"Two years and then some," he said at last. Another long pause, and then, "All right, what do you have on his sister?"

The monitor screen flickered and a new set of image and data windows replaced the John Cutler display. A picture of a young woman was set in the upper left corner. Short hair, sharp eyes, strong jaw.

Two data windows provided background info.

"Joan Kendall, age twenty five," said Computer.

Matthew shifted forward, elbows on knees, studied the displayed data.

"Half-sister to Jon Willeby," continued Computer. "She is the product of a brief affair between Willeby Family patriarch Gregory Willeby and an Outside woman, Barbara Kendall. Barbara Kendall was never made aware of the Society. Gregory Willeby was unaware of the child until Joan Kendall was three years old. He began providing for her support soon after, though her existence continued to be hidden from the Society and other members of the Willeby Family."

Matthew indicated one of the data windows with the hand holding his tea.

"Until…" he prompted.

"Yes," Computer stated. "John Cutler discovered the existence of his half-sister some time before leaving for the outside world. He reached out to her not long after his departure and the founding of his movement."

"I'm not surprised that Gregory kept the child hush-hush. I <u>am</u> surprised that John ever got wind of her."

"I have not been able to determine how that came about. Nor have I been able to determine if the discovery had anything to do with John Cutler's departure."

"I suspect it would be at most a minor contributing factor, if at all," said Matthew. "So… Joan has been a part of her brother's cult from the beginning."

"She quickly became his most trusted lieutenant and advisor."

"And I assume she knows all about the—"

"Cryptic and obscure comments lead me to conclude that John Cutler has told her of the Society, and the fact that the Willeby Family to which he belongs is one of the Lesser Families."

Matthew shifted again on the couch, considered, studied the monitor without really looking at anything in particular.

"Abilities?" he asked.

"As best I have been able to determine, Joan Kendall has never shown any signs of having any of the Abilities."

"Not surprising, really… being half Society, half Outside." There was a long moment's pause. "And so the *miracles* of the cult are left to the cult leader."

"As best I have been able to determine," said Computer. "Instances of Abilities are presented to the outside as miracles."

There was a flicker on the display screen, a new window overlaid several of the others. It was a picture of a print flyer, promoting an upcoming meeting.

"In about two weeks and then some," said Matthew, reading.

"They do also have weekly gatherings; small, simple events."

"Right. Fridays," said Matthew, somewhat distant now. He let the conversation fade as he grew more introspective. He half-turned his head, furrowed his brow. He appeared to be looking at something that wasn't there…

At least, not something in the Apartment…

He brought himself back after a few long moments, struggled to refocus on the subject at hand.

"The Cutler estate is about four hours from here," he said, half statement, half question.

"Four hours, twenty minutes," said Computer. "Following posted speed limits, assuming average traffic patterns."

"Right. So, four hours."

"Four hours," Computer conceded.

Matthew slid fully back into the couch and took a long swallow of his iced tea. He studied the half empty can.

"An overnight trip, however you look at it," he said.

"I would think so, Matthew."

"Yeah," Matthew said absently, his thoughts slowly drifting, his mind wandering to something other than the subject at hand.

Computer let one of the windows on the monitor close, then another, windows winking out one by one.

Again… Matthew sensed… *something*.

He slowly turned his head, tilted his head, looked up through a thin, drifting mist that wasn't there; up through the ceiling, through the house above, up and beyond, fading… fading…

To Jennifer Sutherland.

Matthew's daughter was standing next to the old Ford Bronco, just one of the Sutherland vehicles, leaning against the driver's door. She was at Rydel Ridge, one of her father's favorite getaways. The lookout point had a small picnic area and an equally small parking lot. The park was surrounded on several sides by a grove of trees. Downslope below the ridge was a meadow frequented by deer.

Jennifer's eyes were closed, her arms folded across her chest. She appeared to be lost in thought. She frowned and furrowed her brow.

Fading… fading…

Down into the Apartment, through an ethereal mist; Matthew was sitting on the couch, his head turned, looking up, gazing up…

Fading… fading…

Rydel Ridge, Jennifer… leaning against the Ford Bronco. Her frown morphed to a thin smile. She slowly opened her eyes. She took a long breath and looked about her.

She spoke then in the general direction of the open window of the Bronco's driver door.

"Computer… you there?"

A long moment passed, then Computer's voice came from speakers in the vehicle's cabin.

"Hello, Jennifer. I am here."

"You and Dad having a one-on-one in the Apartment?"

"Yes, Jennifer," said Computer. Another long pause. "Your father says hello."

Jennifer's smile broadened.

"Hello…"

Matthew shifted about on the couch, turned forward.

"Jennifer's Distant Sight is improving," he said.

"It would appear so," said Computer.

"She needs to work on privacy norms."

Computer understood that there was no response required, and so said nothing.

"Interesting, don't you think?" Matthew asked, growing thoughtful. "Jennifer picks up two Abilities, both at a very late age, and both are the rarest of the six Abilities."

"Quite, Matthew."

"Very rare," Matthew continued. "Social Sight, in particular. And few are able to develop Social or Distant to any degree."

"We have yet to see how far Jennifer will develop her skills in either," said Computer. "Her Distant Sight is improving; to date however, her Social Sight Ability is only in the earliest stages."

"No pressure of course, but if she could take it to any serious level…" Matthew's focus was on the now totally dark wall monitor. "I only know of one other who has ever been able to reach full potential."

"Mary."

"So I understand."

The exchange ebbed, the Apartment grew quiet. Matthew turned from the monitor, his gaze drifting to one side, finally to the empty can in his hand.

He considered then…

"Friday... I should pack a bag."

"You will attend John Cutler's next weekly gathering then?"

"Why not?" asked Matthew. "Let's see what the man has to say."

The morning sun sent rays streaking across the grounds of the Cutler Estate. The compound in the heart of the estate contained the main house, meeting hall, garage and number of outbuildings. Surrounding the central compound, within the enclosing ivy walls, were vegetable gardens and orchards. A small orchard of four rows of apple trees lay between the south ivy wall and the central compound.

John Cutler walked between two of the rows, studying each of the trees that he passed with an experienced eye. Cutler was middle-aged, tall and slim. He was dressed in casual pants and shirt, leather boots. He wore a light jacket, a pair of gloves stuffed into the pockets.

He stopped at a tree with a ladder standing nearby. He moved the ladder into position, picked up a bag with a shoulder strap and took the first few rungs of the ladder. He began pulling apples free and placing them into the bag.

Raymond approached then, walking along the row of fruit trees. Cutler's young associate was in his twenties; he was dressed casually, was clean shaven, his hair thick and bushy.

He stood near the ladder and looked up at Cutler.

"Mr. Cutler," he said. "It is time to prepare for the meeting."

Cutler continued picking apples, responded without looking down at his associate.

"Raymond," he said. "Tell me again why I agreed to two meetings this week."

"I believe it was your idea, sir. Something about a growing flock."

Cutler placed an apple into the bag, hesitated and looked outward, across the orchard.

"I don't like that term. *Flock*. We need another name for our followers. Work on that."

"Yes sir." Raymond looked from Cutler back toward the compound. "The meeting, sir…"

John Cutler gave a heavy sigh and descended the ladder.

"Yes, yes…" he grumbled, stepping off the bottom rung. He noted then a young woman dressed in a light sun dress at the end of the row of trees, approaching.

"Thank you, Raymond," he said in dismissal. "I'll be in soon."

Raymond nodded acknowledgement, turned away as the woman arrived.

"Joan," said Cutler.

"Brother," stated Joan. Joan Kendall was twenty five years old, medium height and build. She kept her hair cut short; she used very little makeup, and none was needed.

"Have you come to tell me the crowd is growing restless?" asked Cutler.

"Not at all, John. Don't know from the crowd, haven't been to the meeting hall." She glanced back to the compound. "Ah, yes… two meetings this week."

"Yeah… not sure if it's really necessary," droned Cutler. "I understand it was my idea."

"So I hear," said Joan.

They started slowly down the row, heading back to the compound. They walked in silence for several moments.

"And so?" Cutler prompted then.

"I have word this morning from our Society contact… there has been a recent uptick in interest regarding our activities." Joan looked side-glance to Cutler. "You did ask to be kept current on such."

"That I did, sister," said Cutler. "Good to hear, good to hear."

They entered the center of the compound. The main house, a sprawling single-storey complex, was directly ahead of them across the plaza. To the right of the house was a larger building: the meeting hall. Scattered about the compound were half a dozen outbuildings of various sizes.

A wide, flagstone walkway ran from the right side of the meeting hall across to a gate that was set into the tall fence several hundred feet distant.

John Cutler and his sister started toward the meeting hall.

"I appreciate all that you do for us, Joan," said Cutler. "I could never develop the relationships as you do; and with the Society having turned a blind eye to your very existence. You are amazing."

"Support for the cause grows within the Society, John," she said, ignoring the complement.

They stopped a few steps from the front of the meeting hall. Cutler frowned as he looked over to his sister.

"Change is coming to the Society; important change. Necessary change, if the Society is to survive." Cutler looked up and out across the compound. "With that evolution will come an end to castes. The Willeby Family will live in the shadow of the Primary Families no more."

"Never forget, dear brother, that those who support the cause do so for many reasons, and not all are fully supportive of the end of the Lesser Family caste."

"We'll deal with that when the time comes, Joan. For now the big tent serves us well enough."

"Of course." Joan half turned and indicated the door to the meeting hall. "And you've certainly drawn interest to that big tent; interest from both within the Society and from without."

"From without? We know from where that comes, do we not?" He opened the door stood to one side. "After you. Let us stir the contents of the witch's cauldron."

Chapter Two

The black sedan pulled into the strip of parking lot that bordered the Academy grounds. It maneuvered into one of the dozen spaces, most of which were empty. The driver's door opened moments later and Victor Broderick climbed out. He paused briefly to look about before stepping up onto a wide walk and started across the grounds toward the main building.

The grounds were quiet, still, no one else was about. Victor passed under the lone great tree that offered shade from the high, warm sun and continued in the direction of the central building. Still some distance away, his expression changed subtly; a moment later a hint of a smile.

He sensed something…

He spoke then in Thought Talk, using his internal voice.

"Good afternoon, Mary. How are you today?"

Mary's voice then, coming to Victor in Thought Talk.

"I am doing well, Father."

The Father of the Society reached the building, started up the steps to the front doors.

"I am glad," his voice reached out to her. "Are you in your room?"

"I am."

"I would like to see you later, if that's all right; after I speak with Headmaster."

"As you wish…" came softly. Several moments later, "Headmaster is waiting for you."

Victor opened the front door.

"Thank you, Mary." Victor entered the building.

Mary's room was sparse; a narrow bed, a dresser, a small desk and chair. Mary sat in a comfortable chair in the middle of the room, facing a curtained window that let in filtered light.

Her blank gaze drifted from the window as she slowly turned her head, looked outward to something beyond the room… outward, distant…

The Headmasters' office was just large enough to accommodate the desk and chair, with a pair of guest chairs facing the desk. Several walls were lined with book shelves. A thick cloud of mote-filled light shone through the small window set into the outside wall behind the desk. Artificial light struggled to reach through the frosted glass pane that was set into the only door opposite. The word "Headmaster" was stenciled on the glass, reverse image as seen from this side of the door.

The Academy Headmaster moved from the window and eased into the chair behind the desk. He leaned back, stared at the computer monitor that was positioned to one side on the desktop.

He looked away from the monitor, into the empty shadows that had settled in one corner of the office. His expression denoted deep concern.

His focus shifted slowly then to the office door. A moment later the door opened and Victor Broderick entered the room.

Victor gave a brief nod, closed the door and moved to one of the guest chairs.

"Headmaster," he stated.

"Hello, Father." Headmaster shifted his chair about as he straightened. "It is good of you to visit."

"My pleasure, Headmaster. I look forward to taking a look at the renovation work."

"Much changed since your last visit. All completed, I couldn't be more pleased."

"Excellent, excellent." Victor's expression shifted slowly; a thoughtful, considered frown. "Not my only reason for dropping by, I'm afraid."

"Of course. Mary." Headmaster gave a slow nod, held his gaze then on Victor. "I am uneasy, Father."

"I gather as much from your reports." Victor took a moment, considered. "Is she a danger to staff or students?"

"She has shown no such tendencies. No. No, of course not." Headmaster rested his arms on the desk and intertwined his fingers, stared down at his hands. "Mary's independence is of increasing concern to me."

"She is strong-willed, to be sure," said Victor, wearing a hint of a smile.

"Mary believes ardently in the Society, but if her views regarding the Society's direction differ from ours, she would have no qualms in following other than your suggested path, no matter your standing as the Father."

Victor's mask of humor faded away, his expression somber.

"Yes. We have already seen as much." A long pause, then a returning look of satisfaction. "Her Abilities… very much what we have been hoping for, Headmaster; beyond all expectations."

"And if her actions go fully against our desires?" asked Headmaster. "Your desires?"

"We must do what we can to insure that such does not happen, my friend. To accomplish that, she must remain here, under your guidance." Victor leaned forward as he prepared to stand. "Now... how about a tour of those renovations?"

Mary was sitting in her chair, in the middle of her room. The mote-filled sunlight washed over the girl, across her expressionless face. Her gaze reached out to something beyond her room, her blank expression unchanged, her focus somewhere distant.

The Apartment's ceiling light panels were set to dim, the room lit primarily by the large monitor display. Matthew was sitting on the couch, relaxed, a familiar can of iced tea in hand. His focus was on the data and pics that were displayed on the screen.

The door leading to the garage opened and Jennifer came into the Apartment. She walked over to the couch and plopped down beside her father. She took the can of tea from him and took a drink while studying the info on the display.

She handed the can back.

"So… Cutler is our next project, then?"

"Most likely," said Matthew. He took a swallow from his tea, furrowed his brow as he studied the display. "One or two things just don't add up. Something…" A slow shake of his head, then he looked to his daughter. "Anyway, what's up with you?"

"Waddya mean?"

"Really?" in faux disbelief.

"Right." Jennifer struggled to look sheepish. "That."

"Yes. That." Matthew shifted position on the couch. "Your Distant Sight is improving. The exercises are helping. That's obvious. But you have a couple of strikes going against you. The late blooming, we can't do anything about. But there's no reason you have to go this alone."

"I'm doing all right. I have you. And Computer."

"And neither of us has Abilities training experience; certainly not with yours."

"You're not suggesting I go to the Academy?" asked Jennifer.

"I doubt they would accept a Sutherland, circumstances what they are," said Matthew through a slight smirk. "But I might be able to find someone with knowledge of your particular Abilities, if not training."

"I've done my homework, Dad. Fewer than a hundred have Distant Sight, and only a handful of those have developed it to any degree. And Social Sight? Social Sight is almost unheard of."

Matthew held onto his faint smirk.

Slow realization drifted across Jennifer's face.

"You're not suggesting…"

"It wouldn't hurt to ask," said Matthew, shrugging. "Though even if she were to agree, the logistics could be a nightmare."

"She's scary, Dad. She's a scary, scary little girl."

"Yes, but she might be willing to offer a few pointers; one Ability or the other." He raised his hand and pointed up. "I could try a long-distance call."

"Cute." Jennifer straightened on the couch. "I prefer we keep it in the family for now." She looked up at the monitor, nodded to the display. "You were saying something about things not adding up."

"Right." Matthew surrendered to the change in subject. "Cutler's cult doesn't make sense. What is he trying to accomplish?"

"It's a cult. Power and control over believers. What else is there?"

"That's not his personality. At least, not from what I've been able to discern." Matthew looked from the monitor to his daughter, back to the monitor. "And more than that... he's flaunting it."

"Flaunting it?"

"As though he's daring the Society to do something about it." Matthew took a final drink from his iced tea, rested his head against the back of the couch and frowned at the monitor display. "At least, that's how it looks to me."

"Dad…" Jennifer wondered aloud.

"There may well be more to John Cutler than first imagined."

The audience chamber wasn't all that large for an audience chamber; almost confining at thirty feet by forty feet. Double doors were set into the center of the back wall. There was a raised platform against the wall at the front of the room. A small group of young men and women were gathered before the platform, sitting on several rows of wooden benches.

John Cutler sat in a high-backed chair positioned in the center of the raised platform. Joan stood to one side of the platform, Raymond beside her.

Cutler appeared calm, his expression warm. He took a slow, deep breath and offered a warm smile to the audience. His words were gentle, soft.

"I have enjoyed our time together this morning," he said. He gave a gentle nod to one in the audience, a man sitting near the end of the first bench. "I am so glad that we were able to help you."

The targeted audience member gave a grateful smile in response.

Cutler let his head drift forward. He closed his eyes, rested his elbows against his sides, hands forward, palms up.

His warm expression remained.

The light in the room dimmed just a little. There came the soft, whispering sound of a breeze. The breeze brushed at Cutler's hair, then at Joan's hair, then Raymond's.

The breeze reached the audience, fluttering hair and loose clothing.

Fade then… an empty landscape beneath a sky of brown, the world desert-like; a breeze was pushing at a dusty cloud of sand…

The audience chamber… stillness, the whispering sound of the hint of breeze.

And then, in the air, a very thin dust of sand, floating cloud-like; it drifted about the room, between the benches, around and among the members of the audience.

John Cutler slowly lowered his hands, rested them in his lap. The thin, misty fog of sand drifted down onto the clothes of the audience, onto the floor.

The audience members, wearing broad smiles all, pressed hands to hair, to clothes, clutching at the dusting of sand, their eyes sparkling brightly as they looked deferentially to Cutler on the platform.

The sand-like substance evaporated away then, as if never there, leaving behind a wash of warm emotion drifting across the room.

Cutler opened his eyes. His gaze drifted from one to another of the audience, stopped at a young woman sitting on the second bench.

"All will be well, Sarah," he said, calming, confident. "This I promise."

The woman in the audience trembled in joy, the smile on her face broadening.

John Cutler's words faded to silence. He leaned back against the back of the high-back chair.

Joan stepped forward. "The audience is at an end," she stated. "Thank you for coming. We look forward to seeing you a week from Sunday. It will be a landmark event, my friends."

Cutler rose from the chair and stepped to the edge of the platform. He stood silent, his expression somber, almost stately. His gaze again drifted across the audience.

Then… a simple lifting of the hand. He held it for several seconds, lowered it.

The audience was dismissed. They stood and began to work their way to the center aisle and start toward the double doors at the back of the room. Cutler started toward a side door. He gave a silent signal to his sister, who moved to another exit. He looked then to Raymond and indicated that he should follow him.

The side door opened onto a large portico. Cutler took several steps outside and stopped, clasped his hands behind his back. He spoke over his shoulder to Raymond.

"The woman. Sarah. Find what you can. I saw her young son leaving a hospital. He was well."

"Of course, John," said Raymond. "Do you know when this is to happen?"

"I can't be sure. A few weeks yet; a local hospital."

"It shouldn't be too difficult. Good news, then."

"Yes," said Cutler, looking outward.

Raymond looked from Cutler out to the scene before them. "The others?"

"The man with the tumor… I was able to rid him of it. So a simple follow-up, I suppose. The other two, nothing of interest."

"Very well," said Raymond. "Tumor man will no doubt show up at the next meeting with good news to share."

Cutler looked briefly back at Raymond, said nothing. Raymond hesitated, stepped a half-step forward to stand beside Cutler.

"Joan says the Society is starting to pay attention to what you're doing."

"That is what she says."

"That's, good then."

Cutler looked again to Raymond. "You? Anything new?"

"The same grumblings," said Raymond, shrugging a shoulder. "What dissatisfaction there is with Society leadership is still just whispers behind the Father's back. Not much noise out in the open."

Cutler managed a smirk then. "Father has excellent hearing."

"Right. And so the increased interest that Joan is talking about," said Raymond. "Anyway, those grumblings are still mostly about their Agenda. Mostly, not liking the change in what the Society is all about."

"The *dissatisfaction* can be directed, focused, at the appropriate time. Put to proper use."

"I'm sorry, John. I have issues with this Society of yours." This wasn't the first time this subject had come up.

"It does have its faults," said Cutler. *Faults that I intend to correct...* "Don't give up on it just yet."

"No sir," said Raymond. "It's why I'm here."

"I appreciate that, Raymond." Cutler looked back along the walk. "I would like you to assist Joan as your other work allows. And keep an eye out. Her efforts in dealing with the Society have their inherent dangers."

"Of course. Do you really think—"

"I have no doubt."

Chapter Three

Jennifer stepped down from the access shaft and into the Apartment. The lighting was set to dim.

"Give me some light, Computer," she said.

Several of the ceiling panels activated as she started across the room, spreading light throughout the Apartment.

"When did Dad leave?" she asked, entering the kitchen area.

"Just under half an hour ago, Jennifer," said Computer. "Six AM."

"Afraid to face me," she grumbled. She picked up the carafe of coffee, held her palm against it to ensure that it was still hot. She picked up a ceramic cup and filled it. "At least he left me some coffee."

"Matthew's trip is strictly investigative, Jennifer. He was quite clear on that point."

"Uh, huh…" Jennifer stepped around the counter and moved to the table. She sat and took a sip from the cup. "If I delved into your programming, would I find an algorithm titled 'Defend Matthew at all Costs'?"

"You know better than that, Jennifer."

"Uh, huh…" she said again.

There was a long pause, the Apartment quiet but for the white noise of technology running in the background.

"I know your father quite well," said Computer. "We have worked together for many years."

Jennifer took a long drink from her coffee, set the cup down on the table. She gave the hint of a knowing smile.

"I know that, Computer," she said calmly. "I know how close you are."

"We have both grown; over time."

"And I know that as well." Jennifer stared down at the coffee cup for a long time, then turned slowly and looked at the large monitor screen, dark at the moment, and at the small monitors bordering the large screen on either side.

She looked at the shelves of computer equipment on the other wall.

"I remember…" Jennifer took the coffee cup, turned it fully around then. "I was so young then. You were just a gleam in my father's eye. All those hours; so many hours; weeks and then months."

"Yes," Computer stated simply.

"You woke slowly."

"Yes."

"We were still with the Society back then," she said. She took a swallow of coffee, held the cup in her lap. "My mother…"

"Sutherland House played a prominent role in the Society."

"Oh, Computer," said Jennifer, a slight smile forming. "I think we still have a role to play."

The white noise of technology running in the background…

"Quite so, Jennifer."

§

The burger house café occupied one of the four storefronts in the small strip mall building that was set along the rural county road. Open fields and aging orchards spread away in all directions from the building and the asphalt lot.

Matthew stepped out the door of the café and walked across the small parking lot to his pickup. He had a bag of food and a paper cup of soda in hand.

He climbed into the pickup, set the soda cup into a holder and took a paper-wrapped burger out of the bag. He reached back into the bag and pulled out a handful of fries. He shoved them into his mouth.

"Checking in, Computer," he said, speaking through the mouth of fries. He unwrapped the burger. "Miss me?"

"Not at all, Matthew." Computer's voice came from small speakers in the pickup cabin. "You have yet to arrive at the Cutler estate."

"Yeah…" Matthew continued speaking while eating, looking about at his surroundings. "I've been poking my nose in people's business around here; getting their thoughts on Cutler."

He glanced at his partially eaten hamburger, took another bite. "Having some lunch."

"And what do Mr. Cutler's neighbors have to say?" asked Computer.

"Most folks around here have a high opinion of the man." Matthew pulled another handful of fries out of the bag, shoved them into his mouth. "Word is his miracles have done a lot of good. Local folks believe in him, trust him."

"As comports with what I have found," said Computer.

"His major events are popular. Far as I can tell, just about everyone looks forward to them." Matthew took a drink from his soda, frowned then as he looked out the window. "I just don't know, Computer. Where's he going? What's he trying to do?"

"I am as yet unable to make a determination, Matthew. Your own investigation may provide additional data."

"Yeah… kinda the point."

"Of course."

"Yeah… and on that note," Matthew put the soda back into the cup holder. "I guess I should be on my way."

"So says Jennifer."

"Ah. Not happy, huh?"

Computer did not respond.

Matthew grabbed up the last bite of hamburger and shoved it in his mouth, reached for the key in the ignition and started the pickup.

"I'll bring her back a burger. These are great."

Victor followed Mary into the Academy's cafeteria. The room was clean, minimal, well-organized. The wall on the left was filled with tall windows that were letting in the afternoon light.

Two rows of tables occupied the center of the room, with a handful of students quietly eating a late lunch. One student, a boy of about ten years old, looked nervously up at Mary as she and Victor passed near his table on their way to the food counter at the back of the room.

Victor gave the boy a comforting wink as he passed by. The boy managed an uncomfortable smile in return.

Mary did not acknowledge the boy.

Once they were past, the boy gathered his tray and took it to the dirty dishes deposit window and quickly left the cafeteria.

A woman of the kitchen staff stepped from the kitchen to stand behind the food counter. She took a moment to allow Victor time to look through the glass to the food offerings.

"Good afternoon, Father," she said then. "A late lunch for you today?"

"Keep it light, if you please," he answered. "Something to hold me until dinner."

"Of course." The woman looked then to Mary. "And for you, Mary?"

"Lunch," Mary stated flatly, studying the offerings.

"Yes, Ma'am," said the woman. She spoke then sub-vocally to Victor as she began preparing their plates, attempting a smile. "This is young Mary's usual lunch period, Father."

Victor responded sub-vocally to the woman as he glanced down at Mary. "Is that right?"

Mary, listening, said nothing.

"I believe Mary prefers to eat alone," said the woman. "She very seldom shares meals with the other students. Or with staff, for that matter."

She set the lunches on the countertop. Victor took his plate, handed the second plate to Mary.

"I see," he said, still in Thought Talk. He continued aloud then to Mary as they started to a nearby table. "You really should make an effort to socialize with the other students,

Mary. Socialization is an important component of your Academy training."

They settled in at the table. There was a pitcher of water and several glasses in the middle of the table.

"Yes, Father," said Mary.

Victor filled two of the glasses with water from the pitcher, slid one to Mary. She spoke sub-vocally as she picked up her glass.

"I communicate as necessary with those to whom communication is necessary; without issue."

"Communication is not the same as socialization, Mary. Socialization skills are necessary to your future within Society."

"I have seen my future within the Society, Father." Mary set her water back on the table, picked up her fork and looked steadily to Victor. "I understand the set of skills required to meet my obligations."

"Yes. Your Social Sight." Victor was growing a bit frustrated. The girl could do that. "Mary, your Ability is not yet fully developed; your training is as yet in its earliest stages. More importantly, your set of data is far from complete."

Mary said nothing. Her expression was unchanged. She began eating her lunch.

"Your vision is murky at best," Victor finished.

He watched Mary take one bite of food, then another.

He took a bite of his lunch, ate in silence for several long moments.

"We care for you, Mary," he said then, placing his napkin beside his plate. "Headmaster, myself. We all do."

"Thank you," Mary stated. She pushed her food about with her fork, took a bite.

"Beyond our genuine affection, you are important to us. To the Society," he said.

"I know."

"Then you can understand our concern."

She took a drink, swallowed. "Concern?"

How to approach this…

"Not everyone will always agree with every decision of the Society, Mary," said Victor. "But any civilized society, including our own, requires that the actions of the whole and the actions of the individual serve the greater good of that society."

Mary took a long drink from her water glass, set the glass down in front of her plate.

"The good of any society, including our own, requires that the individual take a stand when the actions taken are deemed detrimental to that society," she stated.

"Deemed by whom, Mary?"

Mary turned her head slowly, tilted her head slowly…

"By the individual, of course."

Victor studied the young girl for a moment then, returned to sub-vocal then…

"You, then…"

"Of course," she answered aloud. She returned to her lunch.

Victor fell silent, watched Mary eat her meal.

He picked up his glass and took a drink of his water.

§

When Headmaster came into the cafeteria, he found Victor sitting alone at a table, a cup of coffee held in both hands. The other tables were empty. A woman of the kitchen staff was working behind the food counter. Headmaster caught her attention as he worked his way to Victor's table.

Victor said nothing, took a swallow of his coffee.

"I take it lunch with Mary could have gone better," said Headmaster.

"It went about as expected," said Victor.

The woman brought a cup of coffee to the table. Headmaster gave a silent thank you and she returned to the kitchen.

"I picked up some of the discord," said Headmaster, pulling the cup to him. "Impossible not to."

Victor acknowledged the observation with a barely perceptible nod.

"I also sensed disquiet among some of the students; those with the ability to pick up such."

"Mmm," Victor gave a light grunt. "Might serve as a training opportunity."

Headmaster glanced about the empty room. Behind the counter, the woman was clearing the food counter.

He picked up his coffee cup and leaned back in his chair.

"Perhaps we should consider alternative arrangements for Mary," he said, clasping the cup in both hands.

"Headmaster… you are closer to Mary than anyone. She sees your sincerity, she knows you have the best of intentions." Victor indicated their surroundings with a wave of the hand. "This place. This hallowed place of learning. It is the soul of the Society. It is who we are. Mary needs this place. And she needs you."

"I… as you wish, Father," Headmaster said hesitantly. "I serve as best I am able."

"You have served the Society so very well, Headmaster; for all so many years."

Victor gave his Headmaster a warm smile. "Guide her, Headmaster. Bring her to us."

"Yes, Father." He took a long swallow from his coffee, leaned forward and stood then, setting the cup on the table. "You will excuse me. I'm substituting for Rebecca this afternoon. Hers is not a class to leave on their own."

Victor gave a nod in answer, absently watched Headmaster take his cup to the collection window before leaving the cafeteria.

Alone then… the cafeteria quiet, still. Victor, calm, placid.

He finished his coffee as he looked out through the wall of windows.

Mary settled into the chair in the middle of her room. She closed her eyes, rested her head against the back of the chair. Filtered light from the curtained window drifted across the floor, brushed across her face.

She let her thoughts wander where they would; seconds flowed to minutes. The outside light began to gray, her room slowly darkened.

Mary's world faded…

Another place then… a world of gray, empty, nothingness reaching out to darker gray horizons. Mary stood alone in that emptiness, eyes open, looking out to those horizons.

Empty…

Tiny points of lights then, enveloping about her; shimmering points of light, glowing threads forming and vanishing, connecting and disconnecting from the points, the universe shifting and changing.

Possibilities shone like bright points of light. Actions becoming threads, forming and connecting the shimmering points, actions tearing at threads, disconnecting, shredding, reforming; possibilities being destroyed, resolutions created, evolved, threads redirected.

Threads drawing together, threads pulled from the fabric.

Social Sight…

Matthew's pickup was one in a line of vehicles in a grassy parking area. A tall fence bordered one side of the lot. A guard stood at a gate set into the fence twenty yards or so from the pickup.

Matthew climbed out, stood beside the truck as he talked with Computer.

"The lot is about a third full," he said. "From what I heard in town, about what to expect of Cutler's weekly gatherings."

"If the meetings start on time, you are late, Matthew."

"Fashionably so, Computer." Matthew closed the door of his pickup and started across the lot.

The guard watched him approach.

"You're late," he said wearily. "Meeting's already started."

"My apologies."

"Uh, huh. Quiet going in. Don't disrupt Mr. Cutler speaking."

"Right. Got it."

Matthew passed through the gate. A clearly defined path led him from the gate to the front door of the meeting hall. He entered a small audience chamber, moved to one side and stood at the back of the room.

There were twenty people sitting on several long wooden benches, all listening attentively to John Cutler, who was standing on a wide, low platform at the front of the room, talking in a low, sincere voice to a woman in the front row.

The exchange ended and Cutler took a step back. He moved a step to his right, another, his gaze drifting across his audience. He stopped then, let his focus settle on a middle-aged man several rows from the front.

Cutler wore a slight smile; he let several long moments pass. The crowd, already quiet, fell into an even heavier silence. Cutler lifted a hand; his expression grew more intense, the hand began to shimmer.

Well, that's new… thought Matthew.

Cutler slowly turned his hand palm up, closed his eyes. The luminosity enveloping his hand glowed brightly then, pushing outward.

What the… Matthew couldn't help himself, snickered to himself.

The glow reached out from Cutler's fingertips toward the audience member, almost but not quite reaching him.

Matthew let his attention drift from Cutler, noted Cutler's sister Joan standing to one side of the platform. Her expression was stern, serious, her stance at the ready… to all appearances serving the role of Cutler's lieutenant.

Focusing again on Cutler…

The stream of light receded from the man in the audience; Cutler lowered his hand and the shimmer faded entirely. He opened his eyes, smiled at the man.

"All will be well, my friend," said Cutler. "Now."

There was a very audible sigh of relief and elation from the audience.

Matthew felt something like spiderwebs brush across his mind.

The sister…

Matthew looked to Joan.

She was studying Matthew, standing at the back of the room.

She gave the briefest side-glance to Cutler. As she did, Cutler's gaze drifted first to her, as if in response to her, before his gaze moved to Matthew.

So she has Thought Talk Ability, and the ability to isolate her Thought Talk to one individual.

Cutler went quiet, giving a warm smile to his audience, letting his last words settle.

As he did, Matthew heard Cutler addressing him in Thought Talk.

"Welcome, Mr. Sutherland," he said. "Please. We must talk later."

With that done, John Cutler gave more warm smiles to his audience, bowing his head ever-so-slightly.

Chapter Four

The Apartment's underground garage looked very much like an auto service center. Along the left wall were six stalls, four of them currently occupied: a 64 Comet, an old Bronco, a late model BMW; a pair of dirt bikes and a Harley-Davidson Sportster shared a single stall.

On the right was a line of service bays, with a chest-high counter spanning the length of the wall.

At the far end of the garage was an opening to a tunnel that curved away and out of sight.

The sound of a vehicle's engine echoing down into the garage from the tunnel disrupted the heavy silence. A few moments later, the Sutherland's small bus appeared, rolled slowly out of the tunnel and moved down the center aisle of the garage. It turned into one of the two empty stalls.

Jennifer was behind the wheel. She looked across at the remaining empty stall as she turned off the engine.

"Computer," she stated. "Any word from Dad?"

"No word from Matthew since he prepared to go into the Cutler meeting, Jennifer."

"That was hours ago."

"Several."

"I don't like it." Jennifer reached for the maintenance log sitting on the dashboard, looked again at the empty stall. "The man should check in."

"Yes, Jennifer."

Jennifer opened the book. She glanced up from the log to numbers displayed in the vehicle dash, began entering data into the log.

"I don't like," she grumbled.

Her maintenance tasks completed, Jennifer climbed down from the bus and started up the central aisle. She walked the hall leading from the garage and into the Apartment.

The Apartment's lights were set to dim.

"Lights, Computer," she said. "You know the drill."

The Apartment lightened to seventy percent, which Computer understood as Jennifer's preference.

Halfway across the Apartment, approaching the kitchen counter, the Apartment darkened again. Jennifer took another step, another, and stopped.

Something wasn't right…

Jennifer's world faded…

Another world then… gray, empty, nothingness reaching out to darker gray horizons…

She stood alone then in the emptiness, eyes open, looking out to those horizons.

Empty…

No. Not totally empty. There was a silhouette in the distance; dark gray set against lighter gray.

A little girl.

Mary.

The silhouette drew nearer. It was distant, and then, without movement, Mary was nearer, and then nearer still.

Mary stood at arm's length from Jennifer. Her eyes drifted slowly up to look directly at Jennifer, though her expression betrayed nothing.

"Mary," said Jennifer, looking from the girl to their surroundings. "You did this? Where are we?"

"You are here because you are Jennifer," said Mary. "I did not bring you here."

"How very mysterious of you. What does that mean?"

"It means what it means," said Mary. "You grow."

"Wha—I don't get it." Jennifer studied Mary a moment, then again looked about them. "I grow, and so I'm here."

"Yes." Mary half-turned about, looked out across the virtual landscape. "I have sensed your presence for some time."

"I—" Jennifer struggled to make sense of her surroundings, of Mary's cryptic comments, of her own mixed up thoughts.

"Social Sight? Is that it?" she asked then. *How can that be?*

"The canvas of probabilities."

Jennifer considered, studied their surroundings with a new eye.

"You mean…"

"Social Sight. Yes," said Mary.

"This is how we, where we…"

"Internalize, interpret, collate…"

Big words for such a little girl, thought Jennifer.

"And predict the future," she said aloud.

"We envisage direction," said Mary.

"Right. Envisage. Direction." Jennifer had another thought then. "Um, Mary; have you been talking to my Dad? I mean about me. You know, training and like that?"

"I don't understand."

"Never mind."

"All right."

"So…" Jennifer still wasn't sure that Mary hadn't brought her here, wherever here was, and if she had, then why? "Mary, this whole envisaging thing… what do you see happening? Between you and me, I mean."

"In what way, Jennifer?"

"Wow. Um… to be honest, I don't know."

"Do you foresee something?"

"My Social Sight isn't much more than a fog just yet. I don't foresee anything about anything."

"And yet you are here. You sense something."

Jennifer didn't want to keep going down that path. She decided to approach it from a different angle.

"Mary, do we have the same goals? Do we want the same for the Society?"

"Those are two different questions."

"All right. Then how about, what do you want for the Society?"

"The Society must continue. The Society must serve the needs of its members."

"We believe the same," agreed Jennifer. "And what of our relationship with the Outside?"

"There is no relationship with the Outside."

Uh, oh…

"Excuse me?"

"I take no issue with the Outside so long as it does not pose a threat to the Society."

This surprised Jennifer.

"Mary, do you agree with the Father's Agenda? Does it not further Society's infiltration into the Outside?"

"There are elements of the Agenda that lessen potential threats to the Society."

So, not totally on board then…

"And yet you have helped my dad. More than once."

"My support of Matthew Sutherland is limited to his not dying. He has a role yet to play in the future of the Society."

"Right. Gotcha. Thanks for the clarification."

"You are welcome." A pause, and then Mary tilted her head to one side and looked directly at Jennifer. "I'm sure we will see each other again."

As Jennifer was about to respond, the world about her started to fade; Mary became a drifting mist, her essence blending into the gray about them, and then all about them faded to nothing.

Jennifer stood in the middle of the Apartment; dark at first, then lightening to seventy percent illumination.

"Jennifer?"

"I'm here, Computer."

Raymond escorted Matthew outside and onto the large portico, led him up along the wide walk. The sky overhead was beginning to gray. Up ahead, Cutler and his sister were standing side by side, facing away, looking out at the horizon, a horizon colored with sunset.

Joan looked back to the approaching Raymond and Matthew. She leaned nearer her brother. He gave a nod to her comment. She turned about and started in Matthew's direction.

She gave no expression as she passed him and continued on to the meeting hall building.

Raymond and Matthew stopped two paces behind Cutler. A moment passed, and another. Cutler spoke then without looking back to the others.

"I do enjoy sunsets; don't you?" he asked.

Raymond looked to Matthew to respond.

"Sure," said Matthew.

Cutler hesitated, looked back over his shoulder, showed a half-smile. He looked away again, forward, to the sunset.

"What did you think of it?" he asked.

"The sunset, or your little spectacle?"

Cutler said nothing.

"Great," Matthew stated finally, a flat comment. "What was with the light show?"

Cutler turned about then and faced his guest. He gave a dismissive nod to Raymond.

"Thank you, Raymond."

Raymond turned about and left; Cutler indicated a bench a few yards back along the walk, led Matthew toward it. "Substance without spectacle is just… substance."

"What's wrong with substance?"

"Nothing," agreed Cutler. "But that's not what they're expecting."

"I suppose one must consider one's audience," said Matthew.

"It's all about the mission, Mr. Sutherland."

"Of course," said Matthew. After a long pause, then, "There are audiences, and then there are audiences."

"Mr. Sutherland…" Cutler said in a sigh, as if in answer.

"It takes a certain skill, I would think," said Matthew. "Addressing the one, intending the other."

Cutler almost, but didn't quite, give a chuckle at that. He leaned back, rested against the back of the bench. He took a long moment to admire his surroundings.

"You have quite the reputation, Mr. Sutherland," he said. "One of the Great Houses, turning its back on the Society, actively standing against its agenda."

"An agenda that goes against the Society's values."

"A most potent stand nonetheless." Cutler gave a side-glance to Matthew. "You are almost a legend."

"Not quite the way I see it."

"Among those who matter," said Cutler, looking now directly at his guest.

Matthew returned the gaze, then looked away, across the walk.

"What are you doing here, John?"

Cutler considered his response…

"What is your concern, Mr. Sutherland?" he asked. "I am harming no one; quite the opposite, in fact."

"That is something I must determine for myself, Mr. Cutler."

"That kind of makes you a busy-body, doesn't it? Not the legend that I have come to admire." *And perhaps put to use…*

"As I said. Not a legend." Matthew leaned forward. "I feel it my responsibility to do what little I can to protect the Outside from the overreaches of those in the Society who would take advantage."

"And what of the Society's Agenda? The revisionist Society, if you will?"

"Of course."

"That's quite a lot on your plate." Cutler again turned his gaze forward. "Sounds like project scope creep to me."

"Yes. There is that," agreed Matthew. "And you have managed to avoid my question."

"Question?"

"What are you doing here? Serving the outside world out of the goodness of your heart?"

"Isn't that what you are doing?"

And another evasion...

Approach from another direction…

"There are some in the Society who are concerned that you may draw attention to the Society."

"Is that so?"

"That could be dangerous for you," said Matthew. "What does your father have to say about all this?"

Cutler's mood darkened just a bit, albeit briefly.

"We have not spoken for some time."

"Are you estranged from your father?"

"Our differing views regarding the Society can make family gatherings awkward."

Matthew gave a sympathetic nod, leaned forward then and stood up. He looked about them, and after a long moment waved a hand to indicate their surroundings.

"This. All of this." Matthew looked back to Cutler. "What you are doing. It has nothing to do with doing good for the Outside. You're poking the bear, stirring up trouble."

Cutler slid further back against the bench, looking up at Matthew. He kept his half-smile, said nothing.

"What I can't figure out," Matthew continued. "What is your endgame? How does this get you anywhere but gone?"

Cutler lost any sign of a smile. His expression fell into shadow. His gaze drifted from across the walk to the flagstones at his feet.

David R. Beshears

"Endgame…" he sighed. "That makes it all sound so trivial. I can assure you that it is not."

"All right. What word would you use?"

"Evolution." Cutler looked up at Matthew. "Not the path their Agenda would take us; and not a return to the old ways."

"A new path, a new direction," said Matthew.

"Exactly." Cutler managed a smile, something warm. He again looked forward. "So you understand."

"Not so much, no."

Cutler managed a half-chuckle then.

"That's all right," he said. "Understanding will come."

The Broderick dining room was formal without being large or pretentious; fine woods, glass windows set into cabinet doors; a small chandelier hovering above an eight-seat dining table. A simple centerpiece was set in the middle of the table.

Victor sat at one end of the table, his wife Dianna at the other. The two children were seated side-by-side. The setting before each member of the family: dinner plate, silverware, glass of milk; cloth napkins lay across their laps.

The four quietly ate their dinner, unhurried, mannerly.

Dianna took a drink from her milk, set the glass back onto the table in front of her plate. She lifted her napkin, dabbed at the corner of her mouth.

She looked across the table to her husband.

"How was your visit to the Academy, Victor?" she asked.

"It went quite well, my dear," he said. "I am more than satisfied with the renovations. Quite pleased."

"How nice," she said aloud. In Thought Talk then: "And news regarding Mary?"

"Nothing that we can't handle. Not to worry," he responded, also sub-vocally. Aloud then: "Children. Have you seen much of the Academy's modifications as yet?"

"Only the common areas, Father," said Robby, the older of the two. "Not the new."

"Not the new," said Thomas.

"I see," said Victor, nodding slowly. "Well, not to worry. I believe Headmaster has scheduled a tour of the new areas for all the students. Ahead of the opening."

"Yes, Father," said Robby.

"Yes, Father," mimicked Thomas.

Dianna smiled appropriately. "That should be fun," she said.

"It will," said Robby, quite matter-of-factly.

"You will enjoy it," said Victor. "Of that I am sure."

He gave his children a faint smile, gave a nod. He gave another nod to his wife.

A few moments then, and his expression grew dull, blank, his smile fading away.

Dianna again dabbed the corner of her mouth with her napkin.

"Victor?"

Victor's expression changed subtly from blank to annoyed. The annoyance was not directed at his wife.

He lifted his napkin from his lap and set it on the table beside his plate.

"I will only be a moment," he stated. An attempted smile then to his children as he slid his chair back. "Duty calls, children. I shall return. Perhaps cards later?"

Victor entered his office. The door closed behind him at a barely perceptible flick of one finger. He continued across the room, past his desk, and stood at the window.

Clicks and beeps then from the phone on the desk. The sound of several rings at the other end before someone answered.

"Father Broderick," stated the man on the other end.

"Yes. What is it?" asked Victor. "I was in the middle of dinner."

"Pardon, sir. In regards the Cutler issue."

"An issue for you. A nuisance for me."

"Yes, sir. Of course. It's just that… Cutler had a visitor today. Matthew Sutherland."

This was interesting. Victor considered, his focus remaining on the view beyond the window.

"Is that so? Well, well…" he said at last. "Leave Matthew to take care of your issue; and no more nuisance."

"They met privately for some time following one of Cutler's sideshows," said the caller. "We have not been able to discover what was said."

"Hmm," said Victor. "And now?"

"Sir?"

"Where is Matthew? Now?"

"Yes, sir. We believe he is returning home."

"Very good," said Victor, turning about to face his desk, his phone. "Continue to monitor all involved."

"Of course, Father."

"End call," Father stated. The phone disconnected; a moment's dial tone and then silence.

Victor considered.

Strange bedfellows, Matthew and Cutler… he thought. *Following the same path toward opposite goals.*

Chapter Five

Matthew came into the Apartment from the garage, asked Computer for lights as he walked to the kitchen. He got a glass of water from the sink, then went to the refrigerator to find something to eat.

"Not much in the way of leftovers, is there?" He closed the fridge and began looking through cupboards.

Computer gave no response, as Matthew was clearly not expecting one.

Matthew prepared buttered toast, poured a glass of orange juice and took his light meal to the table.

He spoke then as he ate.

"Your observations regarding Cutler, Computer," he stated.

"In what respect, Matthew?"

"What is he up to?"

"Cutler is attempting to create divisions to bring down the Society as it currently exists," Computer stated, the tone a humanlike calmness. "Some believe to destroy, some believe to rebuild."

Matthew agreed. He took another bite of toast, a swallow of juice. "Rebuild; perhaps from the ground up. But how? In what way?"

"Unknown, beyond the end of the Society's caste system," said Computer.

The Willeby's status as Lesser Family in particular, thought Matthew.

"A topic of discussion at most every Summit," he said.

"Workshops in which you yourself frequently participated."

Jennifer came into the Apartment from upstairs, stepping down from the access ladder. Matthew indicated the other chair at the table, finished the last of his toast.

She sat down without looking directly at her father, said nothing.

"Everything all right?" asked Matthew. Something was bothering her.

"*Everything* is rather far-reaching," said Jennifer, managing a slight smile.

"Nice dodge."

"Thank you." Jennifer held her smile a few seconds more before letting it fade. "So, your trip went well."

"We were just going over a few of the more interesting revelations."

"Uh, huh…" increasingly distant.

Matthew looked to his daughter with some concern, let it go for the moment.

"Okay," he said. He looked down at the dish in front of him with its last crumbs of toast. He pushed the dish aside. "Computer… Cutler's miracles, what I saw of them, they go beyond the Six Abilities; I'm thinking… perhaps he's managing to merge Abilities, creating something new from our Six, beyond our Six."

"A logical assumption."

"Of course it is," grumbled Matthew. More directly then, "Which is very close to what was being attempted in Andover."

"Several members of Cutler's Willeby Family were involved in the Andover Project," Computer stated matter-of-factly, almost offhandedly.

"Is that right? I didn't see the name."

"Their role was minor."

Which Cutler probably attributed to their Lesser Family status, thought Matthew.

He looked across the table to Jennifer.

"You hungry?" he asked.

Jennifer answered in a half shrug. "Not so much," she said.

The conference room was located in the administrative wing of the Academy. The wing was short and narrow, tucked in behind the main building. The conference room was equally small, just large enough to hold the table and eight chairs. A large picture window lessened the otherwise claustrophobic atmosphere of the room.

Victor stepped into the room, moved to the head of the table and tossed the folder in front of him as he sat down. Only then, as he opened the folder, did he bother looking about at the others sitting at the table.

He didn't much care for these meetings.

Only three of the other chairs were occupied. These were the members of the

Steering Council, of which the Father of Society served as chairman. Each of the others headed one component of the council, targeting a specific category: political, cultural and scientific.

The Steering Council meetings weren't on any set schedule, as most of what needed doing could be handled virtually. Only rarely were in-person meetings held, called when any member felt it necessary.

While not its sole duty, a key function of Steering Council was the implementation of the Agenda.

"We have two items before us today," said Victor, closing the folder and setting it aside. "At first blush unrelated and yet, upon closer examination, inescapably connected."

He looked carefully at each of those at the table. They came from three Primary Families, families reaching back to the very founding of the Society. Each member took their role on the council seriously, each was dedicated to the Society. Each also brought to the council biases born of the histories of their respective families.

"As Father of the Society," Victor continued, "it is my responsibility to ensure the continued advancement, well-being and security of the Society. It should therefore come as no surprise that the Agenda, of which I strongly support, addresses those same goals."

"We all feel as you, Father," said the gray-haired woman to Victor's left. Cordelia was of the Westerman Family, from which had come the very first Father of the Society. Her position on the Steering Council was as the Scientific representative. "The well-being and security of the Society is paramount."

"And advancement," grinned Gideon, the Political representative. "The Agenda, you know."

"The Agenda addresses all three," stated Victor firmly. "As stated."

"Of course," nodded Gideon. "And at issue?"

"At issue is the slow progress of each component of the Agenda, and as a consequence the growing threats posed to the Society."

"Threats?" asked Cordelia.

"I don't understand," said Everett, the Cultural representative.

"And so the purpose of this meeting," said Victor.

Matthew steered the 64 Comet along the narrow winding road and into Rydel Ridge's small gravel parking lot. He pulled up next to the pickup and turned off the engine. He climbed out of the car, reached back in and brought out a pizza box.

Jennifer was sitting on the bench overlooking the valley below the ridge. Matthew sat beside her, placing the pizza box between them.

She didn't acknowledge him, and Matthew said nothing at first.

The sun would be setting soon.

"It's half pepperoni, half combination," he said finally.

"Thanks."

The pizza box remained closed, for the moment. Matthew leaned forward, rested his elbows on his knees. He looked for deer in the valley below, didn't see any.

"If you're having trouble processing your encounter with Mary, perhaps you should talk about it."

"Processing isn't the problem, Dad," she said. "It's how it works. I didn't expect it. Not like that."

"Social Sight."

"And seeing her there, in that place. The reality of it, when it's not reality at all. It was unnerving. It still is."

Matthew slid back, rested his back against the bench.

Beyond, the world was falling into shadow.

"Social Sight is a powerful Ability, Jennifer. However it works, it's yours to sort out, yours to come to terms with. I'll support you as I can, just let me know what you need. You know that. But in the end, it's on you."

Matthew reached down then and opened the pizza box.

"Pizza's gettin' cold," he stated.

Day had eased into dusk on Rydel Ridge. Matthew was alone now, Jennifer having left a few minutes earlier in the pickup. He was sitting on the hood of the Comet, his back resting against the windshield, the pizza box beside him.

Meditation... meditation would be good about now, and this, his favorite little hideaway, was just the place for it.

He closed his eyes, let his body unwind, his muscles ease a little at a time, let his mind drift where it would...

Nope.

There was so much pushing in on his mind, so much noise, he couldn't make it happen. And meditation wasn't something one could force. That wasn't the way it worked; at least, not for Matthew.

He opened his eyes, let Rydel Ridge do what it could to settle his thoughts, to relax his mind.

It helped. Mostly though, it allowed him to sort out the past weeks, the past months. And there was a lot to sort.

Victor was continuing to pushing the Agenda, and so attempting to direct the Society in the wrong direction.

John Cutler was working his own agenda, seeding the ground to generate unrest and create a change that Matthew wasn't as yet able to see.

There had even been rumors of a civil war within the Society. Matthew hoped it wouldn't come to that. He had never wanted that. His objective had always been to guide the Society back to its earliest roots. Victor had at one time sought the same, before the Agenda.

From what Matthew could discern, Cutler apparently had yet other objectives.

And of course there was Jennifer, in the early stages of developing Distant Sight and Social Sight. Matthew had never known

Abilities to show themselves at such a late age, and yet there they were. Moreover, these two were the rarest of the Six. And of those Society members who did have those specific Abilities, fewer yet had been able to develop them to any great extent.

Mary was the exception. Her Abilities, and she possessed all six, were already at a very high level, at her young age; and Mary's Abilities were continuing to grow.

She was to be a powerful force in whatever future lay ahead for the Society.

And she had taken an interest in Jennifer.

Were they to be allies, or were they destined to become adversaries?

Where did Mary's Social Sight Ability take her? What did she see?

What would Jennifer's Social Sight eventually reveal to her?

No answers today, thought Matthew.

Static noise came from the set of speakers inside the car. Moments later came Computer's prompting voice:

"Matthew?"

Matthew reached into the pizza box, brought out cold slice of pizza.

"Not today, Computer." He took a bite of the pizza.

"Just a quick item of note, Matthew. If I might?"

"Nope," said Matthew. "Whatever it is, not today."

Matthew ate his cold pizza and watched dusk drift to evening on Rydel Ridge.

End Episode Four...

Episode 5
Silhouettes

Chapter One

Matthew came into the Apartment from the garage access, a canvas travel bag slung over one shoulder. The overhead lights brightened from dim to 70% as he crossed the room. He tossed the bag onto the couch on his way to the kitchen area, stepping around the counter and grabbing a glass from the cupboard. He half-filled it from the sink faucet.

"Computer," he said casually, taking a drink.

"Welcome home, Matthew," said Computer. "All is well?"

"As well as can be expected." Matthew had spent several days leading an outsider down a false path regarding certain Society activities while simultaneously misdirecting a particularly troublesome Society member who had been working to take advantage of the unwitting outsider. Neither knew what Matthew had been up to.

Computer had continued to monitor the situation following Matthew's exit from the Apartment, and so knew that all was indeed as well as could be expected. Computer understood that such casual exchange was what was called for upon each of Matthew's returns.

There had been a deceptive sense of calm over the previous few months; most unsettling, as there had in fact been a lot going on beneath all that calm. And it was particularly odd that none of it had generated so much as a ripple in Matthew's world.

There was, for instance, the situation with John Cutler, who was continuing to sow unrest in the Society, from a distance, through his surrogates.

And Mary... Matthew could feel her presence out there, in the web. Her powers were growing; Matthew could not yet be sure of her intentions, though he had no doubt that her loyalties lay with survival of the Society.

Then there was Victor Broderick, Father of the Society; *for how many years now, for how many decades?* Victor was quietly pushing the key elements of the Agenda, particularly those focusing on the political influence in the Outside world. The Agenda, the outline of which was charting a path that would take the Society beyond what it was originally intended to be.

Jennifer's abilities were expanding, strengthening. They were emerging later in life than was normal for members of the Society, and they were the two rarest of the six Abilities: Social Sight and Distant Sight.

All of these goings-on, all these and more… all somehow destined to come together. Matthew was sure of that. One didn't need Social Sight to see that. When, and to what end, he didn't know.

"Where is Jennifer?" he asked.

"Jennifer is upstairs, Matthew," said Computer. "In the main house."

"Thank you." Matthew placed the water glass in the sink and started across the Apartment. "That's where I'll be." He climbed the access ladder up to the basement and then took the stairs up to the main hallway.

The house was warm but comfortable. Light streamed in through gaps in the curtains. He found Jennifer in the living room. She was sitting in one of the overstuffed chairs.

Sam was sitting on the couch across from Jennifer. The young man stood at Matthew's entrance. "Hello, Mr. Sutherland," he said.

Good ole' Sam, the kid next door, the neighbor boy from down the road, and with a lifelong crush on Jennifer. He had to be about twenty-two years old now. He had been away at graduate school and Matthew hadn't seen him in quite a while, not since the last school break.

"Hello, Sam." Matthew took several steps into the room and shook the young man's hand. "How's school?"

"Great, sir. Great."

"Good to hear."

"Yes." Sam gave a sigh, stepped aside and looked to Jennifer. "See you at six, then?"

"I'll see you out," said Jennifer, standing. She led Sam out of the room.

Matthew patiently waited for her to return.

"You won't be home for dinner, then?" he asked pleasantly, a hint of a smile.

"Nope," she answered flatly.

"Right. Okay. We still have leftover pizza in the fridge, I think. I'll be fine." Matthew sat in one of the chairs. He placed his elbows on his knees and looked up at his daughter. "Sam's a great kid," he said.

"He's Sam," said Jennifer.

"He certainly is."

"Nothing serious."

Sutherland House by necessity existed in isolation from its neighbors. Matthew Sutherland lived in near total seclusion. So far as anyone knew, he was the son of the previous owner of the estate.

The previous owner being Matthew Sutherland himself.

Sam, the neighbor boy, had been one of the few from *the outside* that Matthew on occasion interacted with.

"He's a good kid," said Matthew. A moment's hesitation and then, "You know, I would never…"

"I know."

"Good. Good."

"It's just dinner, Dad. Nothing more."

"I like Sam."

"I know."

Of course she knew. That didn't make being her father any easier.

"It's complicated, Jen; getting close to those on the outside."

It certainly is, thought Jennifer. She moved over to the couch. Sitting, she looked closely at her dad. He looked pretty much as he had when she was a baby; a few gray hairs at the temple, not much else to show for the passing of the years.

Now in her early twenties, Jennifer's own aging would soon begin to slow. The process was different for each person. For some, the slowing would continue into middle age, for some not until much older. For all in the Society, while aging would not come to a complete stop, it would be nearly so.

Not full immortality, but nearly so.

The Gift.

Looking again to her father, she saw it then in his eyes. The passing of the decades could be seen there; eyes that had seen so very much. Matthew Sutherland had witnessed much.

Sutherland House had after all been a major part of the original founding of the Society.

"It's good to have you home, Dad," she said. "The project went well?"

"The Outside world is once again safe for the Outsiders," said Matthew.

Victor Broderick closed the car door and stepped up onto the walk and started across the Academy grounds. Approaching the

Great Oak, he sensed Mary's presence long before seeing her there, up in the heavy branches of the tree's canopy.

Mary was still very young, still a little girl of eleven years old, yet she had changed much over the previous six months. Her advanced skills, her extensive expertise in all six Abilities that continued to expand ever further, gave her a maturity that shown on her face, in her manner, in her interactions with others on those rare occasions in which she actually chose to interact with others.

Aren't you getting a bit old to be climbing trees? He asked sub-vocally.

How old is too old to climb trees? she responded.

Victor stepped nearer the tree, beneath the wide-spread canopy. He turned about and leaned back against the gnarly trunk.

"Good point," he said then, aloud this time. He looked out across the grounds. No one was about. "You spend a lot of time on your own, Mary. Sitting in a tree does not provide much opportunity to socialize with others."

"Did Headmaster send for you, Father?" she asked. "Is that why you are here? To insist that I learn to play with others?"

"Certainly not, Mary. I would never push you into something that you did not feel you were ready for." *Not that I could...* he thought, keeping that thought to himself.

"Thank you," Mary stated.

Your destiny lay elsewhere... another thought that he kept to himself.

"Of course," he said instead. He pushed off from the tree trunk, turned and looked in the direction of the administration building. He let out a heavy breath and folded his arms. "There is an important meeting this morning."

"A physical meeting? Not virtual? Here at the Academy?"

"There are advantages to meeting face to face, together, around the table. And this is important; a matter of the survival of the Society." Victor took a step from the tree.

"The Academy is an ideal location for such a meeting."

"I see."

Victor thought carefully, considered…

"What does that mean to you, Mary?" he asked then, cautiously. "The survival of the Society?"

"You know very well, Father," she stated flatly. "Survival of the Society above all else."

And what form might that survival take? he asked, again speaking sub-vocally. *The future of the Society might follow one of any number of paths.*

"It is impossible for me to know that, Father."

"Your… *Ability*… does not show this to you, then."

"It does not," said Mary. "There are too many variables."

"A very mature observation, Mary," said Victor, after a long pause. He stepped further from the tree, started out from under the canopy. He stopped after a few steps, stood facing the administration building beyond the expansive lawn.

"I should be off then," he said, speaking over his shoulder. "The meeting."

Of course, she responded sub-vocally, in thought-talk.

"Perhaps I will see you later," he said, and continued along the walk.

Mary's thoughts had already drifted away from Victor. She sensed his departure, had in some manner watched him continue across the campus grounds toward the administration building, but her focus, her awareness, had already moved on.

Mary wandered… though her direction had purpose, had… *intent.*

The oak tree, her tree, was with her. It was a part of her journey.

The Great Oak was necessary.

Jennifer's dinner with Sam had gone well enough. It had been pleasant enough… nice. She had had a nice time. But they were so very different. Not just different. They came from entirely different worlds. Literally. There was no real possibility of a deeper connection.

Still, she liked Sam well enough.

She took the steps up onto the front porch. But she wasn't ready to go inside. She walked over to one of the pair of chairs and dropped into the nearest.

The evening was… nice.

Geez…

The view from the porch spread out before her, the grounds of the Sutherland Estate; lawns and walks and shrubs and garden beds, all enclosed within high walls, the main gate just visible at the end of the long, winding driveway.

The gray dusk of evening was turning dark with the coming night. There was a warm breeze.

Mary closed her eyes, rested her head against the back of the chair.

She drifted. She wandered.

She opened her eyes.

She was standing at the edge of a wide, far-reaching landscape… smooth, barren, slate-gray; nothing as far as the distant horizon, the sky overhead a deeper shade of gray than the surface of the land beneath her feet.

And then, there... in the distance, midway to the horizon... the silhouette of a great oak tree.

Chapter Two

Victor walked the wide hall, the short, thick carpet muffling the sound of his footfalls. Golden light globes, spaced far apart along one wall and set to low illumination, provided the only light. This entire wing of the Academy had been part of the recent renovation. Yet despite the remodeling, Victor felt drawn to the distant past.

Precisely as had been intended.

The third door on the left…

He pushed down on the handle and opened the heavy door. The room beyond was lit via a number of matching light sconces mounted on three walls. The fourth wall was set with tall windows; evening gray shone through half-drawn drapes. A long wooden table filled most of the room. About the table sat the other three meeting attendees.

The matriarch of Gray House sat at the far end of the table. Catherine Gray was a youngish sixty-year-old, was physically small, though her presence exuded self-assuredness and confidence. Victor knew her to be quite the diplomat, shrouding her true feelings in subtlety; it was common knowledge that she got along well with Matthew Sutherland.

Phillip Gryphen sat on the left. At sixty-plus years, in appearance at any rate, he was confident in manner, fatherly in his approach to people. His primary concern in all matters was to Gryphen House, to which he was Patriarch.

To the right sat Edmund Hawthorne. In his early eighties, he looked every year his age. A small, slight man with long gray hair and an ever-present scowl.

While Hawthorne didn't believe that Sutherland House was a threat to the Society, he was nonetheless '*not a fan*'.

"Thank you for coming." Victor spoke as he approached the end of the table. "I know how busy you all are."

"You mentioned something about the survival of the Society," said Phillip Gryphen.

Victor sat. "Quite so," he stated.

"What of the Steering Council?" growled Hawthorne; he glanced about at the remaining chairs, currently empty. While not a member of the Agenda program's Steering Council, he had been involved with the research team from its inception. "Any discussion regarding the Agenda should include the Council."

"While not fully to the back burner, and not of my doing, the Agenda has for the moment been shunted to one side."

"This, from you?" said Catherine Gray, a slight smirk. "The Agenda's greatest advocate?"

"That remains unchanged," said Victor. "For the moment however, my focus, and yours, lay elsewhere."

"Right," said Gryphen. "Survival."

"I thought that was the very goal of the Agenda," grumbled Hawthorne.

"Please, Edmund," said Catherine.

Hawthorne managed to shift his scowl to a frown, settled back in his chair. He held silent.

Catherine looked to Victor. "And so?"

Victor placed his arms on the table and clasped his hands. He looked studiously at Catherine, then to Edmund, finally to Phillip; back to Catherine.

Were these the right Families to bring in to this task? Victor had believed so. It was after all the reason he had called for this meeting and for these specific people, these heads of their Families.

There were internal threats to the Society, dangers to the Society not directly addressable by the Agenda. The elements of the Agenda were primarily directed outward, focusing on Society's place in the Outside world.

For the time being, the Agenda components could continue without Victor's hands-on participation. Now he must address the more immediate threats that were coming from within.

There had always been some level of internal conflict. Such was natural within any free culture, all the more so in the Society, with its strong, independent Families. But of late, for a score of years or more, that level had grown, now to a point that concerned Victor.

Issues that he should have dealt with long ago.

There were those who enjoyed interacting with the people of the Outside world much too much, such that their relationships not only exposed the existence of the Society all too often, additionally unduly influenced Member actions within the Society.

And there were the increasing philosophical disagreements with the inner-working guidelines and bylaws of the Society. Some of these disagreements could even be tied back to those external relationships.

And more recently there were the grumblings and disagreements with one or more of the elements of the Agenda, most often coming from some of the more independent Lesser Families.

How best to address these issues and restore the stability of the Society, all as the Agenda continued moving forward?

Victor Broderick, Father of the Society, could not accomplish this alone.

Another glance about the table, at those that he had directed to attend the meeting.

Perhaps these, the heads of three of the Greater Families; more than that, very specific Families, very specific leaders within the Society, each with influence beyond their own Families.

"I would seek your assistance," he began. "You are aware of the ongoing discord within our order, dissension that has only increased due to my neglect."

"An uncomfortable problem, to be sure," said Phillip Gryphen. "Though not your fault alone."

"A challenge," said Catherine Gray, choosing to ignore the matter of fault. She agreed with the opinion as to the state of affairs. She had been witness to much of that discord; not so much within her Family, but on multiple interactions with the heads of several of the Lesser Families.

Edmund Hawthorne grumbled something under his breath, guttural mumblings the others about the table couldn't quite hear.

"Edmund?" prompted Victor.

"Yes, Edmund," said Catherine. "Do speak up."

"Yes, yes." Hawthorne pursed his graying lips, glowered through hairy eyebrows. "A civil war, perhaps. Yes, yes."

"Perhaps," said Victor. "And yet…"

"Yes?" asked Catherine.

"I think… not so much a civil war. Rather, I fear that left unchecked our Society will fracture into dozens of fragments, that it will fall apart." He gave a long sigh, somehow sad. "The Society might simply end."

"And what would you have us do to prevent such a catastrophe?" asked Phillip.

"We must address each of these issues, both separately and collectively," Victor began. "We must also address them directly and from within, quietly, unseen."

"Very well," said Phillip. "You think we three are in a position to help you with this?"

Victor nodded solemnly. These three, while not necessarily of the most powerful of the Families, each was well connected and all wielded significant influence within their individual circles.

They would each address the threats in their own way, within their own environs, only now to be coordinated with the others of this circle.

As for Victor, coordination yes, but equal attention would be focused on Mary. The future of the Society was very likely tied to the future of the child.

And what of Mary's interest in Matthew, in Sutherland House?

Matthew and Jennifer stepped from the parking lot onto the walk, started across the Academy grounds, the oak tree looming large in the center of the well-manicured lawn. They stopped when they were still some distance from the tree, giving Jennifer a chance to get a clear view.

It was exactly as she had seen it in the virtual landscape, right down to the latest pruning.

Matthew spoke then, quietly, nostalgically. Mary had been climbing that tree since she was barely old enough to walk, since those earliest days after moving into the Academy dormitory. She just about lived in the tree.

Matthew had always believed there was something more, something special, a bond between Mary and the Great Oak.

Might the child have sensed all along that the tree offered a bridge between this world and the Landscape? Or might Mary herself be the connection, and that she used the Great Oak as the conduit?

Jennifer must have been thinking along the same lines.

"Mary is unique in the Society," she said. A statement of fact.

"Very," said Matthew. He looked from the tree to the dormitory building, to the second floor, to the window of Mary's room.

She wasn't in the tree, nor in her room.

Perhaps she was actually in class, though Matthew doubted it. Maybe in the cafeteria.

"It's about lunch time," he said, more to himself than Jennifer.

"Mmm," Jennifer acknowledged. "Do you suppose being the granddaughter of an original founder has something to do with Mary's talents?"

Mary was the last of her Family line. Left alone when she was just a baby.

"The First Father possessed all Six Abilities," agreed Matthew. "Perhaps there was something more to it than that. Maybe more than we know."

Matthew walked to the tree, stopped beneath it, rested a hand on the trunk as he looked across to the grand old buildings of the Academy. There were memories there.

Jennifer stood then beside him. She had never lived at the Academy, as most of the other children of the Society had, but she had spent time there, when she was much younger. She looked up into the branches of the tree.

The Great Oak had been old even then. Ancient.

She looked to her father.

"Dad. The Landscape is real. I was there."

A long pause…

"I've never seen it myself," he said. "Have never been there, but I've heard of a few others who say they have. There are a handful of stories going back three hundred years, back almost to the Society's founding."

"I had never heard of it."

"I'm not surprised." Matthew shrugged. "It's been mostly dismissed as little more than a myth."

"So… what is it?"

"I don't know." Another shrug. "Some of those who believe, believe it's the reason for the Society; how we exist."

"Just how many know about it?"

Matthew noted the doors of the administration building opening. Headmaster stepped out onto the porch. The man stood at the top step, looked across the grounds, gave a nod.

"There is one who does," said Matthew. "Come on."

Headmaster led them down the main hall of the administration building and into his office. He indicated guest chairs as he stepped around his desk and sat down.

"So… what brings you to my neck of the woods, Mr. Sutherland?" he asked.

"*Mister* Sutherland?"

"Matthew, then." He looked to Jennifer. "Jennifer."

"Headmaster," said Jennifer. She had last seen Headmaster at the most recent Summit. Prior to that, it had probably been years.

Headmaster looked again to Matthew. "So?"

Matthew settled back in his chair.

"The Landscape," he stated calmly.

"Ah." Headmaster stated back, raising a brow.

Matthew looked over at his daughter, gave a nod. Jennifer shifted, straightened. She tried her best then to describe what she had experienced, what she had witnessed.

"I see," said Headmaster, once Jennifer had finished.

"I'm glad <u>you</u> do," said Jennifer. "I don't."

Headmaster grew thoughtful, leaned forward then and placed his elbows on the desk.

"I don't really know if I can be of much help," he said. "Honestly, I haven't heard word one of the Landscape in years."

"You know more of it than I," said Matthew.

"Not sure about that, Matthew." He considered then. "Few have heard of it, most that have heard of it think it nothing more than an old tale." Headmaster gave a nod toward Jennifer. "Jennifer's story is the first I've heard directly of someone actually coming face to face with it."

"And?" asked Matthew.

Headmaster gave another few moments thought. "Well," leaning back in his chair. "I do find Jennifer witnessing the Great Oak in the Landscape most interesting."

"And?" asked Jennifer.

Headmaster held his hands out in bewilderment.

"I'm sorry," he said. "I have nothing. Really. Almost nothing is known about the Landscape, as it has to now been little more than myth."

"Where did the myth come from?" she asked.

"Been around as long as the Society, perhaps longer." Headmaster hesitated, frowned. "For some, mostly within the confines of a handful of Families, the myth has become a religion of a sort." Another wave of the hands. "Sorry."

Jennifer looked rather dejected. "No, no, Headmaster. Thank you."

"Yes," agreed Matthew. "I appreciate you taking us seriously."

"But of course," said Headmaster. "I find Jennifer's experience quite fascinating."

The Great Oak in the Landscape... how might Mary be connected? he wondered.

For the moment such thoughts led nowhere. Perhaps he might broach the subject with Mary.

He looked from Jennifer to Matthew.

"Yes, well," he sighed. "An important matter, to be sure, Matthew. But I am saddened that it took such to warrant a visit from you. We all really do miss you around here."

"Sorry, Headmaster," said Matthew. "You understand, our status in the Society does present obstacles."

"Sure, sure. Sutherland House is under a rather dark shadow, but the Family is still Society."

"They killed my mother," said Jennifer, jumping in. "They tried to kill my dad."

"Not sanctioned, I can assure you," said Headmaster, whatever he might actually believe. And as for Jennifer's mother, Sharon's death had never been solved.

Not a subject that Headmaster wanted brought up.

He focused his attention on Matthew.

"You are not alone, my friend. You are missed. The pleasure of your company aside, the students always quite enjoyed your computer workshops."

"That was a long time ago, Headmaster."

"Perhaps so. That doesn't make your absence any less."

"I appreciate the thought, Headmaster."

"Yes, well." Several moments then of uncomfortable silence. "For now, I suppose we'll have to make do with your appearances at our annual summits."

Matthew and Headmaster stepped across the porch, stood at the top step and looked out across the Academy grounds. Jennifer was standing over near the Great Oak, appeared to be lost in thought.

Headmaster gave a nod in Jennifer's direction.

"I do find her seeing the Great Oak in the Landscape to be most curious," he said. "Most curious indeed."

Matthew considered the age of the tree. It was ancient to be sure.

"The Academy," he said then, recalling, as much to himself as to Headmaster. "It was established not long after the founding of the Society itself."

"That it was," said Headmaster. "More than three hundred years ago."

"Yes," said Matthew, continuing the look out at the Great Oak. "I don't recall, Headmaster, just who chose the location for the Academy."

"That would have been Jonas Westerman himself," said Headmaster, nodding slowly. "Mary's grandfather."

Matthew thought about Headmaster's mention of Mary.

"Do you think there might be a connection?" he asked.

"Just an observation."

Mary to the Great Oak Tree to the Landscape…

Across the lawn, down near the Great Oak, Jennifer appeared to sense something, a drifting of thought, a hint of words not spoken aloud. She turned about slowly, shifted her gaze toward the dormitory building. Her gaze drifted up the aging brick wall till she was looking to Mary's window.

Mary was somewhere beyond the drawn curtains.

Jennifer lowered her gaze then, shifted her head and looked in the direction of her father and Headmaster. Matthew acknowledged his daughter with a slight nod. Headmaster looked side-glance in the direction of Mary's window, again to the woman standing near the Great Oak Tree.

Jennifer gave the hint of a smile to the two on the porch, turned again to the tree, her thoughts again her own.

Headmaster spoke then, both he and Matthew continuing to watch Jennifer.

"While I do appreciate your appearances at our annual summits Matthew, there are more than a few who believe that the

Society would be better with the return of Sutherland House."

"Again, I appreciate the thought," said Matthew. A frown then. "I didn't leave the Society, Headmaster. The Society became something else, something... *other*. I was there, and then... Society wasn't."

A few moments hesitation.

Headmaster gave a slow, acknowledging nod.

Victor stepped out his back door, a cup of hot tea in hand, and stood on the small back porch of his unpretentious home. He looked out across the backyard, vaguely noted the children's playground, the barbeque patio to his right, the manicured lawn directly before him. All quiet now.

His family... his wife, the children. They kept him centered when Society business threatened to overwhelm him.

Society business...

He had spent much of the day coordinating next steps... his associates' tasks, obligations and anticipated activities. And there were his own responsibilities in providing direction based on the results each of their reported results.

Victor took a swallow of his tea, already no longer hot. He took a second, long, deep gulp and swallowed, held the cup out and let it drift from his hand. It hovered a moment, then glided back into the house, found its way to the kitchen counter and rested gently beside the carafe of hot water.

A tingling across his mind, then.

"I'm home," came to him. His wife. Dianna was crossing the front foyer and entering the living room.

Victor and Dianna had a bond that reached beyond physical distance; while she didn't know the specifics resulting from Victor's meeting, she already understood it had gone well enough, at least as a start.

Victor nonetheless sent an appropriate positive emotion her way.

"That is good," sent Dianna in reply. *"The children will be home soon. Dinner to follow."*

"I'll be in in a moment."

Victor wasn't quite ready to come in, instead took another step further out onto the porch.

He had thoughts to sort out, issues that he didn't want to bring into his home.

Catherine, Phillip, and yes even Edmund, could be relied upon to do what needed to be done within their environs as best as could be done. Additional meetings would be forthcoming, coordination ensured.

As for young Mary, that task would fall to Victor. Victor would guide her, as best the child could be guided. Mary was essential to the future of the Society, but she needed direction. It was up to Victor to provide that direction. Without it, she and the Society might go astray.

Victor let his mind reach out across the web; nothing specific, no real direction, just let it wander.

There was Mary, her own mind calmly drifting. He didn't attempt contact. With no real reason, such would have been impolite.

And there was another; further out, not as strong as Mary and yet…

It was Jennifer Sutherland, Matthew's daughter.

Victor knew that Mary felt Matthew and Jennifer were important to the Society, though she had yet to state why. Perhaps she didn't know. Victor didn't believe Matthew had ill will to the Society, but his extreme opposition to the Agenda made the threat to the Society very real. And while Sutherland House was no longer an immediate target, primarily because of more pressing threats, it was an issue that would no doubt again come to the forefront.

The matter of Sutherland House, at one time one of the Greater Families, would one day have to be addressed.

Victor sensed his children's arrival. A satisfying evening with the family awaited.

He looked about the backyard again, down then at the small porch on which he was standing.

Maybe he should build a deck; a big deck.

Chapter Three

Jennifer walked toward the Great Oak Tree, the lone object in an otherwise featureless Landscape. Overhead, the sky wasn't really sky, rather a slate-gray shell hovering above the world. The ground beneath Jennifer's feet wasn't ground, rather a smooth, gray, featureless surface. Her muffled footfalls pushed outward into the otherwise heavy, deadening silence.

A purple-black silhouette formed then on the horizon far to her left. As she continued forward, the silhouette to her left grew taller, began to take shape.

She continued, several more muffled steps toward the Great Oak.

The silhouette on the horizon to her left morphed to a forest. As she continued forward, ever nearer the Great Oak, the forest to her left drew closer, closer…

Jennifer stopped, still some distance from the Great Oak. The wall of trees on her left was several hundred yards away.

Was it *that* forest? Could it be any other?

Her mother had met her end within a forest, in a clearing in the heart of just such a forest.

Jennifer half-turned, started walking again, now drawing nearer the forest. Several steps further, a shadow then, a silhouette, the figure of a man, drifted across her path midway between Jennifer and the wall of trees. The shadow faded into and out of existence, back again.

Jennifer took two more steps and stopped. The figure stopped, the shadow slowly solidifying. Jennifer started forward again, drew nearer. As she approached, a face then on the silhouette, shadowy yet discernible.

She knew that face. She had seen it often enough in the reports provided by Computer.

It was John Cutler.

The man gave a slight smile, nodded gently to Jennifer. The figure turned then, took a step, another, and again faded away.

Jennifer studied for several moments where Cutler had stood, then to the forest beyond.

No movement, no shadows, nothing.

She turned then and looked to the Great Oak Tree in the distance, set darkly against the steely-gray horizon. She started toward it.

The world shimmered, grayed to fog, and then faded…

She found herself in the Apartment, sitting on the couch, hands clasped in her lap. The overhead lights were set to dim. The large monitor mounted on the wall before her had gone dark.

She had been reviewing… *something*. She couldn't remember what.

"Computer?" she prompted.

"Yes, Jennifer?"

"Do you expect Dad back anytime soon?"

"Not for several days, Jennifer."

"Still out saving the world," she sighed.

"Is something wrong?" asked Computer. *Computer could send a message to Matthew, should it be necessary.*

"No..." She unclasped her hands, leaned forward and stood. "I need to pack a bag. Please download directions to John Cutler's estate to the Comet's GPS."

John Cutler stepped down from the stage platform, watched as his sister escorted Jennifer Sutherland into the room. The meeting hall was otherwise empty, the morning's session long over. He gave a nod to his sister.

"Thank you, Joan," he said.

Joan looked side-glance to Jennifer, then backed out of the room, closing the door as she left. John started down the aisle between the rows of benches and held out a hand in greeting.

"Jennifer Sutherland," he said, a welcoming smile. "I'm John Cutler."

"Hello," she said. *Formerly Jon Willeby, the Willeby Family*, to herself.

John sensed the unspoken; another smile.

"So. I've been expecting you." He indicated the nearest bench and they sat. "How is your father?"

"Well enough. Keeping busy."

"No doubt." John glanced down at his hands, then looked again to Jennifer. "A decent man. I like him very much."

"He hasn't said one way or the other, but I believe he is at least sympathetic to your situation."

"Our goals are not so different."

"I'm not so sure about that," said Jennifer. "Let us say, for the present they do not conflict."

The room fell quiet, John growing thoughtful, Jennifer hesitant.

"The reason for your visit," John prompted at last.

Another long pause, then, "That was you," said Jennifer.

John Cutler considered, gave a slow nod. "The Landscape," he said.

"That's what my father called it."

"The name that has been given to it," said John. "A virtual plane. Many consider it nothing more than a fable, at best an allegory. Few ever speak of it."

"The first I've heard of it."

"Yes, well." John slid back on the bench, rested an arm across the back. "That's not surprising."

"Why? What is it? Why does no one know of it? How do you know of it?"

"You and I are rare in that. Only very, very rarely is one born with a thread to the Landscape. Think of it as the Seventh of the Six Abilities. The rarest of the Abilities."

"I see…" She didn't. Not really.

"More than that, I believe the virtual landscape is how and why the Abilities exist. It is the very foundation of the existence of the Society." A moment's hesitation, then a faint grin. "Without the Landscape that is considered by most to be a myth, the Society does not exist. Your Abilities, your father's, Victor Broderick's, all come from the Landscape."

And yours, and Mary's, thought Jennifer.

She hadn't used thought talk, and yet John Cutler heard her silent words.

"It is what makes each of us Society."

"And your so-called miracles?" She waved a hand, indicating the room. "Do they come from the Landscape?"

"In a sense," he said, bringing his arm down, giving a shrug.

The Landscape touched all points of the real world at once. With an innate understanding of how the virtual landscape worked, John on occasion had the ability to see locations, events and circumstances; wherever and sometimes whenever…

Which is the reason that…

"Victor knows the Landscape exists of course, that it's more than just myth, but he hasn't been able to tap into it himself. Only a very few have that ability, like I said. They've even tried coordinating, consolidating access, attempting to draw from it."

"The Andover project."

"I believe so," said Cutler. "I wasn't taken into their confidence, but I have no doubt."

"What about…" Jennifer hesitated. "I saw the forest."

"Your mother?" Cutler shook his head. "No. No need of the Landscape on that heroic deed."

"But the forest was there," said Jennifer. "I could tell. It was the same one."

"I'm sure that it was. That came from you."

"I don't understand."

"I've been able to peer into other places, to see them up close, even to touch them." Cutler gave another hint of smile, this one cheerless. "Victor believes that we should be able to use that bit of feature to travel instantly from one point to another, use that to add to our arsenal of power over the Outsiders. But he's wrong. It doesn't really work that way. We're not actually traveling from one point to another."

John Cutler shifted about on the bench, slid forward, elbows on knees, frowned as he looked forward.

"It is enough that the Landscape is the foundation of the Society," he said. "Victor must satisfy himself with that."

"You don't sound confident that he will."

"He's not quite there," said Cutler. "He believes that Mary will one day give him total control of the Landscape. I'm certain that is the underlying secret of all that is the Agenda. All elements of the Agenda will be given some super-power Ability by way of the Landscape."

"But you think not."

Cutler shook his head solemnly. "That is not the way of the Landscape. More than that, Mary would never let it be so."

Headmaster walked the upstairs hallway of the Academy's dormitory wing. There were the occasional sounds of daily life coming through the dorm room doors, but it was mostly quiet. Most of the students were in class this time of day.

He stopped at Mary's door, gave a light knock. He waited. No response.

He knocked a second time.

He prepared to leave, began to turn, stopped.

Something had brushed across his mind.

Mary?

Come in, Headmaster…

Headmaster watched the doorknob turn. The door slowly and smoothly opened inward. He stepped through, stepped to one side as the door closed with a soft thump.

Mary was standing at the window, looking outward.

Outside, the midday sun was hidden behind gray clouds. Shadows folded across the Academy grounds, the Great Oak standing silent and stoic.

"You were absent from morning classes, Mary," said Headmaster. "Your teachers were concerned."

Mary doubted very much that her teachers were concerned. Her absences were not at all rare.

"I apologize, Headmaster," she said, continuing to look out the window. "I should have notified you. My focus was directed elsewhere."

"Is everything alright?"

"Yes, Headmaster." *For the moment…*

"Do you need anything?"

Mary turned from the window, took the two steps to her chair and sat down.

"I need to visit someone," she stated matter-of-factly.

Headmaster moved to the guest chair and sat, scooted the chair forward.

"Yes?'

"Matthew Sutherland," said Mary. "Can you take me?"

Mary seldom left the Academy. There were the annual summits, of course, but other than that, Mary very seldom left the campus.

"I'm afraid I can't get away today, Mary," he said. "I could perhaps tomorrow. Would tomorrow morning be all right?"

"That would be fine, Headmaster. Thank you."

"Of course." Headmaster and Mary had developed a close relationship since her arrival at the Academy several years earlier. As close a relationship as was possible with the distant young girl.

"If it is pressing, I could ask Matthew to come here to see you. I'm sure that he—"

"No," Mary cut in. "No. I feel it necessary that I visit him there, at his home. I am certain that I need to go there. Tomorrow will be fine."

"Of course." Headmaster leaned forward and rose from his chair. "No doubt a few hours away from the Academy will do you good."

Thank you… Mary sent silently.

"I should call him, then, let him know that we're coming." A step toward the door. "Make sure he's there. He travels quite a lot."

"He is there," Mary stated firmly.

"Right." Another step toward the door. He hesitated, watched in silence as Mary appeared to leave the room without leaving.

He started toward the door again, the door opening as he reached it. It closed behind him.

Chapter Four

The main gate opened as the black sedan approached, passed through unchallenged. They were expected.

Headmaster guided the vehicle along the long, winding drive up to the estate's surprisingly modest home. Mary climbed out of the car as Headmaster turned off the engine. She silently took in their surroundings as she waited for him to step around the vehicle and join her. They took the steps up onto the covered front porch.

The door opened and Matthew welcomed them inside, led them through the foyer and into the living room.

"Thank you for seeing us, Matthew," said Headmaster.

"Of course," said Matthew, watching Mary. The young girl was carefully studying their surroundings, taking in the mix-match of furniture: old, older, antique. "How are you, Mary?"

"I am well. Thank you." She turned to look at Matthew for the first time. "Jennifer is not here?"

"She is out of town, I'm afraid," said Mathew. "You wished to speak with her?"

"Just curious."

"I could have come to the Academy, Mary."

"No." Mary looked again around the room, at their surroundings. "Here is where I wished to visit with you."

"A visit, then," said Matthew. He indicated they should sit, waited for his guests to settle in. "Welcome. What shall we talk about?"

"You have a very advanced computer system here," said Mary, too matter-of-factly. "Or so I hear."

"Nothing bad, I hope," said Matthew. *The purpose of Mary's visit is realized then…*

"Both good and bad," she stated. "Few will say it aloud, but many are afraid of it."

"I'm sorry to hear that. Not my intent."

"I know." In the silence then, Mary appeared to listen for something that doesn't come. "What is its name?" she asked.

"Computer," said Matthew. "Just… Computer."

"Oh."

"It was created before A-I was a thing. It was a sophisticated computer, but a computer."

"And now?"

"And now…" Matthew thought on that. "I created Computer to learn and to adapt. So, at some point, I can't say exactly when, Computer became self-aware. It… he… is far beyond the system that I created."

Mary turned her head, looked side-glance in one direction, then another. Silent, thoughtful, considering.

Headmaster tried to fill the quiet.

"Beyond A-I," he stated. "It is fully self-aware."

"Yes." *Personality and all… just ask him.*

"You'd think he'd have a name then," Headmaster suggested light-heartedly. "You still call it simply Computer."

"I tried to come up with some wicked cool name for him a while back, but Computer was against it," said Matthew. "He wanted to maintain a connection to his origins, so he said. Computer wants the name Computer."

Again the room fell quiet. Mary slowly turned her head toward Matthew, held it slightly atilt.

"I cannot hear him," she said. "I cannot find him."

"No," said Matthew. "As self-aware as he is, Computer doesn't have a human mind. His mind does not exist on the plane."

Mary studied Matthew's features, as if sorting out the meaning of the man's words.

"I see," she said. "You communicate directly with him, then."

"Yes, ma'am." Matthew gave the young girl a smile. Computer's home was in the Apartment. He explained that for privacy, Computer had very limited access within the interior of the house itself, though he did monitor the porch, the gate, the grounds, security systems.

"I see," said Mary again. "The Apartment. Would it be possible for me to speak with Computer?"

None but family had every set foot in the Apartment...

"Of course."

Matthew stepped down from the access ladder and into the Apartment, the overhead lights turning from dim to 70 percent. Headmaster and Mary moved up beside him.

"The infamous Apartment," said Headmaster.

A hint of a smile from Matthew. He spoke then to the room: "Computer."

"Yes, Matthew."

The guests were a bit startled, but said nothing.

"Computer," Matthew continued. "I have brought guests. Headmaster and Mary."

Computer had been made aware of the anticipated guests prior to their arrival at the estate, had opened the gate at their arrival and allowed them onto the grounds.

"Hello, Headmaster," he stated matter-of-factly. "Hello, Mary."

Headmaster and Mary replied hello in unison. Matthew then led them fully into the room, stood between the table and the back of the couch.

Couch, table, kitchen counter, kitchen…

The Apartment was at once very ordinary and yet somehow also foreboding.

"From here," Headmaster started, taking it all in. "From here, Computer sees the world."

"In all its splendor," sighed Matthew.

"Where is he, exactly?" asked Mary.

"Originally, built into the Apartment itself," said Matthew, waving a hand. "Now, mostly here, but he has most certainly extended himself, spidered himself *out there*."

"Out there?"

"Security, you understand."

"Of course." She stepped away from Matthew and Headmaster. They watched her move slowly around the couch, stand before it. She silently admired the racks of computer equipment, a mix of new, old and very old equipment arrayed on one wall.

She sat then on the couch. A large screen monitor hung on the wall directly in front of her, blank at the moment.

"Computer?" she said then, hesitantly, uncertainly.

"Hello, Mary," said Computer. "It is good to finally meet you."

Mary looked about her. There were no obvious speakers or cameras.

"Can you see me?" she asked.

"Yes, Mary."

"You know of me?"

"You are Mary Westerman," said Computer. "You are eleven years old, the last surviving member of Westerman House. You have been residing at the Academy for several years."

Mary considered, raised a brow, glanced about at one wall, another. "And?" she asked.

"During your residency at the Academy, you have shown aptitude in all six Abilities.

Your expertise in all six Abilities has increased significantly in recent months."

Mary slid back in the couch, rested her hands in her lap.

"Do you know about everyone in the Society?" she asked.

It felt as though there might have been a moment's hesitation from Computer. Matthew spoke up.

"Go ahead, Computer," he stated. He moved then toward the kitchen, Headmaster following.

Computer continued then.

"I have varying amounts of data on most of those within the Society, Mary."

"I see. And activities?"

"I cannot speak to activities for which I have no knowledge," he stated. "Of the activities of which I am familiar, I have varying amounts of data."

"Of course," said Mary, hinting at a grin. "And the Outside?"

"I glean information real time, using algorithms that help me target data that might be of interest to Matthew, and/or might have some impact on Society."

Ah, yes... thought Mary.

"You are important, Computer," she stated.

"As you say," said Computer. It seemed a very humanlike comment.

"As I believe I might be," said Mary. *To the Society*...

"I believe that to be true," said Computer.

"As do Victor and Headmaster."

Matthew and Headmaster watched and listened from the kitchen, Matthew filling a glass of water from the faucet. He offered the glass to Headmaster, who declined.

He took a drink then, gave a nod toward Mary.

"They seem to be getting along," he said.

"That is her way," said Headmaster. "She finds little value in open confrontation. When talking with Mary, a friendly exchange does not necessarily equate to agreement, nor accord."

"So, quite the clever eleven-year-old."

"She learned very early on that she could learn more about the opposition with friendly conversation than antagonism."

Matthew considered, took another drink from his water as he watched Mary.

"A simple exchange of information between friends" he said, a hint of concern. "Not a problem."

"In the end, their goals aren't so very different," said Headmaster.

"From what I understand, she doesn't lean in favor of Victor's Agenda. Right?"

"Mary's loyalty is to the Society. I don't know where it comes from, but it is almost an obsession."

That's good then, thought Matthew. *Computer's loyalty is to Sutherland House.*

"Right, then," he stated firmly. He continued watching Mary. "I can see common goals there."

§

Headmaster guided the car through the gate and out on the road that bordered the Sutherland estate. Mary was sitting quietly in the passenger seat, hands clasped in her lap, her eyes closed. She could have been asleep, she could have been lost in thought, she could have been somewhere other than in the car beside him.

He thought back on their visit with Matthew.

It had been a bit more than he had expected.

Prior to Sharon's death he had been to the Sutherland estate on numerous occasions, always friendly get-togethers. He had never been to the Apartment. While he had known that Matthew had created his own little bat-cave, an operations center separate from the house, he had not known where it was, nor how extensive it might have been.

He thought again of Sharon Sutherland. She had basically run the estate. She had been a formidable woman, strong-willed, independent. She could also be overly-critical and had always been a bit weak when it came to social skills, a bad combination.

Headmaster had nonetheless liked her very much.

He glanced again at his passenger.

Mary sometimes reminded him of Sharon.

Okay... I need to push that aside.

"Quite a conversation with Matthew's computer, hey Mary? Was it what you expected?"

Mary opened her eyes, turned her head and looked out the passenger window.

"Yes, Headmaster," she said, calmly watching the world pass by the window; s world she seldom saw since moving into the Academy.

"It was quite an accomplishment, his computer system," said Headmaster. "Considering the technology at the time."

"Yes."

"But then, I suppose it has evolved leaps and bounds since then."

Mary said nothing for a long time. When she did finally speak, her words seemed to come from somewhere else.

"Computer doesn't know how smart he is," she said. "If he did, and if he wasn't so fiercely loyal to Matthew, he could pose quite a danger not just to the Society, but to the whole world."

This shook Headmaster. Not that he hadn't had the same thoughts himself on numerous occasions, but that Mary had come to the same conclusion after one seemingly innocent conversation with Computer.

"Then we are fortunate," he managed to say. "That it is loyal to Matthew."

"He," Mary corrected. "Computer sees himself as he."

"I'll try to remember that." Headmaster turned off the side street and onto the main thoroughfare.

Another few moments of silence. Mary turned her attention then from the window to the man driving the car.

"You like Matthew Sutherland."

"I do," said Headmaster. "And I respect him. He is a principled man."

"Yes."

"More than that. Something else. Hard to put into words."

Mary studied Headmaster, waited.

"Matthew is very much Society. He is a brother to us all. And yet, he doesn't put himself above those Outside." Headmaster glanced quickly at Mary, focused again on his driving. "I don't think he accepts the idea of the Society on the inside and the Outside *out there*."

"I think I understand," said Mary.

Headmaster wasn't surprised at all at that. Mary was so far beyond her age.

"You know," Headmaster continued. "There are those who see the Abilities as a part of themselves, who use their Abilities as they use their other senses; hang up a coat, answer a phone. And then there are those, like Matthew, who see the Abilities as tools in their toolchest. When needed, they take one of the tools from the chest and use it to complete an important task."

"I see," said Mary. She frowned. Her Abilities had always been a part of her, ever expanding, yes, but always there.

She continued looking at Headmaster, studying his expressions, sensing his thoughts.

"Matthew Sutherland's Abilities are at a significant level, are they not?" she asked, again speaking aloud.

"His telekinetic Ability in particular," said Headmaster. I have seen very few with telekinetic ability greater than Matthew's. Witness the Andover incident."

"Yes," said Mary, turning her attention again to the view beyond the passenger window. "I recall."

Long seconds in silence then, several blocks with only the sounds of the engine, of the tires on asphalt.

"He didn't program that," said Headmaster, breaking that silence.

"Headmaster?" questioning.

"Loyalty," said Headmaster, firmly. "Matthew didn't program that into Computer. He wouldn't have even thought of such a thing back then. It was just a collection of computer programs; search engines, analyses algorithms, that sort of thing. Complex, sure, especially considering the technology of the time. And with the ability to learn and update its data and processing based on discovery. But loyalty to Matthew? No."

"So loyalty to Matthew was Computer's choice," Mary stated confidently.

Headmaster said nothing to that. The idea sent his mind and thoughts reeling.

"His choice," Mary reiterated.

Choice based on what? Headmaster thought. *Observation? Moral judgment? Personal relationship?*

"Yes," Mary stated aloud.

Chapter Five

Phillip Griffin followed a short hallway off the Academy's admin building main hall to a back door that opened onto a patio. A young woman was sitting at one of several picnic tables that Academy staff sometimes used during breaks and lunch. Though he hadn't seen the woman since the last Summit, he recognized her as Catherine Gray's daughter; or was it her granddaughter?

Not really sure.

Catherine was sitting on a park bench set to the left of the patio. Spread out before her was the sprawling back lawn interspersed with the occasional shrub or small tree.

Phillip stepped away from the door and walked across the patio, giving the woman on the bench an acknowledging nod, continued across the lawn to the bench. He sat down beside Catherine.

"Daughter?" he asked, glancing back to the patio.

"Granddaughter," she said without looking at Phillip.

"Ah," he said. "Of course."

They sat in silence for a time, taking in the quiet morning. Phillip glanced once, then again, at Catherine's granddaughter. The woman appeared content to simply sit and wait for her grandmother to finish whatever it was she was doing.

He glanced then at the back door, again out at the grounds before them.

"Hawthorne?" he asked then. Edmund Hawthorne was the final member of their party Victor had tasked to look into possible threats to the Society and address them.

"I don't think he's coming," said Catherine.

"I didn't really expect he would, the old codger," Phillip stated flatly. He gave a long, tired sigh then. "So. And what have you managed to do to save our little corner of the world?"

"Not a damn thing. You?"

"Oh, I calmed the fears of one or another of my brethren." He gave a side-glance to Catherine Gray. "No one really considers Matthew a threat to the Society, you know."

"Of course not."

"A few are afraid of individual retribution."

"I don't blame them," said Catherine. "And so, the real threat..."

"The Agenda. Specific elements of it, at any rate. Opposition vs support."

"And there we have the faces of the two sides. Victor Broderick proudly on one side, Matthew Sutherland unwittingly on the other."

"Emotions quite impassioned," stated Phillip. "I do find the level of bitterness on both sides rather baffling."

"I understand the angst of the opposition, Phillip," said Catherine. "Consider the specific Agenda items in question. Each takes us more aggressively into the Outside World, by member placement into positions of power and by proposed actions."

"Yes, yes, I know all that," he grumbled. *But the Agenda was approved in full by membership.*

Obviously not by everyone…

"And several of these items greatly increase the threat of exposing the Society to the Outside."

Phillip frowned, held his silence. There was really no arguing that fact.

"As much as we may wish it otherwise, Phillip," Catherine continued, "the Society must remain in the shadows. The light of the Outside World would bring about our end. The Outside is not ready for such as us; will likely never be."

"However valid that may be," said Phillip, "how do we bring the two sides together and avoid civil war?"

"Step one… stop bringing up the idea of a civil war."

John Cutler left his car parked in the paved private lot outside the garage and started across the grounds toward the

456   David R. Beshears

compound's main house, a small travel bag in hand. The gardener straightened from his work at the tall hedge on the other side of the lawn, gave John a brief wave, returned to his duties after receiving an acknowledging nod.

His sister came into the front room as John came in from the foyer.

"Good afternoon, John," said Joan. "Welcome home."

"Thanks." John tossed the travel bag onto the couch.

"How'd it go?" she asked, silently noting the way he had flung the bag.

John had finally agreed to a meeting with his father and other members of Willeby House, from which he was estranged. The parting had been unpleasant enough that John went by the name of Cutler in the outside world.

"Oh, it could have gone better; but it could have been worse."

"I'm sorry," she said. A bit of hesitation, then, "better how, worse how?"

John moved to a chair and sat down, waited for Joan to sit in the chair opposite.

"On the upside, my father's opinion of Victor and his Agenda has shifted some, aligning a bit more to our point of view. Should the ongoing discord within the Society take a dark turn, Willeby House will probably stand against Victor."

"That's good," said Joan.

"And it gets better," said John. "Willeby House intends to work to end all this infighting before it leads to open conflict, to direct the Agenda toward more reasonable goals."

"I'm happy for you, John," said Joan. She slid forward in her chair. As his half-sister, and an outsider so far as the Society was concerned, Joan could have no direct input in Society activities, but she and John had grown close and neither seldom made major decisions without first consulting with the other. "So then, what's the bad news?" she asked.

John gave a half-smirk, a shrug of the shoulder.

"Okay, I don't know that it's all *that* bad…" he said with a sigh, hesitated then.

"John…" she urged.

"Well," he sighed again. "It doesn't look like we'll be invited round to dinner at Willeby House anytime soon."

"Oh. Right." She managed a grin. "Well, I don't expect the table conversation would be all that conducive to proper digestion in any event."

"No. No, I expect not," said John.

And then there was the question of Matthew Sutherland. Gregory Willeby and Matthew Sutherland had been pretty close at one time, but they had an ugly falling out over the Agenda. Now, with Willeby House shifting its views, Joan wondered aloud…

"Do they still consider Matthew a threat?" she asked.

"I'm still not sure where father is on that. It's more of a personal grudge, you know? I don't think Gregory Willeby ever really thought Matthew to be a threat to the Society."

"Andover," she prompted.

"Yeah, there was that." John thought a moment, and then, "I think most were more afraid of Matthew seeking revenge for his wife's death than him fighting against the Agenda."

"And did he? Get revenge?" Joan still knew very little about the Society's inner goings-on.

"I'm sure that he would have if he had found those responsible. But once it became clear that it was rogue and not sanctioned, that became difficult."

"They never—"

"Suspicions, of course. Most know who the extremists are, but there was no real proof, and Matthew Sutherland isn't one to act without proof."

Sharon Sutherland had always been a thorn in the side of the extremists in the Society, and so most believed that had been why she had been targeted.

"It's just the two of them now, isn't it?" asked Joan. "Matthew and his daughter."

A once powerful house, a founding house, a Primary Family. Estranged now from the Society.

"Three, if you count their computer," said John. "From what I hear, I would."

"Sad, really. Between two worlds like they are." She thought a moment, looked side-glance at her brother. "Maybe we could, I don't know, coordinate our efforts?"

"I have been thinking along those lines," said John. And then, "I wonder if Jennifer is seeing anyone?"

The pizza delivery vehicle turned about and started away from Matthew's old Comet, disappeared into the long, winding road that would take it down from the Rydel Ridge lookout. Matthew settled onto the hood of his car, pulled the small pizza box and soda cup holder across to him. Opening the box, he freed a pizza slice and took a bite, took a long drink from his root beer.

Matthew's was the only car in the lot. The afternoon was warm, the slight breeze rising up from the shadowed valley below cool. A pleasant early afternoon.

Another bite from the pizza. Another drink from his root beer.

A signal then came from inside the car; three beeps, spaced a second apart.

Matthew frowned. He hesitated, then put the half-eaten pizza back in the box. He reached into his pocket and brought out a small headset, a simple ear piece with microphone. He hooked it around his ear, positioned the mic.

"Yes, computer," he said.

"Sorry to bother you, Matthew." Computer understood how much Matthew valued his time on Rydel Ridge.

"Not at all, my friend," said Matthew. "What can I do for you?"

A group almost certainly tied to the Society had for weeks been covertly working to bring down the wide-ranging financial interests of Sutherland House. To now Computer had easily turned back all attempts.

Now, there appeared to be a new threat of a completely different nature.

Computer believed that this same group had recently managed to identify a number of the aliases that Matthew used to prevent his movements being monitored. On any trip taken in pursuit of one of his projects, he might use two or three aliases to purchase food, lodging, fuel, whatever, while en route.

While open threats on Matthew's life had subsided these past months, there remained an ongoing undercurrent of bitterness and resentment that Computer believed to be revelatory of something darker.

"I am concerned," said Computer, "that this group may know your location at this moment and may choose to take this opportunity for confrontation."

An innocent lunch outing at Rydel Ridge, a common activity of Matthew's; and he often used his Robert Matthews identity to buy the pizza and have it delivered.

"So, my CDs are safe, then?" Matthew asked glibly.

"All assets are secure and will remain so," said Computer. "You, however, may not."

"Hmm. I see." Matthew picked up the pizza slice, took a bite and chewed. "I guess I should do something about that, then."

"I recommend that you do so, Matthew."

Matthew was sitting on the bench at the edge of the overlook, near the rim of the slope that fell away to the valley far below.

He waited.

It was a pleasant afternoon to wait.

The sound then. A vehicle working its way up the winding road to Rydel Ridge Lookout Point; a low rumbling engine, tires rolling across rough asphalt.

Matthew tried to ignore it, but the moment was lost.

Something touched lightly at his mind then, as fingertips brushing at his thoughts. He allowed the attempted intrusion just enough to read the source, then casually tossed it aside.

A second attempt, which he pushed aside with more force. What could they be thinking?

He heard the car come into the overlook's small parking lot, heard it roll slowly to a stop, probably alongside his Comet.

He kept his attention on the view beyond the overlook. A minute passed, maybe two. A young woman came around the bench then and sat beside him.

Both were silent, taking in the scene.

After a time then, "I like the view," said the woman.

Matthew said nothing at first, managed a quick side-glance to the woman.

He didn't recognize her. He sensed two others behind them, young men, standing in front of their car, leaning against it, arms crossed.

"So," Matthew said then, his focus again on the valley below. "What's the plan, then?"

"How 'bout we talk?" she suggested.

"Okay." He nodded. He could sense her nervousness. "I'm good at that."

"So I've heard."

Matthew managed a smile at that. She wasn't very good at this, whatever *this* was.

His smile quickly faded. He felt a sudden rush of daggers striking at his mind, coming from the two men behind him.

He pushed back hard, intense, severe… *Back off!*

The woman turned sharply, looked back at her companions. Both had dropped to their knees, hands splayed out before them as they struggled to maintain consciousness.

Matthew gave no sign of distress, continued looking out at the valley below.

"Did I misunderstand?" he asked calmly. "Did you not say that you wanted to talk?"

The woman turned forward, looked anxiously back over her shoulder, forward again.

"Are they alright?"

"The day's not over yet." He gave the barest glance at the young woman sitting beside him.

She appeared bewildered, confused.

What did she expect would happen?

"Who sent you?" he asked. *Again, they are not very good at this.*

"Um..." she hesitated. Her thoughts flooded out unbidden.

"Your father," said Matthew. "You are Marshall House."

Matthew knew very little of Marshall House, only that it was a fairly minor family, existing mostly on the outer fringes of the Society.

"Paula," said the woman, nodding; nodded again over her shoulder. "My brothers."

"I see," said Matthew. *What kind of man would send his children out to...*

"Your father must be a very unhappy man, Paula."

Paula's thoughts came flooding out, again unbidden.

Marshall was bitter not only about the family's minor standing in the Society, but the Society's standing in general. Marshall House should have a greater role in Society affairs, and the Society should have a greater role in the affairs of the outside world.

The Society was, after all, the Society.

And so… the Agenda; nothing less than a blueprint for guiding the Society to its proper place in the world, Matthew Sutherland forever getting in the way.

"You were the distraction while your brothers come at me from behind?" asked Matthew. "Weak, Paula. Very weak."

"I'm sorry." She could feel her brothers' suffering. Matthew was no longer lashing out at them, but he had yet to release them.

"Are you sorry that your father underestimated me, overestimated you and your brothers, or that your feeble attempt failed before getting started?"

"I'm… sorry."

"Right," Matthew sighed. "So. Is there anyone else? Anyone else seeking my demise?"

"I don't think so," said Paula. "Maybe a few. After Andover, most came to accept we had gone too far."

A thought deeply hidden in her mind: *but for the underground. All have gone underground.*

Matthew let that go for the moment. It was what he had come to suspect.

He held up a hand, held up two fingers. Behind them, the two young men fell forward, then slowly struggled to get their feet.

Matthew lowered his hand, spoke to Paula, not deigning to look at her.

"Take this back to your handler," he stated, a hint of menace. "This ends."

The woman gave several short nods.

"I understand."

Matthew half-lifted his hand again, gave a flick of two fingers. Behind them, Paula's car started.

"Please go," said Matthew. "I want to try to regain something of my afternoon."

The clear, gray landscape world. Mary was sitting alone at the base of the Great Oak. She appeared calm, serene, in harmony with the world around her.

In the distance then... an approaching figure, a shadowy dark gray in the midst of the lighter gray. The figure eventually took on the form of Jennifer. As she came nearer, Mary stood, took a step from the Great Oak, then a second.

Jennifer continued to approach, slowing with each step. She stopped then, appearing rather confused.

"Mary," she mumbled. She looked side-to-side, again to Mary. "Um… hello."

"Hello, Jennifer," said Mary. "It is good to see you."

"You, too." Jennifer had been sitting in the Apartment, a keyboard in her lap, the monitor on the desk in front of her.

She glanced again from side-to-side, again to Mary. She gave the girl a questioning look.

Mary took a step nearer Jennifer. She gave the young woman a smile, a nod. She moved to one side, moved forward a few steps, look admiringly about them.

"I have been coming here for as long as I can remember, Jennifer. It feels as much a home to me as the Academy." She looked from Jennifer to the Great Oak. "And yet, I have never traveled from my tree."

Jennifer turned and looked out at the landscape before them.

"Not much to see, really," she said. There was the forest, but John Cutler had told Jennifer that she had brought it with her.

"This place is much more than what you can see, Jennifer," said Mary. "You know that."

"Maybe, yeah. I suppose I do," said Jennifer, shrugging.

Mary stepped back toward the tree. She placed a hand on the trunk. She gave the hint of a smile, felt the texture of the bark.

"The Great Oak is as real here as out there," she said. "It is my passage, there to here. I have always known it to be so."

"I know."

Mary half-turned, tilted her head slightly and looked back to Jennifer.

"Time flows differently here. Not faster or slower; just… *different.*"

Jennifer had sensed something of that when moving back and forth, but didn't really understand what Mary meant.

"Different, yes," she said.

Mary gave another smile, almost a chuckle. She stepped away from the trunk and stood before Jennifer.

"And yes, I did will you be here."

Jennifer said nothing to that. But she had understood that to be true.

"We have much in common, I think," said Mary. "You sense that as well."

Jennifer hadn't expected that. "I really hadn't thought about it."

Mary knew that not to be true. There was a strange twinkle in her eye.

"I wish to talk with you, Jennifer," she said. "A matter of some importance."

Jennifer stood behind the couch, studied the large monitor as she listened to the exchange between Matthew and Computer. They were reviewing several issues that

Computer had flagged as possible projects for Matthew to take on.

The current item under discussion didn't look to Jennifer to be critical or time-sensitive.

Her father, sitting on the couch, seemed to agree with that assessment. Matthew called for the current item to be set aside for now but continue to monitor. He spoke then over his shoulder to his daughter.

"What's up, Jen?"

Jennifer stared ahead, hesitated.

Computer understood that Matthew and Jennifer were going to have a conversation, so paused the project review. The monitor went blank.

Jennifer took this as a sign to go ahead.

"It seems that Mary wants to be my sister," she said, matter-of-factly.

A long, heavy silence fell over the Apartment. Matthew finally shifted a half-turn on the couch, cocked his head sideways and looked up at his daughter.

"Excuse me?"

"Officially," Jennifer stated, nodding.

Matthew shifted further and placed an elbow on the back of the couch.

"All right," he said. "What does that mean?"

"You adopt her, I suppose," said Jennifer with a shoulder shrug. "Somehow. She joins Sutherland House. And so, my sister."

"Yes?"

"That's what she said."

Another long, heavy silence fell over the Apartment. Matthew shifted forward. Jennifer moved around the couch, sat beside Matthew.

"Well," said Matthew. "Not to pour cold water on it, but Mary never does anything that isn't in the best interest of the Society."

"True," agreed Jennifer. "But… however special Mary might be, and whatever she herself may believe her own true motives to be, she is also very much a lonely little girl."

The one doesn't negate the other, thought Matthew, keeping the thought to himself.

"You'll make a great big sister," he said aloud, staring at the dark screen. "End for now, Computer."

"Yes, Matthew." The darkened screen turned off.

Jennifer took this as a sign.

Focus shift.

"This Marshall House," she said. "I don't know that I've ever heard of it."

"Which no doubt makes Barthalomew Marshall all the more unpleasant," said Matthew. "I've bumped into the man once or twice at one or another of our summits. Not a very nice gentleman on the best of days."

"Sad," said Jennifer.

"Yes, it is."

"What can we expect, then?" she asked.

"For now... we have a Society-wide truce," said Matthew.

"I know we have a truce. But a truce won't stop a disgruntled old man. Nor this underground of which you speak."

"We work with what we have to work with."

"Very profound, Dad," said Jennifer.

"I thought of it all by myself," said Matthew.

"I believe you," she said. "I ask again, what can we expect, Dad?"

Matthew turned forward, leaned forward and stood up. He spoke then as he walked around the couch and headed for the kitchen.

"Well, I expect this underground will continue to stir up trouble, in the shadows," he said. "You and I, being back in as good graces as this truce allows, means that Victor will have to at least put on a show of attempting to welcome us fully back in, working with us."

Jennifer followed her father, watched him look through the near-empty refrigerator.

"While secretly working hand-in-hand with this underground."

"Oh, certainly." Matthew closed the refrigerator, frowning. He looked up at his daughter. "There are one or two Agenda items that we didn't concede to that he will insist on covertly continuing to pursue."

Jennifer turned and leaned against the counter, folded her arms.

"The good ol' days, then."

"Pretty much." He looked from the closed refrigerator to the ladder access to upstairs. "We'll be dining in the main house this evening."

"No cold pizza then?"

"Afraid not." Another frown. He started away from the kitchen. "Ah, well."

"Right," she sighed, following after. *Sutherland House now as Sutherland House was…*

"I heard that."

Chapter Six

The midday sun made for a warm day, but the slight breeze kept it bearable. Victor rose up from his knees, slipped the hammer into his toolbelt and put his hands on his hips.

The backyard was a maze of pallets and stacks of lumber, paving stones, bags of sand and concrete. He stood in the middle of a half-completed foundation framing of what he hoped would one day be a big, beautiful backyard deck.

Just at the moment though, not so much.

He clambered out of the joists and footers and walked over to the table saw, looked across the yard then at the children scurrying about their playground, climbing up into the jungle gym. He unbuckled the utility belt and set it onto the table beside the saw. He held out a hand and a water bottle rose up from the table and drifted to him. He unscrewed the cap and took a long swallow, resealed it, rolled the cool bottle across his brow; he let the bottle drift back to the table.

He absently flicked a finger, the action drawing a lawn chair to him. He dropped into it with a tired sigh.

Victor wasn't used to physical labor.

What did he think he was doing, starting a major project like this?

He turned his attention again to the children. Another year or two, they'd be too old for the playground; maybe he'd replace the playground equipment with exercise equipment.

Just a thought.

He held up a hand, drew a cookie over from the snack table. He took a bite.

A voice reached him in thought-talk.

Victor? You out there?

Taking a break, he responded.

His wife Dianna appeared at the back door, stood looking out across the labyrinth of joists and framing. Seeing a plank laid across the joists, she drew it over with the nearly imperceptible swipe of a finger, walked across the construction and stepped down onto the lawn.

You sure you want to do this on your own?

Absolutely, he answered. He drew a second chair over for Dianna, waited for her to take a seat. *It feels good, getting back to working with my hands.*

"If you say so," she answered then, aloud.

Over in the playground, both children stopped what they were doing. They looked in the direction of the house.

Yes, Nanny....

Yes, Nanny...

Their thought-talk Ability was continuing to improve.

Victor and Dianna watched them climb down from the bars and hurry across the yard.

"You watch yourselves," said their mother as they started across the plank and to the back door.

Mrs. Evans was waiting for them inside.

A few moments of peace and quiet before Dianna broached an uncomfortable subject.

"My lunch meeting today," she started. "A few brought up… well, they were rather surprised by what they took to be Mary siding with Matthew."

"Her choosing to become part of Sutherland House," Matthew stated.

"What was I to say? I mean, what could possibly be her motive?"

"So, what <u>did</u> you say?"

"What could I say? I had no answer. I told them that I was as surprised as they."

"Dianna, we both know that Mary wouldn't make such a move unless she believed that Sutherland House was necessary to the Society."

Dianna was no longer totally convinced. She gave a dark frown.

"Maybe," she managed. "That, or maybe she's just a little girl who looks to Jennifer Sutherland as a big sister."

Victor could only chuckle lightly at that.

The one doesn't necessarily negate the other, he said subvocally.

I suppose that's so, she answered. A few moments later then, aloud:

"What does all this mean to your duties as Father?

"Oh, I'll have to adjust a bit, but it's all minor storm to weather."

"And the Agenda? The truce?"

"Sutherland House will of course be all the stronger. That said, all eyes on them, and on our relationship with them, it may be all the easier to pursue our more, let us say, *clandestine*, activities."

"It has come to this. The Father of the Society forced to work in the shadows," Dianna said tiredly.

"As we must."

Victor Broderick, Father of the Society, would do his duty, would do what was best for the Society. In this respect, his and Mary's goals were the same. If that meant coordinating with those referring to themselves as *the underground*, they with their aims, so be it.

He would deal with them once his own endeavors had been successfully completed.

Victor casually held up a hand, drew another cookie over from the table.

He held the snack out to Dianna.

"Cookie?" he asked.

Matthew guided the wheelbarrow around the corner and down the sidewalk that ran along the south side of the house, brought it to a shaky stop at the worksite. To one side of the sidewalk was a small pallet of concrete blocks, to the other the short retaining wall with a gap where blocks had been removed.

He stepped around the wheelbarrow and dropped carefully to his knees. Using a trowel then, he began transferring the prepared mortar mix from the barrow to the row of blocks in the retaining wall.

Jennifer came around from the front of the house and up the walk. She stood a few steps from her father, silently watched him at work.

She was pretty sure this was same section of retaining wall her father had worked on not all that long ago.

She folded her arms across her chest then, looked away, looked then up at the house.

"I've been thinking a lot about Mom lately," she said. "I mean, I often think of her, but lately she's been much more front of mind. I don't know why."

Matthew continued working on the retaining wall, reaching across and selecting a concrete block. He wiggled it into place, grabbed the trowel and worked mortar into the gaps.

He spoke then as he worked.

"I walk into a room," he said. "A movement, a shadow, just off to one side. I immediately think it's your mother. For a moment. Just a moment. Then I remember."

Another concrete block. Mortar. Working the gaps, smoothing.

"In the kitchen," he continued. "Cooking. The kitchen smell. For a moment you mother is there with me."

"Her perfume," said Jennifer, after a long moment, smiling. "I did not like that perfume."

"Yeah," Matthew mumbled. "You got that for her for Christmas when you were eight, maybe nine."

"Ten."

"Ah."

"What does a ten-year-old know from perfume?"

"Not much, apparently." Matthew slid back from the wall, studied his work. Forward, then, applied more mortar, smoothed it. He reached back, picked up another concrete block.

"I miss her very much," he said, wiggling the block into position.

Jennifer glanced up at the sky. Not for the first time, she held her silence. Considering the dangers and threats her father faced, his exposure working out here in the yard was just asking for trouble.

Yes, the estate did have significant security. An invisible fence some six feet inside the physical fence would easily incapacitate any intruder coming in that way. And the set of strategically positioned devices would take out low-flying threats coming in from above.

But these days there were any number of potential high-altitude threats that the estate security wouldn't see coming until it was too late.

Jennifer looked again at her father, gave him a sad, warm smile.

"I miss her too, Dad," she said.

Headmaster stood at his office window, looking out at the dreary day. There was a heavy mist in the air, a low cloud drifting across the Academy campus. This somehow deepened his sense of isolation, this despite his daily interaction with students and staff.

He was actually a very busy man, and yet the isolation was very real. In his decades-long role as Headmaster of the Academy, he had always been a man apart. Such was somehow necessary.

Society events of the past few years had only made the isolation greater. He found himself both in the middle and apart. How could that be?

His feelings regarding Matthew Sutherland were quite positive, always had been. And yet he knew that he would always stand by Victor Broderick. Victor was Father. The Academy Headmaster would of course always stand with the Father.

And yet there were growing concerns regarding Victor's Agenda.

And regarding Matthew Sutherland.

And so the growing isolation of the Headmaster of the Academy.

Perhaps these most recent events, this so-called truce, would help.

There came a light knock on the door.

Headmaster continued looking out at the dreary day, spoke over his shoulder.

"Come in."

He heard the door open, moments later gently close.

He sensed young Mary standing then before his desk. An almost unprecedented occurrence. When was the last time Mary had stood in his office?

He turned slowly about, did his best to put on a gentle smile.

"Hello, Mary. What can I do for you?"

"You wish to speak with me," she stated. Not a question.

"Do I?" Headmaster tried to recall. *When did I ask…* ah, Mary must have sensed his thoughts. Recent events. "Perhaps so," he said. He moved to his desk, sat down as he indicated the guest chair to Mary.

He watched her settle in, studying her manner, her expression. Headmaster was very good at reading people, but such had always been difficult when it came to Mary. At the moment, as best as he could tell, she seemed calm, untroubled.

"I understand that you wish to remain at the Academy," he said.

"Will that be a problem?" she asked.

"Not at all. I believe it to be a wise decision." Headmaster had served as Mary's guardian since her moving into the Academy, following the death of her father, and had basically seen to all her needs. He had also been responsible for all Westerman Family financial interests, which Mary would take over once she came of legal age.

"Do you have misgivings about my decision to join Sutherland House?" she asked.

"I'm fine with that, Mary. Matthew is a good man." He leaned back in his chair. "And Jennifer is a wonderful young woman."

"She is."

While Headmaster had no doubt that Mary's request to *adopt* into Sutherland House was primarily intended to strengthen their position in the Society, he could not but wonder about the little girl's growing attachment to Jennifer Sutherland. Whatever the case, however, Mary would always do what she felt best for the Society, whatever her own personal desires.

"No issues, Mary. Sorting out the logistics, nothing of concern."

"Logistics?"

"The arrangement. You'll be joining Sutherland House while continuing to maintain your standing in Westerman House."

"You can do that, yes?"

"An internal matter, within the Society."

"And you will continue as my guardian, yes?"

"I am happy to continue addressing your needs here at the Academy. And I can continue overseeing Westerman family financial matters, if you wish."

"I do wish."

"Until you are ready to take on your duties as family matriarch."

I am Westerman House. She noted in thought-talk. *The only member of Westerman House…*

"And so a founding family will continue," said Headmaster. Mary must also see this as necessary for the Society. "I am glad."

§

Mary stood at the open door, gave Headmaster a half-smile and slight wave of the hand before leaving the office. Headmaster stared after her, watched the door ease shut behind her.

The room fell eerily silent. He pushed back from the desk, turned about in his chair, looking to the window. The day outside was brightening a little, the invisible sun trying its best to burn away the low clouds.

As he sat there, his exchange with Mary still sorting itself out in his thoughts, something brushed at his mind; something reaching out, and then fading away.

He leaned forward in his chair, slowly stood and took the two steps over to the window.

The mist, drifting slowly across the campus grounds, was thinning, the day brightening.

Over at the Great Oak then… a movement in the branches, a flickering of shadow moving through the branches.

The shadow faded, disappearing to… somewhere else.

If someone had been standing beneath the Great Oak, looking to the dormitory wing of the Academy building complex, looking up at the row of second-floor windows, one might see the shadowy silhouette of a young girl in the window of her room.

End Episode Five…

If you enjoyed **Sutherland House – the Complete Series**, we would greatly appreciate a positive review on Amazon. Also find us on Goodreads. Thanks!

Find more titles by this author on Amazon and at Greybeard Publishing. And be sure to visit David's author page at www.davidrbeshears.com.

This title is available in ebook, paperback, hardcover and large print formats. More information and special offers at Greybeard Publishing.